Nicole -
May you
find the be[illegible]
between
the lines -
♡

Our Invisible String

a year long journey
through the stages of forbidden Clove

~JULIANNA WOITE~

[illegible] 2023

Julianna Woite

LIVE YOUR HISTORY

www.juliannawoite.com

ISBN: 9780578379777

First edition

So long as men can breathe or eyes can see,
so long lives this and this gives life to thee

William Shakespeare

Contents

Acknowledgement

In one way or another, everything on these pages was inspired by something one hundred percent real.

They are a collection of moments, woven together to tell a story.

I certainly didn't do it alone,

and everyone who pithed in knows exactly who they are.

So, this is for you who lent your experience, your memories,

your creativity, and your names,

for all who listened frequently and inspired often,

and for the one who walked with me until we finally found the ending.

You hold the key – not fade away

Prologue – Turning the Key

"An invisible thread connects those who are destined to meet, regardless of time, place and circumstance. The thread may stretch or tangle, but it will never break"

~ Ancient Chinese Proverb

* * *

Stages of Forbidden Love

In 1969 I read the most amazing book. It was called *On Death and Dying* by Elisabeth Kubler Ross and I picked it up on the recommendation of a friend. As someone who had lost my father to cancer as a child, I had always been uniquely fascinated with the grieving process and had spent a great deal of my life volunteering to help others who had suffered a similar loss. Although I was only fourteen years old at the time of his death, from the minute we received his diagnosis, I knew that I wanted my father's struggle to mean something. For me, giving back was the natural way to do that. The instant I was old enough I turned my application in to the local human services agency and at the age of sixteen, I started volunteering at a day-camp program for children like me. The camp had started as a group for kids who had lost their fathers in the Korean War. Eventually it grew to accepting kids who had a serious medical condition or had lost a parent or sibling to a serious medical condition. I must admit that the program was really ahead of its time, and I was proud to live in a community that embraced difficult issues such as this. Nevertheless, it was through this program that I began to appreciate my natural resiliency as well as the cruel fact that not all people are born with that. In all honesty, I handled the death of my father pretty stoically, but I quickly learned that not everyone is equipped to do that. I suppose some of my resilience stemmed from the fact that my father was a funeral director. Growing up around death gives a kid a unique perspective. You learn very quickly that death, no matter how premature, is a natural part of life and that a proper funeral is a true celebration of that life. In my head, as long as people lived vibrantly enough to earn a good funeral, the pages of their calendar didn't really matter. Then again, I was the only kid in school with a casket key collection, so I knew my outlook on things was probably a little skewed!

Anyway, volunteering with the children at the camp remains one of the most rewarding things I have ever done and is directly responsible for my decision to pursue teaching as a career. I graduated from Bennett High School in 1958 and immediately enrolled at Mount Saint Joseph's Teachers College on Agassiz Circle. Inside that iconic brick building, I collected the knowledge and the skills I would need to change the world. I actually liked the school so much that I taught there part time in later years. It was Medaille College back then and became a University not long after I retired. Pretty cool circle of life! Nevertheless, I also served forty years in the Amherst Central School District, and I never looked back once. I like to think I have my father to thank for that.

So, like I said, when a colleague began telling me about this groundbreaking book, I knew I needed to grab a copy. Little did I know that opening that book was about to change the way I looked at everything. Little did I know that those pages were about to take me on a journey through time, a journey that would force me to confront the past and open an old wound just long enough to help make sense of it.

According to Kubler-Ross, there are five stages of grief: denial, anger, bargaining, depression and acceptance. I think by now most of the population is familiar with those stages, either through a school curriculum or via their own self-help journey. But let me tell you, in 1969, this was mind-blowing stuff. Even more mind-blowing was the lightbulb that went off in my head as I learned about them. The more I read, the less I applied these stages to traditional things like death and illness. For me, everything I read became about a boy named Jack...about me and Jack...and our woeful tale of forbidden love. For the first time, I saw everything so clearly, and applying the stages really helped to explain the course of our relationship. While what Jack and I experienced was pretty extreme and, dare I say, rooted in true love, I began to realize that everyone at one time or another has probably had to endure these stages with regards to a failed romance. At the very least, most people will admit to having endured a forbidden crush. Let's face it; we've all had them, the great love of our lives that - by some burden of birth - is destined to never be more than a fantasy. Whether it's the boy who likes boys - not girls, the heartthrob teacher, the second cousin thrice removed, or (God forbid) the stepbrother, WHY you can't be together is irrelevant. Whether the roadblocks are religious, chronological, or genetic makes little difference. The underlying problem remains the same. You are never going to be together. Ever. What ensues is the romantic version of the stages of grief...grief for this relationship that will never be. Yes, that crush will cycle through denial, anger, bargaining, depression and finally, acceptance. What Jack and I experienced was no different...it was just a little more intense.

It is often said that with age comes clarity. I'm not sure if its clarity that has driven my sudden urge to talk about 1957 or the general feeling that having reached my 80s, I no longer give a crap. They say crustiness comes with old age too. Regardless, I have decided to finally open up about the most fulfilling and heartbreaking year of my life. It was the year that Buffalo celebrated its 125th Anniversary, the year Elvis sang at Memorial Auditorium and the year I discovered that love is love. I guess I'm hoping that in telling it, my story will help some of you find answers or at the very least, peace. I know what you're thinking. You are wondering why, if I intended to tell you this story, I already spoiled the ending. Why have I told you that Jack and I don't end up together? Here's where you need to jump on board with the theme of this story. I didn't actually spoil the ending, because this story is not about the ending. This story is about the journey. There are a lot of times in life when your fate is sealed and a lot of times when you might not have been dealt the hand that you were expecting. The true human experience and the true test of one's character can be found in how we deal with those moments. How we bounce back from adversity, how we deal with disappointment and how we find beauty between the lines will become the things that define us. Even under the best of circumstances, matters of the heart will test our faith and redefine our limits. When our heart finds itself attached to something it can't have, that's when we need to face them with compassion, rationality, and a pretty solid sense of humor. Sometimes the ending simply doesn't matter. It's like Buddy Holly preached. If your love is real, it won't fade away.

What follows is an account of my personal journey through "the stages of forbidden love," a process that literally took an entire year of my life. Even sixty-four years later I can recall almost every minute of 1957 with complete clarity. I can see the cherry blossoms that adorned Jack's park-like street and smell the paint we used to make crafts at the children's center. I can taste the M&M's we shared, hear the Frank Sinatra songs we sang, and remember the frustration we felt living within our limits. But more than anything, I can feel the wind that blew through my hair as we cruised in his Chrysler convertible; I hope I can feel that forever. So, with that, I will do my best to tell you our story and I will try not to leave anything out. Like they say - truth is often stranger than fiction and once you get to know me, you will realize that I am nothing if not strange.

STAGE I – DENIAL

Everyone wants to believe that they are a fundamentally good person, and when something happens that challenges our good opinion of ourselves, denial is a likely defense mechanism. The differences between who you want to be and who you fear you actually are can be crippling. No one wants to look in the mirror and see a reflection they can't reconcile. By denying our feelings and living our illusions, we think we are maintaining control. Admitting that this thing might be beyond our control…well that is not a conclusion we come to willingly… or at least not without a valiant fight.

The forbidden crush is a complicated conundrum. Most people believe that they have a certain ownership over their feelings, and, therefore, should be able to nip this pesky crush in the bud. This, my friends, is rarely the case. At first, one might try projection, i.e.: "Come on Rosie…I KNOW you like Jack." Whether or not Rosie likes Jack is irrelevant. If YOU believe she does, you can try to transfer all your feeling over to her, i.e.: "Let's go to Jack's, Rosie. I KNOW you want to" or "Don't Jack's eyes look amazing in that blue shirt? Come on Rosie…I KNOW you think he's cute." Yes, in the beginning, living vicariously through Rosie might seem like a stellar idea. Sure, you might be a little jealous if they actually start dating – and sure, you might be a little psychotic if she breaks up with him – but all of that is better than admitting the truth. Being a psychotic friend is way better than being a fundamentally psychotic person.

If transference and projection don't work, repression is a likely alternative. You figure if you can just shove those feelings down deep enough, they are bound to be extinguished. You very clearly know that perusing these feelings is impossible, so you very clearly know that you can't admit you're having them. You tell yourself that it's a phase, a stage, nothing more than an illusion. You convince yourself that you are more powerful than these feelings...which sometimes you might be. In this case, however, I was not; most definitely not.

The funny thing about denial is that it isn't all about you. Once you get past your initial hesitation and admit that you have actual feelings for this forbidden person, you may also have to wrestle with that person's perceived feelings for you. It's bad enough that you have this inconvenient crush on something harmful, there is no possible way you can allow yourself to believe that those feelings are being reciprocated. In a desperate act of self-preservation, you will convince yourself that he is not flirting with you, that the dreamy look in his eye is nothing more than a speck of dust and that he is only talking to you to be polite. Let's face it; fighting off your own feelings is hard enough, having to willing turn down his affections would be crippling.

January

"The very first moment I beheld him, my heart was irrevocably gone."
Jane Austen

* * *

The Best that Never Was

Leave it to Buffalonians. If time has proven anything, it is that we are nothing if not resilient. We are also nothing if not proud of our history, so I guess I shouldn't have been surprised that Buffalo wasn't going to let a little thing like a global pandemic stop it from celebrating our county's bicentennial. EC200. That's what they called it. Two hundred years ago, - April 2, 1821, - Erie County was officially created and, despite Covid-19, Western New York planned to spend an entire year celebrating itself. I mean have you seen those videos of the Buffalo Bills Mafia? Yeah. Buffalo knows how to celebrate itself!

Now, I have always been a student of history and I would normally relish any opportunity to reconnect with some wholesome Western New York nostalgia. For some reason, though, this EC200 celebration was getting under my skin. I was finding it all oddly reminiscent. Seeing the bustle, the pride in local history, it was all taking me back...back to 1957...back to

Buffalo's 125th Anniversary Celebration and the defining year of my life.

I guess everyone gets to a certain place in their life where they look back and try to find clarity. They want to know what it all meant…what it was all for…and what they might leave behind. They evaluate experiences, second guess decisions and rank their adventures. While I don't pretend to have much more clarity than the next person when it comes to most of those things, there is one topic about which I remain unequivocally certain. It might seem strange to say, but when looking back at my adventures and trying to decide between the "best of this" and "the worst of that," one contest will always seem clearer than the rest. It is the story that defines me and its ghost will always sit atop any list I make. I know it will sound crazy when I tell you, but I guess I will just consider that part of the charm. I've learned that life doesn't always make sense, and when we open ourselves up to that, we find the most beautiful things in the most bizarre of places. I've also learned that not all endings are the ones we hope for, but if we are persistent, we might find another layer…and it is in this layer that the magic lies. So, while I have been lucky enough to have been happily married for more than forty years and to have children and grandchildren that I genuinely enjoy, I also have a secret and I wear it around my neck every day. Hanging from a silver chain, a paint-splattered key guards my secret and - strange as it seems - I believe that it is this secret that has enabled me to be the wife and the mother that I have grown to be. Through my secret, I have loved and been loved in a way that defies reason and it is this brand of love that guides me through everything. So yes, when I am looking back and ranking the things in my life, the category of love will always have an easy yet unusual answer. Without question, I will profess that my all-time most memorable love affair is the one that never actually happened ….and the contest isn't even close.

It's funny to think how something that never technically existed could hold such a major place in my life, but I guess when it comes to matters of the heart, some lines can just be fuzzy. Although the relationship may have lacked the traditional definitions of a love affair, like the title, the commitment or the physical contact, this bond was real in every way that mattered, and that was always enough. We both knew from the beginning that a romantic relationship couldn't happen, and we probably both denied our feelings for a lot longer than we needed to. In the end, knowledge and denial were never powerful enough to make our connection go away and we somehow found ourselves caught up in the most magical and incomprehensible love story. Yes, it was wrong and yes, it was impossible, but it was also spectacular! In some weird way, an intangible affair has the power to unleash love in its truest form - without judgements and without expectations. What we shared was so pure in its secrecy and so honest in its silence that I don't think anything was ever quite able to match it. This affair was found inside a look and confirmed inside a smile. It thrived between the lines and quickly snuggled into its unique place inside my life. For something that wasn't supposed to be anything, it somehow became absolutely EVERYTHING!

I'm no idiot. I know that something that is rooted in deceit and secrecy should not be considered beautiful, but if you consider the year, the society we were living in and that these restrictions wouldn't even be a factor today, it all gets a little easier to digest. We were victims of time. Two chronologically misplaced individuals thrust into a storyline they couldn't escape or control. I suppose there will always be a small part of me that is bitter about that, the part of me that wonders how the universe could have screwed this up so badly. There are still days that I can't understand how any supreme power could take two people so clearly destined to be together and needlessly keep them apart. But lamenting our fate is pointless. I learned a long time ago to be grateful for what we were given and not to resent what we could never have. At times it's hard not to wish that we would have had more, even though I know for certain that what we did receive was far more than I ever dreamed or deserved. The fact remains that even within its limits, this love story changed everything. It doesn't take a genius to see that my life is divided into two very clear halves, before 1957 and after 1957. It was the year that guided me through the "stages of forbidden love" and saw me stronger for it. It was the year that built me up, tore me apart, and taught me who I was; it was the year that year created me. Even more than that, it was the year that cemented one of my life's most basic truths: *Loving someone is never wrong - the fuzziness lies in where we draw the lines.*

Crashing into Oz

I guess if we are starting at the beginning, I should properly introduce myself. I was born with the name Josie Johnson, which I sometimes let people shorten to Jo-Jo, and in 1957, I was a sixteen-year-old protestant living in a modest neighborhood in Buffalo, NY. I was the oldest of three spunky girls and lived in a beautiful old Victorian house in one of the older neighborhoods in the city. While my house wasn't new or flashy, it had an old-fashioned charm that I genuinely loved and I would have chosen it over any of those old mansions over on Delaware Avenue. Considering we never could have afforded one of those mansions anyway, my affinity to our neighborhood was pretty handy. My family was by no means poor, but with my mom cutting hair following the death of my dad, the depth of our wealth and the color of our collar became pretty clear. Before his death two years ago, my dad had worked for a small funeral home in town and made a respectable salary. He had taken up the profession following his return from WWI where he spent most of his time on an island in the Pacific. It was on this island that he learned to care for American soldiers killed in action and the mortuary sciences soon became his specialty. Almost immediately, dad knew it was his calling and treated his profession and his clients with a respect and humility I found tremendously inspiring. As for my mom, she never wanted to give up on the "Rosie the Riveter" dreams she had during the war and was never content to be a full-time housewife. Luckily, even after my sisters and I were born, mom had always cut hair on the side, partly to give us extra money and partly because she genuinely enjoyed it. Once Dad was gone, Mom's hobby became Mom's job and her extra "hair money" became our only means of survival. I guess someone was really looking out for us when they put that idea in her head. Anyway, these days Mom made the bulk of her money servicing the socialites from the Country Club of Buffalo and had become a very sought-after stylist. All those ladies at the club passionately depended on my mom and her "vision" to set them apart from the rest. My mom had a true gift for knowing what styles would be most flattering for someone and her clients spoiled her as they became more dependent on her talents. Don't let their affinity fool you;

however, they were NOT her friends. They would gossip with her during their appointments and be very friendly with her at events in town, but they felt their superiority acutely and we all knew that she was only one mistake away from ruin.

As for my sisters and I, we learned to be pretty self-sufficient. As our mom's schedule tightened, I frequently found myself doing the shopping, running errands, and picking my siblings up from school. With me being in our local Bennett High School and them still in the elementary building, I got out about an hour earlier, which gave me just enough time to take the bus home and grab the car from my mom. I had only been driving for a few months, but I already knew that having my license was life changing. Don't get me wrong, I didn't like having the car because it made me cool or because I was living iconic teenage adventures. No, I liked having the car because it came in handy as I ran the errands for the day. I mean I really wish I could tell you that my afternoons were filled with milkshakes at Parkside Candy and teenage hijinks at Delaware Park, but that just wasn't my style.

Being born naturally conservative, I was, and probably still am, one of the least adventurous people you will ever meet. I had always considered myself a card-carrying rule follower and I genuinely found comfort in adhering to details. I didn't like to deviate from expectations and shied away from anything even remotely considered a risk. I was, for all intents and purposes, a certified goody two shoes. If I'm being honest, I will admit that prior to 1957, I lived a bland but satisfactory life, free from drama, but completely void of passion. Although my soul was secretly filled with poetry and music, I spent my days walking in a black and white world, frantically trying to maintain the illusion I was living. You see, at my core, I am a bona fide people pleaser and to that point I had always done what was expected. Since the expectations in our family and our city were pretty clear, I quickly learned and settled into my "place" in the hierarchy of Buffalo society. You see, I wasn't rich or cool enough to travel with a clique or be invited to the popular parties, but I had become good with that long ago. Dakota Rose Frazier and I had been best friends for almost as long as I can remember and to me, one true friend was always worth more than the glitz of popularity. I was usually too conservative and sensible to be on the front lines of adolescence anyway. I had spent most of my life watching the action from the sidelines and had become proficient at vicariously living my dreams through others. This wasn't a problem, really. I was actually pretty content with my piece of the world and never gave much thought to the pieces I was missing. Yes, I, Josie Johnson, probably could have won an Oscar for the skill with which I executed my supporting role in life. I had mastered going through the motions and had almost accepted that this reality was all I was ever going to get, which it truly might have been if it weren't for Jack.

Jack Riley was a local football star whose parents had put him in private school at a young age. Jack came from "old money" and his family owned a factory and a few of the major restaurants in Buffalo. Even as a small child his athletic potential was staggering, and his family had always made the decisions and followed the connections that would ensure his continued success. Being devout Catholics, the Rileys lauded the benefits of Jack's catholic education to anyone "unfortunate" enough to be enrolled in public school and shamelessly bragged about his athletic accomplishments to anyone who would listen. Due to some power-play over the "lacking" conditions of the Canisus High School athletic facilities, however, the Rileys pulled Jack from Canisus the summer before his freshman year and hypocritically enrolled him at Bennett High School, home of All High Stadium, the most prestigious facilities in all Western New York. If I'm being honest, transferring to Bennett was pretty common back then. From a teenager's perspective, it was "cool" to go to Bennett. You have to remember, the 1950s was the birth of rock and roll and Bennett students were notorious for hosting rock and roll dances at hotels and country clubs. We might have only been a public school, but parents took notice of our academic excellence and our extra-curricular activities made us the envy of kids across Western New York. It was actually a well-known joke that students who lived in the suburbs or another area of Buffalo could weasel their way into Bennett by using the secret phrase "I want to take Hebrew" or "I want to take Russian." You see, Bennett was the only school offering these languages so an applicant could have permission to enroll just by making this request. I never knew what Jack's parents said to get permission to register and I honestly, don't know whether Jack had any say in it, but I do know he would have been too polite to say anything even if he had disagreed. Nevertheless, although I had always known of the existence of Jack Riley, I hadn't had much contact with him before he transferred to Bennett. Jack's social circle was vastly different than mine and running into him around the city was usually not an issue. Obviously, all of that changed over the next few years.

The first time I came face to face with teenage sensation Jack Riley, I knew he was special. But what I couldn't possibly have known back then was how or why he was special. You can't blame me for that though. At no point in my education had anyone warned me about magic like this. How could I possibly have known that standing before me was no ordinary boy...no simple sum of his parts. I don't think I realized it at the time, but from the moment I saw him I was falling.... falling headfirst into a fairy tale that had been written to turn my life upside down. It's true. Just the act of looking at Jack that day was already starting to change me. In all my life I had never seen anything like it. Even from a distance the lightning that danced in his eyes was enough to stop anyone dead in their tracks. Looking at him was like Dorothy getting her first glimpse of Oz. One minute you are spinning in a tornado of your own making and the next, there he is - a Technicolor boy - triumphantly glowing against the black and white backdrop of your everyday world. I remember trying not to look at him. Every part of me could feel I was on the precipice of something I didn't understand. I tried to save myself, but his colors pulled me in like a magnet. He was mesmerizing - and I wasn't sorry. In any other world, I might have been tempted to fall in love with Jack Riley. Given the unchanging existence to which I was born, however, there was no way that was ever going to happen.

I know it's going to sound silly to you, ludicrous even, but in cities across America in 1957, things weren't like they are today. There were unwritten rules, family expectations and lines of convention that you just didn't cross. Kids obeyed their parents and parents slaved to please society. Appearances were important and conformity equaled survival. I'm not going to go as far as to say my neighborhood was built on prejudice, but they certainly followed a pretty strict set of unwritten rules as far as society was concerned. I know that sounds daunting, but it was all very cordial actually. Everyone was genuinely friendly to each other and from birth you were taught to respect and to be kind to your neighbors (Buffalo is called "The City of Good Neighbors" after all). Any relationship deeper than that, however, was limited to your own kind. Catholics married Catholics, Protestants married Protestants and no one of any religion dared marry beneath their station. Looking back, it's easy to see how crazy that was, but when something is all you know, questioning it doesn't come as naturally as you would hope…and fighting it can be damn near impossible.

So, you see, as far as Jack Riley was concerned, I knew I needed to get him out of my head immediately. Regardless of any bizarre things that may have happened to my constitution the first time I saw him, any sort of friendship between us was very unlikely and anything deeper than that was firmly out of the question. If his status as a Catholic didn't squash our possibilities, the mounds of money in his closet certainly did. There was absolutely no way Jack and I would ever be anything more than cordial schoolmates and I needed to be okay that. My mom's job depended on it.

So, as anticipated, in the fall of our freshman year Jack Riley settled into Bennet High School and took up with exactly the people you would have expected him to; his blue blood and his jock persona left little room for experimentation. By the end of our sophomore year, "Quarterback Jack" had firmly cemented his rank as one of the bigger men on campus, but despite his status, Jack always remained humble and never resembled anything close to a snob. At his core, you see, Jack was an old soul. Although he hadn't seen much of this world during his sixteen years, he walked around with the kind of class typically reserved for a man twice his age. He was half Frank Sinatra, singing with his martini, half James Dean traveling *East of Eden*. As all special people, he was burdened with a tremendous blindness to his own worth and a suspicion of anyone who tried to convince him otherwise. In a way, this cluelessness only served to feed his allure. He remained confident without arrogance and sweet without suspicion. Being a teenage boy, however, Jack was also a living, breathing paradox, embodying the perfect combination of Victorian gentleman and immature momma's boy. He was charismatic yet he was cringeworthy. He was suave yet he was clumsy. Most notably, although he was notoriously clueless, I would come to suspect that he was actually an evil genius. In my opinion, Jack Riley was the Webster definition of perfect and following a state championship run during the football season of our junior year, most of Buffalo probably agreed with me. Jack and his teammates gave our little nook of the state something to be proud of and it was no surprise to anyone when Bennett High's football team was chosen to ring the bell in Niagara Square as we ushered in 1957. Happy New Year!

The Soundtrack

It was only January, but the birth of 1957 was already creating a palpable buzz around the city. This year, you see, not only marked the 125th birthday of the City of Buffalo, but it was also the official kick-off celebration for Buffalo becoming a "World Port" on the Erie Canal. When digging for the canal started in 1823, it basically put Buffalo on the map. By the time the canal opened in 1832, the population of Erie County had increased one hundred forty five percent and commerce from the Erie Canal led to Buffalo being the eighth richest city in America by the turn of the century. The following year, Buffalo pretty much reached its peak when we hosted the prestigious Pan American Exposition of 1901. Although our fair city played host to over eight million visitors from around the world, the success, was tragically overshadowed by the assassination of President McKinley, while visiting the expo. Buffalo may have been known as "The City of Light," but that singular event cast a shadow that we have never quite been able to crawl out of. This year, however, our celebration of the 125th Anniversary and World Port Celebration was bringing some notoriety back to Buffalo. Even the New York Times had published an article boasting how the celebration was "the biggest event here since the Pan American Exposition of 1901" and it was expected to attract millions of visitors. Yeah. The eyes of the world were on us again – and this time – we were going to crush it!

Back in my small corner of the world, I was just trying to survive the 11th grade. Although the winters could be dull and seemingly endless in

Buffalo, there were a few things that I always looked forward to. Winter Homecoming, for one, was always an adventure. I wasn't particularly into basketball, but high school games had a certain energy that I really loved. Add to that the pep rally, Winter Fair and Snowflake Ball and even I couldn't deny that Bennett's Homecoming week was filled with possibilities. Possibility for what, you ask? Well, I wasn't really sure...but I could feel the possibility, nonetheless. So, with that attitude, I enthusiastically attended each and every homecoming event, and while I might not have been in the nucleus of every function, I still enjoyed my chance to cheer everyone from the sidelines... literally and metaphorically. Like I said, I wasn't cool enough to travel with the cheerleaders or be invited to the popular parties, but that was okay. My social circle was small but loyal and made up of a charming array of misfits. While we were nowhere near being part of the popular crowd, we didn't have to sit in exile in the cafeteria either. To be honest, my friends and I were just painfully middle class. The beauty of the middle class was that it gave me liberty to befriend anyone in school without judgement. It wasn't absurd for the popular kids to be talking to me and it wasn't social suicide to hang with the music geeks, the rebels, or the mathletes. Being part of the invisible middle class was oddly liberating. I knew who I was, and I knew where I belonged...or at least I thought I did.

Despite my initial feelings of possibility, by the night of the Winter Ball, I was pretty certain that this Homecoming was going to end in the same lack luster fashion as all the rest. I would go to the dance, have an amiable time, and be home too early to admit out loud. Let's face it; I was the queen of mediocre and dutifully resigned to everything that came with it. To be honest, there was a brief moment last summer where I actually thought things might be different this year, but I didn't like to think back to that too often, and I was obviously very wrong anyway.

It all started with my best friend, Dakota Rose Frazier. Let's just say that there were a few weeks where I thought Dakota Rose might be breaking into the popular crowd, and I was more than a little excited about what that would mean for my "best friend" privileges. You see, Dakota Rose's family had money, but not "old money" like most people in Buffalo. While going to school to become a pharmacist, Mr. Frazier had perfected use of the Wild Prairie Rose, state flower of North Dakota, to make medicine. He discovered that its essence helped relieve stress and improve people's emotions. Needless to say, Mr. Frazier marketed his discovery and made a literal fortune with the drug companies. The Fraziers even named their first born – Dakota Rose – after the discovery.

Anyway, with their fortune only decades old, the Fraziers were seen as part of the "new money" population, and this was a very grey area for many things. Sometimes when the country club ladies would talk about the Fraziers, the words "new money" would be whispered with an eye roll or said as they covered their mouth. It was kind of the same way that you talk about someone with a disease. Technically they were "allowed" to socialize with the upper class, but no one ever seemed too thrilled about it. At some point, it was even decided that the name "Dakota Rose" sounded too "hillbilly" and the next thing I knew, my best friend had been rebranded as "Rosie." Nevertheless, Rosie's boundaries were different than mine and for a few weeks last summer I actually thought I saw something developing between her and Jack Riley. Their families had attended a couple of Country Club events together and after that, Jack had invited Rosie to a few outings with his group of friends. For some reason, I found myself overly interested in everything concerning Rosie and Jack and I was her biggest cheerleader as she decided on whether she should actively pursue him (which in 1957, didn't consist of much more than some flirty sentences and possibly leaving a sweater in his car). Needless to say, things between Jack and Rosie didn't develop and I was pretty disappointed. Okay, maybe disappointed is an understatement. Maybe I was psychotically heartbroken and cried like there was a death in the family. "Teenage hormones," my mom would say. In my own head, my complete and utter overreaction was due to the fact that Rosie dating Jack would have given me a better social circle. I guess looking like a grubby social climber was more comforting than admitting my real issue. Admitting that this had more to do with Jack than it did with popularity was too painful to explore.

Zipping up my dress for the Ball, my summer memories were interrupted by a song on the radio. I wasn't surprised to hear an Elvis Presley song. It had just been announced that Elvis was performing in Buffalo's Memorial Auditorium this April and all of Erie County was in a frenzy. His songs were on the radio non-stop, and I had probably heard his new hit "Love Me Tender" a million times this week alone. For some reason though, it seemed to be speaking to me differently right now and I couldn't process what I was feeling.

Confused and a little annoyed, my body was frozen. The more Elvis sang of his devotion, the more I found myself fighting off a hurricane of reservations about this dance - and I couldn't shake the feeling that something was missing. Not missing from my outfit or from my purse but missing from my LIFE! Oh, I was perfectly used to not having a date and wasn't particularly surprised or disappointed at the idea of going to this dance as a group, so that couldn't be it. By the time the song ended I was both annoyed and anxious. The last two minutes had left me with a pretty weird premonition, but I was much too stubborn to listen to what I feared it was telling me.

So, with that, I headed out into the January darkness with a cute new dress, a corsage I bought for myself and a smile full of optimism. If I was being honest, I would have admitted to struggling with some nagging thoughts, warning signs if you will, that were relentlessly carrying on behind my brain. The kind of intuition that tells you that life as you know it is about to change. The kind of premonition that zeros in on that pesky hole you've begun to feel inside your heart and says "Hey – I think I found a cure for that." Unfortunately, I listened to no such voice and heeded no such warnings. Looking back, I can tell you exactly what this was, but at the time, I was clueless. How could I have known that the hole I was feeling was for Jack, and that I had missed him before we even officially met?

Walking into the Snowflake Ball, I couldn't help feeling a little hesitant. For as long as they have existed, school dances have always gone in one of two directions - because everyone knows that there is rarely any in-between where adolescents are involved. Buying a ticket to a school dance was like signing an acknowledgement that you were either about to have the time of your life or you were going to spend most of the night outrunning your teenage demons. Let's face it, school dances are usually entirely fueled by two equal ingredients: hormones and drama.

Remaining optimistic, my friends and I laughed and danced and tried to enjoy all the perks of being young and invisible. Was there a teenage demon in the room with me? Possibly, but I was in no mind to acknowledge it. Every teenage girl has demons...the girl who is wearing your dress better... the boy who got the solo you wanted...the teacher who you swear fails you for fun. Part of growing up is learning how to recognize your demons and stay two steps ahead of them. I had always felt a little beyond my years with some things and knowing how to avoid conflict was typically one of them. Tonight, however, was looking like judgement day for me. Although I had been doing my best to outrun the thoughts and fight off the feelings, tonight would be the night everything would crumble. After sixteen years of drama free mediocrity, tonight I would finally find myself unable to outrun my demons.

"Oh my gosh," Rosie squealed from her red taffeta dress, "Look at the stage!"

I might not have realized it at that moment, but what I turned to face was one demon I wasn't going to be able to outrun. His name was Jack Riley and he had just stumbled on stage to sing a song with his side-kick Sean Harrigan. Jack and Sean's bro-mance was pretty legendary and all eyes were on the stage, positively stoked to see what nonsense they were going to come up with next. Stepping in on the band was not unusual for these two. They were charismatic and harmless, and the teachers never saw a problem with letting them push some of those boundaries. It's a good thing the bands they hired liked high school football.

Rumor was that Jack and Sean were going to sing "Anything You Can Do I Can Do Better," from *Annie Get Your Gun*, which I knew was probably going to be hilarious. Sure the movie was a few years old, but everybody still loved the song and Jack and Sean singing it to each other had gut buster written all over it. If you don't know the song, it's sort of like a verbal show down and the idea of those two bantering back and forth while trying to out-do each other was pretty engaging. Calmly sitting at a table with a few friends, I sipped my Coke-a-Cola and tried to convince myself that I didn't have butterflies. Sure, there was something odd going on inside my stomach, but I was really trying to blame it on the carbonation and the caffeine. The idea of having a physical reaction to seeing Jack on stage was not something I was going to admit without a fight. Just like I wasn't going to admit how positively dreamy he looked in his red bow tie. So, stubborn and naive I looked up at the stage, confident in my ability to have only appropriate thoughts and reactions. And then it happened. The music started and everything came to a screeching halt. I could hardly believe my ears. Oh, good lord. What was I hearing? This was not from a musical. Oh no. This wasn't even a duet. Oh jeepers! This was a possible disaster. This was rock-n-roll ... Yes, it was the new Buddy Holly song, "Not Fade Away," and heaven help me, I had very little control over my hormones where Buddy Holly was concerned. While the rest of the world was powerless to the raw sex appeal of Elvis, I was much more enamored with the paradox that was Buddy Holly. His signature horned rim glasses made him look like anything but a rock star, but his bluesy hiccup vocals and mad guitar skills proved otherwise. Elvis may have had the girls, but Buddy was the first white performer to play the legendary Apolo Theatre. Yeah, he may have looked like a nerd, but Buddy Holly was BAD ASS – and played by his own rules. There was no denying it; I had a serious crush on Buddy Holly. What's worse, seeing Jack sing his song with a little tinge of rock and roll swagger, I feared that Buddy Holly might not be the only one I had a crush on. Oh, why did Jack have to choose THIS song? Within an instant, I was powerless. With a deep breath, I looked to the stage and realized I was staring straight into the eyes of my own teenage demon.

As expected, Jack and Sean singing to each other was indeed hilarious - those boys were really in the zone and that same chemistry that made them such a threat at quarterback and wide receiver made them the most undeniably charismatic comedy team of the night. I can't say that anyone in the room was surprised by this. Those two goofing around was just part of Bennett's culture, and everyone was pretty used to it. There was something different about Jack tonight though. I couldn't put my finger on it, and I wasn't sure if anyone else was seeing it, but whatever it was made me feel like I was seeing him for the first time.

As I sheepishly watched Jack serenade Sean, who was milking all of the absurd and sarcastic emotion out of this song that he could, something even more unexpected happened. I immediately swore that I must have imagined it, but for a split second, there was a small possibility that Jack looked at me. I knew it wasn't anything anyone else would have detected and even I didn't see it so much as I FELT it, but I couldn't shake the feeling that it had happened...and that it meant something! I was speechless. I knew it was wrong and I knew it was impossible, but for some crazy reason, I also knew that we had just made a connection. In all honestly, from that moment on, my world never spun the same. Not fade away.

Oh, this was NOT good. I knew that I should be laughing along with everyone else, but for some reason I wasn't. I was just watching Jack... stunned...paralyzed...captivated. This may have been a spoof, but at that moment, something about it felt very VERY real. This was one of those times in my life where I wondered if anyone else in that room was seeing what I was seeing. Jack was so perfect, mythical really. Could everyone else see that too? Did time seem to be stopping for anyone else? Was it REALLY hot in here? Why did there seem to be so much less oxygen in the room than a minute ago?

My thoughts were spinning. I knew I shouldn't...strike that...I COULDN'T be feeling what I was feeling but admitting that didn't seem to help it go away. Could I be falling for Jack? Crazy!! I mean I had always secretly admired him from a far, but who would blame me for that? He was pretty freaking amazing. I bet ninety percent of the girls and sixty percent of their moms secretly felt the same way. But this, oh this was over the line. I couldn't have actual feelings for Jack. That was just as stupid as it was improper. First of all, we weren't even friends. I mean, here we were, at the same school dance, and chances are we wouldn't even speak to each other the entire night. Why on earth would I be crushing on someone I barely even knew...not to mention someone who was so clearly off limits? There was no way I, of all people, was that irrational. This could ruin my family!

Not fade away.

As I continued wrestling my thoughts, the song mercifully ended and Jack disappeared into the crowd. Naively, I thought that the end of the song would mark the end of my struggle. Oh was I wrong. If only it could have only been that simple. Unfortunately, nothing about me and Jack was ever going to be simple, and this was the night I first felt that. Before I could even catch my breath, the band began the next song, and everything changed. What ensued can only be described as a "moment." Call it a moment of truth, a moment of clarity or a moment of my life. Whichever moment you want to christen it, it was a whopper, and it was about to change me forever. The funny thing about moments is that they are rarely splashy. Unlike the movies, they don't come with explosions, violins, or dramatic rain scenes. Moments quietly sneak in when you're not looking, slap you across the face and then leave as quickly as they came. This moment was no different.

The minute I heard the first line I was frozen. *Love me Tender*. Sweet holy Moses! It was Elvis*!* His same gushy rock and roll ballad that gave me the feels in my room earlier that day was echoing through the gymnasium and this time I knew it was talking directly to me. It spoke of love…dreams… fulfillment. I looked up and saw Jack across the room. If I didn't know better, I would have sworn that he was being highlighted by his own personal ray of sunshine. He was so much more vibrant than anyone around him. His smile was brighter, his eyes were bluer and his whole aura glistened with the perfect amount of pixie dust. Standing paralyzed in the middle of the Snowflake Ball, that song and those lyrics grabbed me by the throat and unapologetically threw me to the ground like a rag doll.

Lightbulb. I had feelings for Jack. Dammit. I legitimately had feelings for Jack. I didn't want to. I knew I shouldn't. I knew I couldn't. But I did. Heaven help me. I did, and there was nothing I could do about it. The more those lyrics sunk into my skin, the more I just wanted to be near him. I had no grand illusions of actually talking to him, but I desperately needed to be near him…to breathe him in. Watching him from the shadows, the song taunted me, magnifying my internal struggle and my sudden unimaginable pain. Good God he was perfect. How had I never noticed before? For the first time in my life, I was feeling things I didn't quite understand. I was powerless, and it was sort of intoxicating. Yeah. *Love Me Tender*. And then all at once there was movement among Jack's crowd and I saw Jack walking, almost dancing in my direction. I instinctively held my breath. Maybe I hadn't imagined that moment we shared during his song... maybe he HAD looked at me. A sudden rush of pleasure and panic crashed through my body. This was all so foreign to me and the idea of trying to talk to him from beneath the weight of these new feelings was more than a little intimidating.

Watching Jack walk toward me was simply iconic. God he was beautiful, but more than that, there was something about him that made me feel at home. For as terrifying as this was, there was also something very soothing about being in Jack's presence. Looking back, I think I started holding my breath when he was about ten feet from me. My mind was so busy thinking of something to say that I somehow completely forgot how to breathe. What happened next, I still feel as vividly as if it just happened five minutes ago. As Jack approached my personal space, I congratulated myself on remembering to exhale. Taking another deep breath, I looked up to meet his gaze, but instead of being greeted by Jack's eyes, I saw those eyes looking dead ahead. It was then, from my own personal hell that I watched as Quarterback Jack walked directly past me (and this torch I held for him) and headed out into a night full of possibility. He didn't even acknowledge me.

And so, with Elvis's "Love Me Tender" as his soundtrack, Quarterback Jack and his followers flagrantly cascaded past me, his cluelessness the final dagger to my suffering. Alone on the dancefloor, my entire world was upside down. In that moment, the moment I admitted my feelings for Jack, I discovered levels of hopelessness I never knew existed. The strange thing though, was that hopelessness wasn't all I felt. Backward as it may seem, in that moment I felt so much more than pain. I also felt an odd contentment, a little excitement and lots of things I couldn't yet wrap my head around. Reeling in the middle of the Snowflake Ball, I began to sift through layers of feelings that I never knew could exist. I felt overwhelmed as I struggled to collect myself, but through the pain and the confusion there was one thing that was becoming blatantly clear. If I knew nothing else from this epiphany,

I unquestionably knew this: Jack Riley made me feel alive.

By school on Monday, everything in my world looked different. Suddenly the math wing became the wing with Jack's locker, the music wing became the wing where Jack had band and the library became the place we would both cut through on our way to third period. Maybe it was a coincidence or maybe it was the result of my epiphany, but I swore that Jack suddenly started to notice me. For no good reason, our eyes would meet over the historical fiction section, and I could still feel the weight of his gaze as I passed through Shakespeare. Some days he would throw me a smile as he turned into the band room and never before had we managed to be at the same cafeteria trash can at exactly the same time every day. Although I wasn't ready to admit it, I could feel the fates beginning to manipulate us. I just wasn't exactly clear on why.

For the rest of January, I struggled with my new reality. Echoes of the Snowflake Ball haunted me when I closed my eyes and no amount of denial seemed to make my unspeakable pain and longing go away. For as much as I hated myself for feeling this way, for as ashamed as I was with my inability to stop daydreaming about him, I also began wrestling with a completely foreign level of happiness. Nothing in my life had ever made me feel as good and as bad as Jack did. What on earth was I going to do about this? (And how could I make sure that I never had to hear "Love Me Tender" ever again...?)

February

"The ultimate lesson is learning how to love and be loved unconditionally"
Elisabeth Kubler-Ross

* * *

The Valentine

By February, I had decided to be logical about this. Okay, so I had a crush. Big deal! I had developed and survived a bunch of other crushes and there was no reason to believe that this one would be any different. The fact that this crush was socially forbidden and basically had the ability to obliterate my family was obviously a problem, but my awareness of this had to be a good sign, right? Oh, I was well aware how disastrous this could be, and I wasn't just being dramatic either. In 1957 Buffalo, my pursuing Jack Riley would be nothing short of scandalous. There was no way that his catholic country club parents would allow him to be romantically linked to someone of my stature, not to mention my religion. Sure, they were friendly with my mother as she set their hair and "couldn't live without her" before any large social gathering, but the thought of their hairdresser's daughter being at that gathering with one of their sons, would spell disaster. There was no doubt in my mind that my mother would be blackballed. I had seen it happen. To everyone else, I was one insignificant teenage girl, but to me, well I knew that I was exactly one decision away from being the financial ruin of my family.

So, like I said, I had a crush. Big deal! Everyone says that admitting your vice is half the battle, so I was trusting that this would run its course like the others, and I would be on the road to recovery any day now. Sure, this situation felt a little different, but I just couldn't focus on that. I couldn't think about the way he looked at me or the ridiculous chemistry that seemed to pass between us. I couldn't admit that the fates seemed to be pulling us toward each other or that in some weird way I could feel the universe rooting for us. Nope! A crush was a crush and I had been around the block enough to know that those never ended with a bang, just a whimper.

Ironic then that this story was not playing out the way I was used to. First, the object of my crush was usually fundamentally fictitious.... someone who physically existed but interacted with me only in my mind. We've all had those crushes...the projection kind. You fall for a face, or an image, and spend the rest of your days assuming what that person is actually like. Basically, you find an attractive body and systematically project the perfect personality onto it. You then engage in a completely fictitious romance inside your own mind. I was a pro at this. With the scrutiny of a rocket scientist, I could concoct plans and manipulate situations where my crush and I could be in the same physical place at the same time. It was sort of like making a date that my crush had no idea he was attending. Then, in anticipation of seeing my crush I would plan fictitious talking points and daydream about different fairytale adventures we would have. In the world of the crush, the anticipation was undoubtedly the most rewarding part.

Unfortunately, I had been around this block enough to know that reality was never anything like my fantasies. Instead of being riddled with flirting and fun, in the real world, I knew that those times my crush and I were together would pass by rather uneventfully. My crush would appear, mundane things would happen, and life would move on. In my mind, things with Jack were going to be no different. Let's face it, he was in the starting lineup and I was a certified benchwarmer. This, I believed was my lot in life.

I was destined to worship from afar.

How then, did I find myself here… trapped in the back seat of a Chevy… desperately trying not to touch Jack's leg with mine? Why was I laughing with a car full of kids… and what on earth had Jack just given me? If it looks like a Valentine and reads like a Valentine, what is the square root of panic?

To answer these questions, we need to back up a little. I guess it really all begins with some innocent community service. At Bennett High, you see, completion of twenty hours of community service was mandatory for all football players. You have to understand, these kids were nothing short of gods in our community and the school felt a certain responsibility to make sure they gave back to it. The athletes had the entire year to accumulate their hours and the diligent kids picked away at them every month. After some inconspicuous investigating, I found that Jack Riley was entering our second semester without a single hour logged. Spotting an opportunity, I had spent the last few weeks frantically pulling strings and trying to get Jack an offer at the children's center where I worked. Like I mentioned, it was an organization for kids who had a serious medical condition or had lost a parent or sibling to an illness or the war. I worked after school with a small staff of permanent employees but most people at the center were volunteers. That is how I had started too. Never actually expecting my scheme to work, I nonchalantly mentioned the opening at my center on a day when Jack was within ear shot.

"Excuse me, I couldn't help but overhearing that your center had an opening," Jack said casually.

"Yes," I said quietly, nearly choking on my own surprise. "I can get you the paperwork if you want."

"That would be great. Thanks." Jack said smiling at me in a way I couldn't even process.

The following day I presented Jack with the volunteer paperwork and was dumbfounded when he eagerly accepted it. What on earth was I doing??

Jack began volunteering in the beginning of February and within days had established a rapport with the kids and the staff that was oddly impressive. I hadn't truly expected Jack to accept the position and when he did, I certainly hadn't expected him to excel! You could see on his face that he truly enjoyed working with the children, and it was clear that the kids adored him. Despite his uncanny maturity, Jack had this beautiful childlike quality about him. He was a Peter Pan in a world where other kids were trying way too hard to grow up. He knew it too. Regardless of his popularity, Jack was never pressured to compromise his values or his irresistible innocence. People accepted him for who he was. It was part of what made him so special.

As luck would have it, the Valentine's Day celebration was scheduled to happen during one of Jack's shifts. Knowing this, I quickly volunteered to coordinate the event and went completely overboard in the planning and the purchasing. Everything I bought and everything I organized hinged on the "Jack factor." It's not like I was planning the party FOR him, but I was unabashedly planning the party AROUND him. Each craft and each game was scrutinized under the microscope of "what would Jack do?" and (more importantly) "what would I get out of it?" I planned games that I wanted to see him play and I bought crafts that I wished he would make for me. There was an impressive selection of all his favorite candy and decorations that blatantly confessed the words I would never be able to say. I knew that planning this party was the closest I would ever get to having Jack as my valentine and I unapologetically squeezed every bit of satisfaction out of it that I could.

As party day rolled around, I struggled to keep myself in check. For as excited as I was, I knew how these events ultimately turned out...completely uneventful. I knew that crushes were about anticipation - not reality. My rewards had already been reaped in the day dreaming. I couldn't allow myself any unrealistic expectations about the event itself. Honestly, I should just consider myself lucky if he actually showed up. I wasn't even allowed to be having this crush for heaven's sake. It's not like there was any possibility of actual chemistry today.

When I spotted Jack coming thought the door, he was predictably adorable. He had on a bright blue Superman tee-shirt and "valentine red" Converse high tops. He sure knew how to dress to impress eight-year-olds! The boys immediately smothered him to talk about superheroes and comic books and the girls coyly followed them around with varying degrees of sheep eyes. Taking up my usual role as photographer, I snapped some pictures for the bulletin board and was immediately struck with one of the images. Jack was bending down in a crowd of kids, patiently trying to build a car out of blocks. Next to him squatted a precious little girl named Zoey, whose look absolutely captivated me. The way that little girl was looking up at Jack... like he was some mythical combination of Santa Claus and almighty Jesus... well that look just about summed it all up. Those little eyes said everything I was feeling. It was an innocent look of pure wonder from someone who knew that this moment might be the best one she would ever get.

As craft time approached the tables were covered with endless possibilities for the children to explore their creativity. There were hearts in various colors and sizes, paint, stickers, glue and glitter. There were, of course, samples to copy or the opportunity to create your own masterpiece. Even if my motives for planning the party were questionable, watching the kids enjoy the activities proved extremely rewarding. In fact, I had become particularly connected to a little boy named Troy and I was confidently expecting him to make me a Valentine today. Honestly, Troy was one of the cutest things I had ever seen. He was six and blonde and thought he was my boyfriend (he had asked me to move in with him just last week). If I couldn't have the valentine I secretly wanted, I couldn't deny that having Troy was a solid second.

Disappointment is a complicated emotion. As the day wore on, I tried to remind myself that I hadn't actually expected anything memorable to happen with Jack...and to this point I hadn't been wrong. He was busy, I was busy, and I hadn't even been able to enjoy his mere presence the way I wished. To made matters worse, little Troy had blown me off for a pig tailed seven-year-old named Maggie. It shouldn't have bothered me, but it did. I was probably self-aware enough to know that my disappointment had less to do with Troy and more to do with Jack but being unable to attract a six-year-old was absolutely killing my ego.

Trying to get over myself, I joked with Troy about how he had just thrown me over for another girl. As Troy giggled adorably, Jack suddenly caught my eye. Apparently, he had been watching us and was smiling at me with an impish twinkle that I would come to know very well. While I teased Troy about my perilous lack of valentines and my prospects of becoming like the old maid in our card game, I couldn't shake the feeling that Jack was up to something. I could see him working diligently at the craft table and he kept looking up at me with those eyes that were quickly turning my legs to spaghetti. When I finally wrapped my brain around what I was seeing, I was positively dumbfounded. Jack was walking toward me…and he was not empty handed. Immediately nauseous, I frantically tried to collect myself. I was about to have "a moment" and I refused to ruin it by accidently saying something psychotic. It was at that moment, without a word, that Jack Riley first handed me his heart. Okay, so it was made of paper and very haphazardly glued together, but to me, that heart was everything. There was a red heart, framing a white heart and he had scrawled my name across the middle in blue marker. Fumbling for words I giggled my way through a variety of sentence fragments that ultimately made no sense at all.

"Oh my g- ha ha ha. You're so - ha ha ha. This is - I just - ha ha ha."

It was completely humiliating, and I didn't even care. Jack Freaking Riley had just made me a valentine. If I died in the next fifteen seconds, my life would still have been well spent. Mercifully, Troy walked over to inspect the valentine and the tension was broken.

"Thanks for preserving my honor," I said, smiling at Jack. "This kid's a heartbreaker."

Laughing, Troy opened his hand and offered me some sweaty M&M's.

"You can still have these, Miss Josie," he said adorably.

As soon as I politely declined, Troy turned and ran, leaving Jack and I haplessly alone. What Jack said next, I would remember forever, partly because of what he said and partly because of HOW he said it.

"It's okay, Josie," he proclaimed matter-of-factly. "…I got you."

"I got you," I repeated in my head. Truer words had never met my ears. For better or worse, legally, or illegally, he most certainly had me. Obviously, Jack was just using it as an expression, but to me that sentence was everything, and for a few seconds, I couldn't help letting my thoughts run wild. What if there really was a deeper meaning to his word choice? What if there was a hidden message? What if "I got you" secretly meant "I want to have you?" Snapping out of it, I immediately laughed to myself. I knew that there were a few solid reasons why my thoughts were ridiculous. First, I was just plain old Josie. People like Jack didn't pine over people like me. Second, Jack realistically couldn't "have me". I mean that didn't seem to be stopping my renegade emotions, but there were some pretty big differences between me and Jack... like, I don't know...how about the fact that he had about thirty other girls waiting in line for him and my dance card was embarrassingly free. Yeah, this is preposterous, I thought. Snap out of it!

Jack was simply being nice and that was just fine with me. The last five minutes of my life had already exceeded any pipe dreams I ever had. Let's face it, holding that valentine in my hand made me feel like a storybook princess. Somehow, I had managed to escape the tower, outrun the dragon, and not make an ass of myself doing it. Wow, I thought, so this is what living feels like!

For the remainder of the event, that valentine never left my hand. Sure, I was a little self-conscious about it, but not nearly enough to actually put it down. Hell, I was two seconds from asking to have it surgically sewn to my skin! As I cleaned the tables and said goodbye to the kids, I tried to treat Jack as nonchalantly as before, but I just couldn't. We had experienced a moment – and things felt different. Heck, things WERE different. I couldn't help but notice that Jack was purposely hanging around me, engaging me in banter that somehow rolled out of me effortlessly.

"Do you want to finish these?" Jack playfully asked referencing the six M&M's left at the bottom of the candy dish.

"Only if you let them melt in your hand first!' I said with just the right amount of sass.

For some reason, talking and joking with Jack came as naturally as breathing. Good God, there were brief seconds where I even felt cool.

"Good," Jack said sarcastically, "leftover sweaty M&Ms are my favorite!"

The next thing I knew, Jack was chewing, and I was downright belly laughing at the hilarious faces he was making. God knows what else had been in that bowl and how many kids had actually manhandled that candy.

And then, out of nowhere, something even crazier happened.

"Hey, my friends are picking me up in a few minutes," Jack said smiling. "Do you need a ride?"

In the distance, I was pretty sure I heard the crackling of hell freezing over.

The next thing I knew, I was in the back seat of Sean Harrigan's car with Max Murphy and Jack, who despite being the tallest, graciously offered to sit in the middle. His quirky friend Denny sat in the front, changing radio stations with mind-numbing speed. At that moment, my life was a total fog. One minute I was scrubbing glue off a table and the next I was at Freddy's Donuts with four boys - four POPULAR boys. Yes, sitting in the car, my thoughts were spinning. It's amazing the flurry of thoughts that can run through someone's head at moments like these and I was being peppered with an irrational batch of them. I was consumed with how soft Jack's jacket felt…how good he smelled and how just the prospect of our shoulders touching was sending 10,000 volts of electricity through my body.

"I wonder what his favorite donut is…that's a really big watch…do you think he can hear how hard I am breathing?"

Oh yeah, my brain was on overload, and I was probably only seconds away from complete spontaneous combustion. But wait…there was also something amazing going on here. Regardless of how renegade my thoughts were, my actual behavior was completely under control…so much so that I barely even recognized myself. I couldn't believe it. Being with Jack was like being under the spell of a hypnotist, one who was making me act cooler and much more outgoing than I actually was. Or maybe that valentine had magical abilities. I held it tightly in my hand and looked at it discerningly, seriously trying to figure out whether holding it gave me superpowers.

"You have to try the cream in this donut," Jack said, interrupting my query.

The donut he was eating was some limited-edition maple flavor and Jack seemed to be pretty impressed that he had discovered it. I looked at the half-eaten donut and pondered what my next move was supposed to be. Did he seriously expect me to eat his food? Was I supposed to bite it? Lick it? Buy one of my own? As I glanced from Jack's donut to Jacks' face, I immediately felt my body shift into autopilot. The minute our eyes met, my whole world seemed clearer and the next thing I knew, my finger was in Jack's donut. Wow, this felt so wrong and so right in so many ways. As I licked the cream from my fingertip, Jack smiled with a smug satisfaction. Good God who WAS I right now?

As I climbed out of Sean's car, I felt like a completely different person than the one who climbed in. I had just been on adventure with "the boys" and I had held my own. Sure, I still had this inconvenient crush on Jack, but maybe that was just a steppingstone. Maybe the universe had thrown that crush at me to lead me down a new path...one I never would have explored otherwise. Maybe that crush was going to help me crawl out of my shell and find my tribe. Oh hell, I could figure that out later. Right then I just wanted to happy dance around my bedroom with Jack's valentine and figure out how to never let this feeling go!

In the days following our encounter, I really struggled with my new reality. Regardless of my insecurities, I could feel that I was entering unmarked territory and wrapping my head around the ramifications was going to take some effort. For starters, realizing that I might really be able to manipulate this bizarre plot was a bit daunting. My Valentine's party hadn't just fulfilled my fantasies; it had blown the roof off of them. I had endured a lot of crushes and dreamed up a lot of cockamamie schemes, but I wasn't used to being successful with them...well...not for myself anyway. I was sort of a pro at helping others get what they wanted, but when it came to me, I was usually content to watch life from the shadows. I always believed that I was someone who was built to live vicariously through others. Not the best plan, I concede, but it had gotten me this far. It was safe, it was predictable, and it was easy.

Why ~ oh why ~ then, was this so different?? Why was Jack responding to me and more importantly, who the heck was I when he was around? Being with Jack was changing me. I was feeling things (no, not just THOSE things), things like confidence, like hope! Still, I knew that being with Jack was impossible. No, not just impossible. It was outrageous, ridiculous, and horribly misguided! Beyond the obvious obstacles, guys like Jack simply did not develop feelings for girls like me. Or did they...?

Always Lick the Frosting

I knew that Jack's community service hours were going to be fulfilled by the end of the month, so I spent the next few weeks manipulating the center's schedule and cherishing every afternoon we got to spend together. While working with the kids, we seemed to be developing a genuine friendship and we had even exchanged phone numbers one night so we could plan out sharing rides. Unlike most boys, I found talking to Jack on the phone remarkably easy and our ride conversations usually lasted much longer than I ever anticipated. I tried really hard not to analyze why – why it was so easy and why it was sooo addicting. All I knew was that talking to Jack was my happy place, if for no other reason than the mere sound of his voice. It didn't matter if he was speaking or singing, I had finally accepted that the power Jack's voice had over me was crippling. Even over the phone, the electricity of that voice lit me up so brightly that I practically needed sunglasses. Whether Jack was addressing one person or twenty, it was the kind of voice that made you feel as if he was whispering directly into your ear, and you couldn't help but writhe beneath the palpitations it would cause. Jack's voice had so many dimensions and each layer of it could wrap me up like a blanket. Most of the time, listening to Jack was like watching butter slowly melt over a hot biscuit. His voice was smooth and soft and if I closed my eyes, I could almost feel his words pour over me and trickle down the back of my neck. Sometimes, especially when he was speaking in public, Jack's voice would sound deeper…more textured. And let me tell you, the lower it got, the more electricity it had. Even Jack knew he could make sparks fly anytime he wanted to. Each of these things, however, paled in comparison to one vocal nuance that had the physical ability to leave me helpless. It only happened occasionally and was a trick Quarterback Jack used to try and draw defenses off the line of scrimmage. I know there will be no way for my words to give it justice, so I all I will say is that Jack could make his voice growl with such intoxicating raspiness that shivers would travel down every inch of my spine. You might think I'm exaggerating, but I assure you I am not. The pure animalistic sound of Jack's snarl did things to my constitution that I didn't even try to understand. All I knew was that even across a football field, that sound had the power to send my entire body into the most inappropriate of convulsions, and it was the *best... freaking ... thing... ever.*

As far as the center was concerned, our compatibility as co-workers usually landed us the same assignments and as luck would have it, today's assignment was an especially fun one. It was one of the younger camper's birthdays and the family had sent cupcakes, party games and the child's favorite record to play. Jack and I were left in charge of chaperoning the party and maintaining order amongst this notoriously raucous group of kids. Without a doubt, this was one of those days where I knew I needed to be on my best behavior. This particular group of kids was going to be challenging enough and I couldn't let my irrational feelings for Jack get in my way.

"No goo-goo eyes, no butterflies, no speaking in nonsense," I told myself into the mirror.

I had to be on my game today. I knew I couldn't let him get to me. Knowing and achieving, however, are painfully different things!

Fifteen minutes into the party and I was feeling perfectly in control. Sure, Jack was wearing this cute black tee-shirt with cartoon music notes on the front and yes, I found his eagerness to please the kids with his wardrobe adorable, but I was pleasantly surprised with my ability to keep my gushing to a minimum. Thirty minutes into the party and the kids were on task and seemed pretty happy with the record our birthday boy had brought. Now, in anyone else's world, the category of children's music would have been a safe subject. The album in question was a pure and simple sing-along with a talking sunshine and cuddly farm animals on the jacket. I would come to learn, however, that I was not just "anyone" and my world had already begun to spin differently than everyone else's. As Jack seemed to be focusing on crowd control, I danced along to the record but paid little attention to what they were actually singing about ... something to do with morning chores. Truthfully, most of my mind was still preoccupied with the mere presence of Jack in this room. Suddenly, as the children on the recording sang about milking cows and some other nonsense, my body stiffened. Without looking, I instinctively knew that Jack had snuck up and was standing painfully close behind me. It was something he had done a few times before and I had already learned to recognize the intangible feeling that always came with it.

"Give me your perfect milk, perfect milk," the cartoon animals sang.

Before I could turn my head, Jack's voice, an octave lower and dripping with a smug satisfaction, whispered in my ear,

"What on earth are those animals doing? The sexual innuendo here is too much for me."

The combination of emotions that filled my body in that moment physically dragged me to the ground. Laughing hysterically, I found myself doubled over at Jack's feet, my face buried in my hands.

"How on earth could he say that to me?" I thought. "Did he not know what those words would do to me?"

I felt like my crush was so obvious that even the densest of boys would be able to see it. I knew that Jack was talking about the song lyrics, but he might have well been talking about me, about us. Every move I made was generated by my crush and my impossible desires. I was one big bucket of sexual innuendo. God, Jack was either magnificently clueless or the purest evil genius of them all. How on earth did he expect me to carry on after a moment like that? Between his breath in my ear, the sweet butter of his voice and the flirty undertones of his message, I was pudding. As I listened to the rest of that song – painfully aware of this new interpretation – my head was spinning. While the "outer me" was plagued with the giggles (come on… they kept saying "udders"), the "inner me" fought my demon with whatever strength I had left. All the while, there he was, glued to my side; complacently enjoying the breakdown he had created.

Sixty minutes into the party and my facade was crumbling. I was desperately trying to maintain control of the masses, but my every thought was preoccupied with questions about Jack.

"How had we gotten to this place? What exactly did he mean by sexual innuendo? When had we crossed the bridge where off color jokes were okay? Why, dear God did I feel like he was actually flirting with me?"

As I emerged from my fog, I looked around the room and realized just how out of control things had become. Not only were the kids no longer sitting at the tables eating cupcakes, they were chaotically running about the room smashing those cupcakes into each other's faces. It was complete pandemonium. Good grief! How long had I been out of it? Crap – this was embarrassing. Frantically canvasing the room for Jack, hoping that he would help me regain control of this full-on food fight, I couldn't help but laugh at what I saw. First, I saw Jack, playfully running in circles waving his arms in the air. Behind him was chronically shy Zoey, chasing him with a vanilla frosted cupcake square in the palm of her hand. I knew that I should stop it, but something inside me couldn't help but root for Zoey. On a typical day, Zoey was more prone to sit and watch the action than she was to engage in it. Zoey also happened to have a tremendous crush on Jack. Yeah.... sound like anyone you know? Seeing Zoey let go of her inhibitions and literally chase her dreams, well it filled me with an insurmountable amount of hope. There was something magical about Jack, something that made even the most insecure of hearts feel powerful. There was no way I could squash that.

Knowing that I was in over my head, I probably should have resorted to the "duck and cover" until the fight was over. The kids were clearly past the point of no return, and I needed to make sure that my inhibitions weren't as well. I had barely recovered from our last indiscretion, and I was determined to have more self-control from here on out. I couldn't let him get to me. My feelings for Jack were wrong and I needed to put them in their place once and for all. Yes, the minute that cake got smeared on Jack's face I should have walked away. I should have headed to the sink, grabbed a towel, and nonchalantly handed it to him. Instead, I stood there, looking at Jack, looking at the frosting, and finding myself unable to move.

"Get a towel" I told myself, all the while eyeing the cupcake remnants stuck to his face.

In a very unhelpful manner, Jack just looked at me, shaking his head and laughing. Being caught in his gaze was paralyzing. There was something in the way he looked at me that turned reason upside-down...something in his eyes that cut clean through me and melted me from the inside out. Not all of the time...and not even on purpose...but every so often and always with the same breathless result. It's not that they were prettier than most...bluer than average or bigger than usual. The sum of the parts was ordinary - but what radiated from them was without measure. There was so much going on in that one look...so much that was said without a single word. I wondered if he knew what he was doing...if he knew how I couldn't breathe...couldn't focus...couldn't escape the electricity careening through every inch of my body. Jeepers! His eyes were like kryptonite...if kryptonite was blue and full of calculated mischief. Kryptonite... and I loved every minute of it.

Paralyzed in those eyes, I knew there was no way I was walking away and eventually that frosting sitting on Jack's cheek turned out to be more than I was able to resist. I told myself that I was just being helpful...almost maternal. In a way, I could even have made the argument that I was just doing my job. The instant my finger brushed his cheek I knew I was in over my head - even days later I could recall the entire incident with absolute clarity. I was instantly mesmerized with the feel of his face. The way his stubble felt beneath my finger seemed to sum up our struggle in a way no words ever could. Beneath the stubble, you see, I felt the baby-like softness of his skin... hidden there behind the shadow...just waiting for me to discover it. As my index finger glided across his face he smiled at me – again melting me from the inside out. He smiled at me with the same intoxicating undertone of our last encounter...as if his smile again whispered, "The sexual innuendo here is too much for me."

I could tell from the volcano-like hot flash that I had crossed the line. I then proceeded to enjoy it for a few seconds more than socially acceptable before I stepped back. To this day, I can still feel the internal struggle as I fought ~ and resisted ~ the urge to lick that frosting from my finger. Out of the corner of my eye I could see Jack deliciously licking his own frosting filled fingers. I died a little inside.

After the party, I tried my best to keep my distance from Jack, but as we cleaned up, things just continued to get weirder. Out of nowhere Jack suddenly launched into a detailed explanation of how he wanted to grow his hair longer so he could ducktail it again. He then meticulously described his haircut from a few months ago and asked me if I remembered it. Remembered it?? There was an entire chapter of my diary dedicated to it. That one magical curl of hair that would dangle on his forehead…ugh… . remember it? Are you kidding me??? Good God the way he could make me squirm was embarrassing. From there Jack launched into a series of uncomfortable topics about his appearance, including, but not limited to: his eyes, his lips and his butt (yes, you heard me, his butt). He talked about how he had the Riley eyes and how he could slowly see himself looking like his father. He talked about his eyes' unique blue color and how he felt they were too close to his nose. Now if there was anything on this planet I considered myself an expert on, it was Jack's eyes, and before I knew it I was wholeheartedly participating in the conversation. Although my brain was begging me to shut up (no normal person should know this much about someone else's eyes) I still heard myself commenting on their color and how it wasn't necessarily the way they looked that made them special, it what he did with them. Oh my God. I just referenced what he "did with them". Was I insane? I must sound like the stalker that I truly am.

Unfortunately, Jack seemed to know exactly what I was talking about and proceeded to use those kryptonite eyes to give me a look that turned my entire body to pudding.

"I feel like I have just given you a superpower," I joked, knowing I was in way over my head.

"Oh YEAH you did," he replied winking at me.

"Oh holy hell," I panicked, "what have I done?"

That night I couldn't seem to shake the afterglow of our encounter. I was starting to realize that being with Jack usually had this glorious, albeit peculiar side effect and I was fantastically lost in it. I couldn't help but notice that in the hours and days after one of our adventures I was always filled with the most amazing feelings of fulfillment and simplicity. I slept with a smile on my face and woke to a world that seemed just a little brighter and friendlier than the day before. Every breath I took carried a tingling contentment throughout my body, my skin seemed more radiant and even my stomach was honest to God flatter. Weird but true. Yes, the afterglow was a powerful and unexpected phenomenon and in addition to how much I enjoyed it, I immediately knew that it needed to be respected.

Despite the afterglow, I couldn't help but wonder if Jack tortured me on purpose. Obviously, the taboo of our issue prevented either of us from talking about it, so in all reality, I would never really know. He liked to push my buttons – there was no doubt about that. The incentive behind it, however, was the mystery. The theory of cluelessness is a strong one…he was a GUY after all. If he was oblivious to my feelings, he could likewise be oblivious to how his behavior was coming across. Maybe, the fact that our affair would be so wrong, so impossible, it actually made everything easy for him. He could essentially behave however he wanted and not worry about it being misinterpreted – because no other interpretation would be morally allowed. It was just harmless, innocent fun. If it was so innocent though, how come it never felt that way? This leads to the theory of evil genius. If someone pretends to be clueless, no one ever suspects their ulterior motives. One could, theoretically, chase something they shouldn't with their whole heart, escaping each incident just before things got real, and never acknowledge or reveal their true motives. Maybe Jack was acutely aware of our issue… maybe he was so crazy for me that he taunted his reality and fed that demon on purpose. Ugh. Maybe I just wished that to be true. Regardless of his intentions, Jack's behavior toward me was an intoxicating blend of desire and torture and I think it was the first time in my life that I truly understood what it meant to *feel*. Yes, this whole situation was a rollercoaster, but more importantly, it was an awakening. For better or worse, no one on this planet could make me feel as completely alive - and as completely hopeless - as Jack could.

March

"I was in the middle before I knew that I had begun"

Jane Austen

* * *

The End or Just the Beginning

By March, Jack had completed his community service and spent his after-school hours in the school weight room preparing for baseball season. Jack was the best natural athlete in Buffalo, maybe the whole state, and for as long as he could remember his training always had to take priority. Football was his main sport, but he ran indoor track to stay in shape during the winters and excelled at baseball in the spring. Being a college athlete was a given, the only mystery was what school and what sport he would choose. It was no secret that football was his first love, but those baseball scholarships were pretty compelling. Needless to say, everyone in town liked to speculate about what Jack would choose. Given his size, he probably had a much better chance of playing professional baseball than he did of being a professional quarterback and every table in the corner diner seemed to have an opinion about what he should do. As for me, I was a football girl through and through and knew much more about the game than was considered proper for a girl in those times. Plus, this was nine years before the birth of the Buffalo Bills, so despite being unladylike, it wasn't even a popular local pastime. Nevertheless, I was a big NY Giants fan (they had just won the NFL Championship in December) and I personally would have liked nothing more than to see Jack choose football and give me the pleasure of following his career. I knew our opinions and our logic were irrelevant though. As I would come to learn time and time again, no matter what the obstacles, Jack Riley would always follow his heart.

As far as Jack and I were concerned, we started the month of March as something resembling friends. I honestly couldn't wrap my head around how it happened, but at some point last month Jack and I had bonded. Somehow, despite all the reasons we shouldn't have, Jack and I had become "work friends" and it was starting to spread well beyond the safety of the community center. Jack had started talking to me in school and had even tried to include Rosie and me in a lunchtime game of ping-pong. Even though our ride sharing days were over, Jack would still occasionally call me to commiserate about homework and anything else that was on his mind. I knew it was wrong but talking to Jack was downright addicting. What we were talking about was never the issue. What I loved was the bond I could feel as we spoke. At my core, I loved words and I quickly discovered that I loved the way that Jack used them. There was something oddly poetic about Jack and the things he said made me feel special. Whether we were passing notes in class or gossiping on the phone, our verbal connection was impossibly strong – and it quickly managed to fuel the relationship that was developing between us.

Although I should have found all of this surreal, I actually found it easy. Things between Jack and I were always so natural and being with him was absolutely effortless. I knew it wasn't the crowd where I belonged, and my self-confidence still had trouble wrapping my head around why anyone would want me there, but I had been given a taste of a new life, and I hadn't screwed it up!! Sure, I still had a crazy crush on Jack, but I was starting to realize that casually being his friend was pretty fulfilling all on its own.

Despite my newfound poise, the end of Jack's community service was weighing on me. Aside from desperately missing him every time I was at the center, I also feared all the changes that come with distance. Quite simply, I feared that the conclusion of Jack's volunteer hours would mark the conclusion of our implausible friendship. Let's face it, if I was being logical, I knew that our friendship made no sense, and our relationship had no future. If I listened to logic, I would take a deep breath, sneak one last look at our adventures, and prepare for the end of this amazing ride. Yeah. I knew how this should play out. We would remain cordial, drift apart and eventually become "someone that I used to know." The smiles in the hall and the late-night phone calls would become fewer and farther between... until they finally stopped all together. Eventually, this magical month with Jack would get packed away with my other treasures, and someday I would question whether it truly happened at all. Wow. Logic was brutal.

For as convincing as logic was, I had to admit that if I was listening to my heart, I would hear a completely different story. I don't know if it can be classified as confidence, but this past month with Jack had given me something. Now, at first, this was really hard for me to admit. I had been programmed to believe in certain boundaries and my natural disposition was to blend in whenever possible. I had never dared to dream of fitting in with people like Jack and I certainly never entertained thoughts of forbidden crushes and eminent disaster. But even in the face of all that, every day, every hour with Jack had begun to give me a unique perspective. This ride with Jack was unlike anything I had ever been on, and the more denial failed me, the more I was forced to face some things and to believe in some things. Sure, it was terrifying to admit, but denying it was becoming harder and harder. No matter how much I tried to squash it, logic was being challenged every day and my defenses were wearing down. My heart...heck my whole being was telling me to admit the truth, to see the signs. Yes, if I was listening to my heart, it would tell me that there was something special with this boy, something more powerful than logic. Jack and I had a connection, like we were tied to opposite ends of an invisible string. Lately, so much of our lives seemed to be scripted to keep us together and the chance meetings and odd coincidences were all starting to pile up. Every day, without warning, the universe seemed to pull on that string and yank us closer to each other. Even when we weren't together, I could feel it. I could feel the string and know he was on the other end of it. It was as weird as it was wonderful. I just didn't know if he could feel it too.

The Girlfriend Debacle

It echoed down the hallway, "Breaking News everyone: Jack Riley has a girlfriend!"

In an instant I was pathologically devastated. The idea of Jack with an actual girlfriend was probably one of the most painful thoughts in my universe. I had heard the news from Monica Peabody just before lunch and I spent the entire period pitifully staring at the floor. Of course, I knew that I had to expect this. It's not like we could ever have a future together and, as his friend, I cared about him too much to wish him a life of loneliness and celibacy. At least that is what the rational part of my brain was trying to tell me. On the other hand, the irrational - and arguably more dominant part of my brain, felt like I was on the Titanic. Sure, the girl went to the all-female Nardin Academy and, logically, I knew the chances of ever having to see Jack with her were pretty slim. None of that was making me feel any better though. Just knowing of that girl's existence was slowly killing me. I was numb. I knew I had no right to be, but I was unbearably jealous and hearing the news from someone else really stung me. Obviously, I knew that Jack didn't owe me an explanation, and I was more than a little thankful that he didn't have to see the look on my face as the news hit me. Still, the fact that he hadn't cared enough to break it to me personally was a little disheartening. For some reason, I had expected better.

Despite my expectations and my devastation, what actually transpired over the course of this six-week relationship was rather unexpected. Not only did the presence of this girlfriend not kill me, it actually gave me confidence in this invisible bond that was developing between us. Of course this sounds ridiculous, but it was absolutely, certifiably true – and it all began at a 125th Anniversary event.

Ironically, the first time I laid eyes on "the girlfriend," I wasn't even sure if it was actually her. Jack and I had both made the trek to the Erie County

Fairground for one of several ancillary 125th Anniversary events, but Jack had gone with his crowd, and I had arrived with mine. Although I had heard through the grapevine that Jack was bringing a date to this festival, Jack himself never made any mention of it to me. Knowing how difficult it would be to see him with his girlfriend, there may have been a millisecond where I considered not going, but in the end my curiosity was much greater than my fear. To me, this sort of felt like passing a gruesome car accident and I intended to rubberneck my way through the whole festival if necessary.

Luckily, seeing his car in the parking lot alerted me that Jack had already arrived and, upon entering the events arena, I spotted him a good fifteen minutes before I allowed him to notice me. As I observed him from a distance (yes - that will be our socially acceptable euphemism for "stalked") I noticed an unfamiliar girl that literally followed him from about three paces behind. It was truly impossible to tell if this girl was the girlfriend or just another one from the squad. Jack and this girl were always in the same place but never in any circumstance that would seem "couple-ish." Deductive reasoning pointed to this girl being the girlfriend. She was the only person I didn't recognize. In true cat-fight fashion, I tried to form an opinion of the girlfriend, but I was never able to spot much more than her back. Even from this brief exposure, I was not impressed. What's more, Jack didn't seem to be either. I was beginning to know Jack pretty well and he didn't seem to have the same flair around this girl that he did with me. Or maybe I was just hoping that to be true.

Unable to gracefully hide any longer, I took a deep breath and stepped out of the shadows. Jack spotted me in the crowd almost instantly, and was instinctively pulled in my direction, as if he too was following our invisible string. Yes, in movie-like slow motion, Jack strolled toward me with his arms outstretched. Impulsively I threw my arms in the air and grabbed him around the neck. To be honest, we didn't really have one of those relationships where hugging was a thing, but today, that didn't seem to matter. As my feet were lifted off the floor, I felt as if I had simply floated off the ground. If I'm being honest, Jack's greeting was pretty overboard. He greeted me with the enthusiasm usually reserved for people who have surprised you or people you haven't seen in ages. Neither of those were the case here, but I wasn't complaining. I was hugging Jack Riley. You heard me…HUGGING!! Returning me to the floor, Jack immediately engaged in the latest school gossip as well as his thoughts on the festival. What Jack was talking about wasn't really the issue here. I was much more enamored with what Jack WASN'T talking about. The longer we spoke, and the longer Jack made no mention of the girlfriend, I began to truly doubt whether that was actually her. Even after returning to his friends, Jack continued to make eye contact with me from across the crowded arena.

Noticing, Rosie tried to gather some facts about the situation,

"So, what's up with Jack today? Did he need something from you? I didn't realize you two had gotten that friendly."

Trying to be nonchalant, I did my best to brush Rosie off, even though we all know I wanted to yell,

"I know right? Did you see how he HUGGED ME?"

Instead, I kept it together and tried to sound uninterested,

"No, he was just saying hi."

Still not moving on, and perhaps using this as an opportunity to bring me back to reality, Rosie continued,

"So did he offer to introduce you to his girlfriend?"

Ugh. My heart sank. Apparently, that was really her.

"No," I answered with equal parts annoyance and confusion, "he never mentioned her."

Even with my fears being confirmed, I was pleased to notice that I was not feeling the jealously I had expected. I guess it was because - regardless of who she was - nothing about the situation actually warranted my jealousy. I mean we all know that I creepily stared at them, but the more I watched, the more I noticed a lack of basic human interaction between Jack and this girl. There was no handholding, hugging or unnecessary touching; she also continued to walk three paces behind him. And the next thing I knew, the girlfriend bizarrely went home alone after an hour, leaving the rest of their group behind. It was all very…well…okay, I'll say it - it was *weird.*

If we were to assign a point in this story where the affair between Jack and I truly began, this might have to be it. As unbelievable as it seems, the girlfriend probably wasn't even out of the parking lot when I spotted Jack walking toward me. Trapped underneath flashbacks of the Winter Ball, I fully expected Jack to walk right past me, gracefully on his way to something better. Instead, I saw him briefly detour to the snack stand and then continue straight to me, bringing a pack of M&M's and two pieces of pizza. Although I didn't appreciate the significance at the time, those M&M's Jack was holding were about to become our "thing," and I still can't see a package of them without smiling. Even though I didn't quite grasp it at the time, what Jack presented me at that moment was more than just lunch. What Jack extended to me was a peace offering and a silent confirmation of my place in his life. While the pizza may have been nothing more than a sweet gesture from a hungry boy, those M&Ms were not an arbitrary choice and we both knew it. They were a message.... a reminder of the center, our kids and the Valentine's party where Jack had first given me his heart. Without a word, he handed me one of the plates and sat down in the seat next to me. The look in his eyes instantly made me feel at ease and I suddenly didn't care who saw, what they thought or where else I should be.

Over the course of the next forty-five minutes Jack and I sat side by side at that table and felt magic happen. The longer we sat, the more our respective worlds seemed to fade away and we talked, laughed, and dreamt about the future with unparalleled ease. I told him secrets that I would never dream to tell most people and he shared things that normal guys just don't talk about. There was an honesty and a comfort level between us that was impossible to describe. Quite simply...we just...fit! Looking back, it was here with Jack...lost inside the masses... that I first experienced my sweet spot. It was a phenomenon I would only find a few times in my life and anyone lucky enough to have found theirs will know exactly how I felt.

The sweet spot is a truly mythical phenomenon. The easiest way to describe it might be like an emotional narrowing of a spotlight. What starts out as a full and bright stage suddenly shrinks down to a single beam of light... highlighting nothing but the two of you. And oh.... there is nothing like those times when it is just the two of you. Don't get me wrong, you might be in the middle of a crowd, but it is clearly "just the two of you". You feel the world fade away and you snuggle into the comfort of your unspoken connection. It's not about where you are, what he says or even the way he looks at you (okay…maybe it's about that a little). Fundamentally it's about the way that you feel. It's the synchronicity between you and the way you say everything without saying anything at all. Psychologists call it "flow", athletes call it "the zone" and Pacey Witter might categorize it as a kind of "Pinter Moment". Regardless of the terminology, you know the sweet spot is your favorite place to be.

Lost in the sweet spot, Jack and I reached a new understanding that afternoon. Not once in those forty-five minutes was there a mention of the girlfriend and her mere existence somehow seemed irrelevant. Jack seamlessly moved past the fact that he never introduced us and there was a silent understanding that those two worlds should just never mix. Whatever this was that was developing between us was amazingly drama free. We seemed to understand each other on some visceral level and, right or wrong, we both knew that there was an undeniable comfort in that. That afternoon we began to realize that this invisible string that connected us was no illusion. Although we never spoke of it, we were starting to realize that we didn't need to. I could feel that I wasn't in this alone. I could see the way that Jack looked at me and I was starting to hear the words behind the ones he was saying. This was not just some horrible lapse in my judgement. This was a living breathing entity. That didn't make it right of course…but it did make it real.

As far as the girlfriend was concerned, nothing much changed over the next six weeks. When it was just me and Jack, the girlfriend was never discussed and if we found ourselves in the same venue, the girlfriend was outright ignored. Regardless of my natural insecurities, I never felt threatened by the girlfriend, and I almost felt bad for her. When Jack ultimately broke up with the girlfriend, he never even mentioned it…just like he had never mentioned when they started dating, never introduced her and never talked about the relationship's existence. I often wondered if the girlfriend was perceptive enough to wonder about me. Obviously that innocent girl, the one who mistakenly believed that she had hit the jackpot, was just another victim of this impossible situation. Let's not forget that. This was an undeniably impossible situation. Even if those feelings were mutual…which I was really starting to think they could be… they were still forbidden. Regardless of the flowers by the sidewalk, this road was a dead end. Leaving the darkness of denial didn't change that.

STAGE II - ANGER

With the forbidden crush, anger is a very powerful and very dangerous stage. Since your relationship now balances on the boundaries between forbidden, hidden and non-existent, your anger can fluctuate anywhere between self-pity and cannibalistic fury. To be honest, on some days it can be virtually impossible to figure out where your anger is even directed. In the beginning, you are most likely angry with yourself. Once the supreme denial and repression of your feelings has proven unsuccessful you are left with the knowledge that there must be something wrong with you. WHAT on earth do you think you're doing? Has the rational part of your brain suddenly shut off? WHY would you choose to have these feelings that will only end in heartbreak? DON'T you know how many rules you are breaking and how many lives you could be wrecking? Good God - WHY can't you seem to get past this? Screw that devil on your shoulder.

After an appropriate amount of time beating yourself up, you finally decide to admit the truth. Although you are by no means innocent in this whole debacle, let's put the blame where it really belongs - the universe. That's right - if you are being honest, you are primarily angry with the forces that keep you apart. In fact, you find yourself positively indignant that the fates could take something this obvious... this powerful... and screw it up so badly. You are so unequivocally certain that you were meant to be together that you find yourself absolutely baffled that the universe got it wrong. You feel betrayed by everything from your genetics to your birth date and you can't seem to forgive anyone who had anything to do with your life script. This storyline is crap. Screw your place in the space/time continuum.

As if that isn't enough, you can also manage to be angry with everyday life. You find yourself irrationally perturbed with anyone or anything that is allowed to enjoy him in ways that you can't. You are keenly aware that there are places you would be if you were the girlfriend or events you would be invited to if you were a couple. The mere knowledge of these things is outright torture. Just about anything that takes place without you is the immediate subject of your disdain. The simple fact that YOU are not present makes the event completely unsuitable for him and your irrational jealously of anyone present is crippling. It might have been the most innocent encounter in the world, but heaven help a naive fangirl who has a picture taken with his arm around her. The fact that they could be total strangers is irrelevant to you. She is TOUCHING HIM - and you want to rip her skin off. Screw the people who are with him when you aren't.

And then, on the darkest of days, you might even find yourself angry with him! Damn him for making you feel this way and curse him for keeping you on this invisible string. Why does he continue to make your heart skip, your logic freeze, and your insides turn to mush? What the hell is with his mixed messages and his tint of mischief smile? Why does he enjoy flirting with you and what would make him think that was okay? Can't he see that you are sinking? He should be bailing water from this boat not sailing out further. Why would he do this to you? Screw him and his blue eyes (which of course is the problem because BOY YOU WOULD REALLY LIKE TO!!)

April

"Between the idea and the reality, between the motion and the act, falls the shadow"
T.S. Eliot

* * *

The "Death Song" Incident

On April 1, 1957, pretty much every Buffalo girl under thirty was in a flutter. The day we had waited for since January had finally arrived and, let me tell you, there was an energy in the air like none I had ever felt. Elvis Presley – the King of Rock and Roll – had arrived in Buffalo and the very air we breathed seemed different. I had woken up before dawn and could hardly believe that in a little over twelve hours, I would be one of forty thousand screaming fans witnessing history at Memorial Auditorium. As you can imagine, when tickets went on sale in February, the pandemonium was fierce, and the life-changing event had sold out in a matter of minutes. I wasn't even close to getting to the front of the line. Having already mourned my missed opportunity, imagine my surprise last week when I received a sobbing phone call from Rosie. Immediately assuming someone must have died, I was the one who nearly suffered cardiac arrest when she blurted out that her dad had won some lottery at the Country Club and gifted us with floor seats to Elvis! I literally almost passed out.

The next thing I knew it was the morning of the concert and I was both ecstatic and a little nervous. Although things with Jack were way better than they were three months ago, nothing ever seemed to quell the firestorm I still felt every time "Love Me Tender" met my ears. Music, you see, was a very powerful trigger for me, and this song…well this song just felt like pain. For as long as I live, I know that this song will take me back to the exact moment when I knew two things…Jack was prefect…and I would forever want what I couldn't have. Standing in that gym, virtually invisible, is a memory that plays in my head in slow motion, filling me with a magical blend of innocence and hopelessness. Until that moment, I didn't know that I could feel that much love and that much pain in the same instant; even all these years later, that song still possesses the physical ability to rip my heart out. Among my friends, my avoidance of this song was legendary…although not one knew the real reason why. Truthfully, all my friends would get a pretty big laugh out of the way I would dive to change the station whenever it came on. Not one understood the baggage the song carried or the depth of the pain it represented. How could they? To them, it was just a song I psychotically didn't like.

Shaking off my fears, I concentrated on enjoying every inch of this life-altering event. Listening to Elvis records as we got dressed for the concert, Rosie and I danced and sang with an excitement that only comes a few times in one's life. In those carefree moments with Rosie, I could never have imagined what my night would have in store, or that anyone on the planet was actually capable of outshining the King!

Even though Elvis didn't perform until 8:30pm, security started letting people into The Aud two hours early. I still laugh when I think about the look of amazement on the guards' faces. Just breathing the same air as Elvis was making some girls downright hysterical and even from the parking lot, the screams were so ear piercing that you would have thought it was a crime scene. Walking into the venue I felt so honored to be following the velvet ropes to the floor seats. The other girls from my neighborhood were up in "The Oranges" (that's what we called the sky-high balcony with the orange seats), but, thanks to the Fraziers, I was on the floor with the VIPs. From my prestigious spot in history, I squinted at the tiny specs up in The Oranges and tried to find some familiar faces, but I had yet to find any.

After what felt like an eternity, the musicians started to tune. As everyone jumped from their seats in anticipation, I looked to the right of the stage and practically stopped in midair. As hot flashes consumed my entire body, I laughed to myself. While the other 39,999 people in that arena had their eyes glued to the stage awaiting their first glimpse of Elvis, I had just realized that standing a few rows in front of me - tethered to our invisible string - was Jack. It was almost comical. These days our invisible string never seemed to let me down. It was literally the third time I had run into him this week. I mean, Buffalo wasn't huge, but it wasn't THAT small. As the pre-show music began, Jack spotted me too. He looked at me and sort of shrugged his shoulders, like he was also a little baffled by our ability to bump into each other. Studying him from across the rows I was amazed at how far we had come. Although I was still certain that my feelings for him were vastly more intense than his regard for me, I was pretty certain that, if circumstances had been different, I would at least be actively pursuing him. My feelings were real. So why did I have to live in a world where the rest was forbidden?

As the warm-up act began to play, everyone on the floor had already abandoned their seats and formed a frantic mob in front of the stage. In the midst of the madness, I spotted Jack pushing toward me though the crowd, his friends trailing along behind him. Before I knew it, some other friends had found us and we were just one big group, getting ready for the biggest show of our lives. It made me so happy to see our friends getting along. It was like a silent validation that what we were feeling wasn't all that sinister. The next thing I knew, my insides were thrown about my body by the most earth-shaking roar I have ever heard. Looking up, blinded by gold and glitter, I tried to focus my eyes on the icon in front of me. At long last it was Elvis, and the arena was deafening. Dripping with swagger, The King sported a metallic gold and leather rhinestone studded jacket, black pants, and gold shoes with rhinestones on the tassels. His hair was perfectly duck-tailed, and his quivering lip was enough to make anyone gasp for air. To complete the ensemble, his acoustic guitar, adorned with flowers and the simple moniker "Elvis," was draped across his electric body. Looking out at the crowd, Elvis smiled, gyrated those famous hips and the crowd exploded in near hysteria. He tried to calm the screaming, but it was no use. Buffalo was in a frenzy, and he was just going to have to play through it.

I would like to tell you the songs that Elvis played that night and the reaction I had to each and every one of them. As usual, however, the minute Jack and I were around each other, the rest of the world seemed to fade away. Yes, I was living through history, but I simply remained preoccupied with how inexplicably happy being with Jack made me. Continuing to stand together, we listened to every song, playfully mocking everything from the girls who couldn't stop crying to the grown men who seemed a little too enthusiastic about being at an Elvis concert with a bunch of teenagers. Things between us were always so easy. Jack knew that if he kept whispering alternate lyrics in my ear, I was bound to lose it, and I knew that Jack could never resist tempting that childish part of me. We were like puzzle pieces from two different boxes that somehow fit together perfectly. I couldn't explain it, but oh did I trust in it. Undeniably content with his company, I was, at that exact moment in time, uncommonly carefree. Little did I know that things were about to take an unexpected and unfortunate turn.

In hindsight, I should have been preparing for this moment. Unfortunately, being with Jack had made me so happy that I completely forgot about the potential for musical disaster. As the next song began, it only took one unmistakable strum of the guitar before I felt indescribable panic well up inside of me. The moment hit me like a bolt of lightning. "Oh crap," I thought. "This is not going to end well." Also recognizing the iconic notes, Rosie turned to me with raucous laughter and pointed at the stage. Unapologetically, "Love Me Tender," my infamous death song was bleeding from Elvis' soul, and I felt like everyone in Memorial Auditorium was laughing at me. My behavior was predictably psychotic, and I couldn't seem to stop it. I was completely irrational where this song was concerned. Poor Jack looked as if he had no idea what was going on, but mischievous Rosie had no trouble whispering something that must have explained it. For a second,

I panicked that Jack would figure it out. That he would somehow remember the look on my face as he passed me at the Winter Ball and suddenly realize this moment was all about him. Then I remembered; he hadn't even looked at me. He couldn't possibly know. Instinctively, I frantically looked for a path through the crowd. Sure, running out would make me look like a complete psychopath but so would the inevitable weeping and cold sweats that these musical memories were evoking. Sweet Jesus. I was willing to do anything just to make it stop. It wasn't even the chorus yet, but I could already feel those lyrics eating their way through my heart.

When it became clear that an exit was impossible, I quickly decided on a Plan B… just try and play it cool. Rosie and all of the guys were laughing at me - never truly able to understand that I was in serious emotional pain. I tried to look like a good sport, but I felt like I was failing. It was at this point that things took an unexpected twist. Turning my back on Elvis, I smiled in defeat at my sneering friends. Within moments I could feel Jack standing painfully close behind me, undoubtedly biding his time before making the perfect joke. I took a deep breath and waited for the familiar sound of his voice. It was at that moment that something perfectly inconceivable happened. In one magical motion, I felt Jack's arms wrap playfully around me, engulfing me from behind. Before I could even flinch, Jack had spun me back toward the stage and was rocking me side-to-side to the music. I didn't even try to escape. As Elvis continued to sing, there we stood, pressed together like a prom picture, Jack softly mumbling about how "this song isn't so bad after all, now is it?"

On the last verse, Jack capped his performance with the one thing I feared most …he began to sing my death song directly into my ear. As his soft breath danced about my skin I could barely breathe. I could feel his nose brush against my hair and the butter of his voice cascaded through me like Novocaine. My head and my heart immediately engaged in a bloody battle, haplessly refereed by my common sense. What the hell was he thinking? What the hell was I feeling? This could NOT be happening! **S**weet Holy Moses! Why didn't he just rip my heart out and slap me with it??

For as playful as it began, the mood shifted in an instant. As his arms began to squeeze me in a way that felt dangerously close to crossing the line, Jack suddenly let go and jumped backward... like squeezing me had zapped him with an electric shock. I couldn't turn to look at him. I was filled with awkwardness and dreaded any sentence that might escape my lips. We had just had a moment. We both felt it. Whatever this was between us was growing – and we were both completely unable to deal with it. I could hear my friends laughing and hoped that no one there had the sense to read the confession I could feel escaping from my face. I had no idea what this was between us - but it was something - and, God help me, I had no intentions of stopping it. If there was one thing I wanted, it was for Jack to love me tenderly. Thanks a lot, Elvis!

The Kiss of Death

By the time baseball season rolled around I was torn between my anger at the universe and my unshakable happiness at having someone like Jack in my life. I was definitely in over my head and hiding it was becoming increasingly difficult. Accepting that there were things against which I was powerless was extremely frustrating. Ever since the Elvis concert, whenever we were together, I worried about what my face looked like, what story my eyes were telling and whether anyone would notice how I could barely breathe. Although I never would have believed it possible, Jack's friends were remarkably cool with me and, having already known Rosie from their society parties, started including my friend group in some of their adventures. I guess on a small scale, we were starting to make progress. On my end, this promotion in the social hierarchy was noteworthy but we all know that the company I was keeping was irrelevant. All that mattered was that I was with Jack and any event that included him either made my days infinitely better - or infinitely worse! Let me put it this way: you know how when someone loses use of one of their senses they report experiencing a heightened acuity in the others? For me, that's sort of what this forbidden crush on Jack felt like. Not being able to talk about our feelings made the looks he gave me almost deafening and knowing I couldn't touch him gave his voice the power to cover me with debilitating hot flashes. Everything about him was magic and his attention filled my heart with an irresistible blend of pixie dust and possibility. That, however, was the irony. If there was one thing Jack and I did not have, it was possibility. With every day that passed I could feel the growth of this bond we weren't discussing and every time we parted I felt the struggle of walking away incomplete. Our limits were as infuriating as they were heartbreaking and I think I brought the stereotype of emotional teenage girl to new heights.

If I was being honest, I needed tomorrow like I needed air. It was Bennett High's Spring Celebration for Bennett Baseball and just the opportunity to watch Jack from those bleachers filled me with an excitement and anticipation like no other. Events like this almost served as refueling stations for me. The anonymity of a crowd, you see, was a gift beyond anything I could describe. For two complete hours I could let my guard down. I could look directly at him, scrutinizing every tiny thing about him, and get lost in the possibilities of what will never be. Events like this were like my alternate reality. There was always something so liberating about being in that crowd. I guess that's because you essentially had an open invitation to love him. That's what being a fan is after all, right? Let's face it, at events like this you were supposed to ogle, be overly enthusiastic and at times, yell irrational things,

"YES!! … That was amazing!! … You're prefect!! Jack! Jack! Jack!!"

Yeah, the zone of "irrational things" was pretty much my home planet where Jack was concerned. Yes. Those games on Friday night equaled perfection.

On the flipside, having Jack in the spotlight was not without its drawbacks. Whenever he took the field, the crowd collectively held their breath, just waiting to see what magic he would inspire next. I was not naïve enough to think that I was the only one in his audience with "impure thoughts". Jack captivated everyone who watched him and on game days I dreaded sitting in that crowd, listening to the desires of others, yet never able to join in on their group therapy. Sometimes, the brighter his star shone, the more I felt like I was losing him. Clearly this was ironic because he was not…nor could ever be…mine to lose. Mine was an invisible burden.

Sadly, amid my overwhelming anticipation, I also struggled with my deepest apprehension. I had been to a few games this season and had noticed an unnerving trend. No matter how big the crowd, Jack had developed this uncanny ability to find me in it. While letting my guard down was liberating, it was also extremely dangerous. Regardless of how much I fought it, every feeling I had for him seemed to seep from my face as I watched him. I was pudding and he could probably see it. At least once a game we seemed to make eye contact and I was painfully aware of the story my face told each time. Usually, Jack just flashed me that heartbreaking smile and moved on. I would then convince myself that he was too caught up in his own performance to digest the story of my face. Or at least I hoped so. Ugh! As the hours ticked closer to tomorrow, I decided to let it go. No amount of apprehension could squash the perfectly fuzzy feeling that the promise of tomorrow had given me. In cases like this, where the anticipation is all you are ever going to get, you need to squeeze every drop out of it that you can. Accept your fate – surrender to your weaknesses – and make the most of your opportunities. Stolen moments are not free – but in my case, they were totally worth the price of that prison term!

The following day, I arrived at the stadium with trepidation. For all of the magic that was to lie inside this game, there was one painful fact that I had avoided right up until the very moment I had to face it. It was indeed the Spring Sports Celebration, and this unfortunately meant one thing: Senior Night. Now, in any other universe this event might seem harmless, boring even, but in my world, it was the social equivalent of torture. Every sport, every year, it was pure torture. Senior Night, you see was a toxic blur of red carnations, Kodak moments and (*just breathe*) kissing cheerleaders. Although I hated to admit it, in each of the years before I acknowledged my feelings for Jack, I was always left with an odd annoyance while watching Jack participate in Senior Night. Of course, I wasn't ready to admit it was jealousy, but I most certainly knew that watching the spectacle didn't feel right. It always opened up some hole inside me that I didn't understand. Even before I knew why, I undoubtedly knew that Senior Night left me heartbroken.

Despite my new friendship with Jack, or maybe even because of it, I really believed that this season I would handle the event so much better. I had seen it before, way too many times before, so I convinced myself that I must have developed a tolerance. I knew the drill backwards and I was banking that this familiarity would equal resilience. Every sport, every season it was always the same thing. In the pregame ceremony each senior cheerleader was paired with an athlete from the team, and because Jack was always a captain, Jack was always one of the boys chosen. Per tradition, the chosen player would give his cheerleader a flower, escort her to center field and give her a kiss before turning her over to her parents (remember – this was the 1950s and mandatorily kissing people on cue was not yet socially unacceptable). Pictures would be taken; fusses would be made and younger cheerleaders would dreamily anticipate their own senior night. It was a formula – almost like a one act play. Jack was nothing more than an actor following a script. It was meaningless and harmless, and I knew I was rational enough to get through it. ~ This, unfortunately, was the greatest lie I ever told myself. ~

The worst part is that I believed that lie right up until the horrifying moment itself. Before I truly had time to prepare, it was happening. The ceremony was beginning, and I was spellbound. Luckily the friends I was sitting with were too caught up in their own conversations to notice any bizarre things that I might be doing. Nervously, I looked to my left and there he was – gorgeous as ever. Jack was standing with socialite Susan VonVandermere and I swear she had a smirk on her face. Still cracking jokes with Max, Jack patiently held that dreaded flower and seemed ready to go on with the show.

"It's okay," I told myself, "you're going to be fine." (deep breath).

Inexplicably holding my breath instead, I calmly watched as Jack and Susan walked toward center field. Always a gentleman, I couldn't help but smile as Jack extended his hand to Susan's father as they approached.

"Whew, no problem," I reassured myself (exhale).

Confident in my resilience, I watched calmly as Jack handed Susan a red carnation.

"See, easy-peasy," I thought (deep breath)

Next, I watched Susan smile all flirty-like and put her hands on Jack's shoulders.

"Okay, not loving it but we can do this," I frantically told myself.

Feeling my heart sinking, I saw Jack look down at that randomly assigned girl.

"Oh sweet Jesus," I gasped

Then, in what seemed to be super-torture slow motion, Jack bent down and softly kissed her.

"HOLY MOTHER OF GOD!"

The shock waves thundered through my body like lightening. My breath was gone, my hands were numb, and I was physically sweating. I knew it was meaningless, scripted, choreographed, and at least fifteen other adjectives that would each fail to make me feel any better. Regardless of the intentions, the sight of Jack kissing a girl…any girl…cut me wide open. The cruel fact was, every season those random and undeserving girls received a gift that I would never get from a view that I would never have. No matter how close we became, and no matter how emotionally invested the two of us were to remain, I had to deal with the reality of what would never be. I would never be close enough to see my reflection in Jack's kryptonite eyes. I would never feel his faint breath on my cheeks. I would never know how soft his lips were or how warm his face felt pressed next to mine. Quite simply, I would never feel Jack's love in the way that I so wickedly wished for. That's right… I said it. *I WANTED THAT*!! Screw the moral compass.

Sadly, the events of Friday night left me a little bitter. I was spiraling back into a phase where I kind of hated all of it. I hated Jack for kissing that cheerleader and I hated that cheerleader for receiving it. I hated Jack for keeping me on this string and I hated myself for not being able to shake the obsession I had with him. I hated being powerless and I hated the reality that this vacuous hole I physically felt inside of me was never – ever- going to be filled. Most of all I hated this burden of birth that kept us apart. Ugh. I also hated that I hated everything. Wallowing was pointless. The end was never going to change so I either had to make the most of what I was given or decide to give it back all together. I was the definition of a lose-lose proposition.

May

"There they were, close together and safe and shut in, yet so chained to their separate destinities that they might as well have been half the world apart."
Edith Wharton

* * *

Feeling Sorry for Myself

By the time May rolled around, I spent a good portion of my days absolutely livid at how things were playing out. What the hell right? In what universe was this absurd situation okay? Just to be clear, by absurd, I didn't mean my scandalous desires...No! I meant my inability to have what I wanted. What kind of world did I live in where I would be deprived of the one thing I wanted so desperately? Why would the cosmos allow me to develop these feelings only to tell me that they were inappropriate? Why would fate keep throwing us together...why would we be victimized by our undeniable chemistry...why, oh why would he keep looking at me like that? Temptation like this seemed cruel and unnecessary. I had always been a good person; I helped others; I stayed out of trouble. This farce felt like nothing short of a punishment and I was furious at the injustice of it all.

To make matters worse, while dealing with my mischievous thoughts about

Jack was hard enough, I also had to deal with the reproachful gaze of my mother. Although being with Jack continued to feel so natural, things at home did not. I don't know if it's fair to call her suspicious, but at the very least my mother was starting to take notice of things, and it was clear that she was not a fan. I mean how could she be? My behavior had the power to blow up her whole world. For as successful as she was, I was the one holding all the cards right now. If she ever truly realized that, then she would be terrified. So, for good reason I could always feel her cold shoulder after our families had been at a 150th Anniversary event and I could sense her irritation whenever I would dare to tell a story that had Jack in it. I mean she obviously knew we were becoming friends, but I feared she was starting to see through our ruse. By ruse I don't mean to make it sound like we were hiding things, because at this point, we really weren't. Our relationship was completely out in the open yet completely contingent upon the lens with which you viewed it. Lucky for us, no one was astute enough to use the right lens. There were times my mom came close though, and it was starting to be a problem. The most vivid memory I have of this occurred after running into Jack at the Broadway Market. We only spoke briefly but we all know my heart was exploding just from the sight of him. Immediately my mother began to hurry me along and annoyingly lurked around me making it impossible for Jack and me to have any time alone. My annoyance was palpable as I tried my best to shake her for even thirty seconds. I'm sure she could tell that I was irritated but ironically it wasn't my behavior that ultimately seemed to concern her. Although I could feel her disgust the entire drive home, it wasn't until we were putting away the vegetables that it all blew up.

"Remember I'm volunteering at the center for Danny Seymour's birthday party tomorrow," I said.

Mom just grunted.

"Danny's mom wanted Jack to come too, so he can probably drive me home."

"....and there it is," my mom snapped.

I was stunned. She said it so quickly and so wickedly. I had absolutely no idea what to say and I'm sure my face looked as bewildered as I felt. When she realized that I was not going to engage, she just rolled her eyes.

"I don't like the way he looks at you," she said coldly.

Now if I hadn't been so shocked I might have had the courage to say what I was thinking. I mean let's be real. We all know my brain was screaming:

"Really? Because I sort of love it!"

Instead, beneath my shock and my guilt, I looked directly at her and outright lied.

"I have no idea what you're talking about," I squeaked.

To top it off, from the other room, my nosy sister felt the need to have the last word,

"Yeah, Josie hanging out with Jack Riley is weird...he's really cute and Josie's just gross."

Great - a full-on ambush - my family sucked. Escaping to my room, I looked out the window and wondered what my father would have thought of all of this. My dad always understood me on different level than my mother and at times like this I especially missed that. Even though I couldn't see it back then, I think my dad always sensed that my heart was too big for such small-mindedness. I wonder if he would have defended Jack and me to my mother; I wonder if he would have fought for us. I wasn't naive enough to think that his being alive would have changed the hopelessness of our situation, but I at least felt like my dad could have been an ally in my pain. Even though he couldn't have changed the outcome, I would like to believe that he would still have been supportive of my feelings.

Oddly enough, I never gave any thought as to what Jack's family might be thinking or saying about any of this. Obviously, if my family was noticing, so was his. In hindsight, my cluelessness was probably best. The truth would have only freaked me out. It wasn't until years later that I would truly realize the firestorm Jack was enduring at home – about me and everything else. Long before the term "helicopter parent" became a thing, Jack's parents were zooming about his business, desperately trying to maintain control of Jack's free spirit. The funny thing is, Jack Riley was and will always be one of the purest and most genuinely good souls I have ever known. Their micromanagement of his daily affairs was not only annoying but entirely unnecessary. Although I will never regret a single word we said or a single second we spent together, I do regret that our affair caused Jack conflict. I suppose that's why he hid it from me.

And so, I trudged through the month of May with the burden of forbidden desire firmly strapped to my back. There were days that thinking about Jack physically hurt. Just the idea of him sucked the breath from my lungs and tossed my stomach like a roller coaster. My days skittered through phases of giddiness and despair with alarming sincerity. There was the span where I traumatically couldn't eat, the span where I dreamily couldn't sleep, the span where I enthusiastically embraced our stolen moments and the span where I vowed to give him up for good. We won't even mention the time I looked for a supernatural solution that would allow us to be together. At present, I was simply trying to find my peace. It might sound crazy, but I was having a hard time understanding what was happening to me. I had never been in love like this before…if that's even what this was. Whatever it was, it was a bewitching like I had never experienced, and I didn't know what to do with it. Regardless of my physiological challenges, at least I was confident that I could master the self-control needed to be around him. I seemed able to squeeze every drop of satisfaction from our encounters yet never worry about crossing the line. Heck, he left me paralyzed half of the time. I probably wouldn't be able to cross that line even if I wanted to! One look from those blue kryptonite eyes and I was frozen. If I was being honest, however, I would admit that this also had its drawbacks. The effect Jack's eyes had on me was both beguiling and infuriating. Although his ability to scramble my brain protected me from my own actions, I feared it would also render me powerless against his. If he were ever to…I would…NO! I can't even entertain that as a possibility.

So, the bigger question becomes whether this dance was going to be enough. Would that look…and everything that fell within it…be enough? Could I continue to confine this fire that just grew bigger and more dangerous as time went by? Would the truths that I felt survive the reality that they could never be said? Could the future we would never have still burn brightly within the opportunities that we would? More importantly, would this dreadfully complicated situation continue to be this easy?

I knew the answer. It was an absolute yes and a heartbreaking no all at the same time. What we were living was our personal Romeo and Juliet - equally beautiful in its prose and parallel in its tragedy. Okay, so we knew we weren't going to die or anything, but we also knew that any delusions of a relationship had to. We needed to accept that anger was pointless, and change was impossible. We needed to find the maturity to be thankful for what we did have instead of being angry about what we did not. I'm not going to lie, sometimes when I was alone, this was really hard. Our circle was indeed infinite, and I knew that the pain was always around the next bend. Unfortunately, I also clung to the realization that "the look" was waiting around the other. Yes, it was a well-documented fact that the minute I laid eyes on Jack Riley all my doubts and all of my anger would immediately vanish. Truthfully, it didn't even take his eyes to numb the pain anymore. I could feel it in the air I breathed, and it smoldered in every message he sent. This... "thing" ...that we shared (I hesitated to call it what it was - that label would force us to carry it like an anvil), well this "thing" was more powerful than the pain. It understood it - even anticipated it - and was able to put it back in the pocket where it belonged. I guess it really just boiled down to one simple thing. In the end, our chemistry was always able to overcome the burdens of our reality. It just didn't always feel like that.

In Memory of Nelson Blocher

Although I never admitted it out loud, the funeral director's daughter in me was ridiculously excited about the highlight of junior year social studies – the annual field trip to Forest Lawn Cemetery. As part of the 11th grade American History curriculum, students spent six weeks studying local history and the unit culminated with an outing to the world-famous Forest Lawn Cemetery. Located just down Main Street from Bennett High, Forest Lawn was a two hundred sixty nine acre park designed by world renowned landscape architect Fredrick Law Olmsted. Part of Olmsted's signature park system, Forest Lawn was a stunning oasis designed to serve both the dead and the living. Complete with man-made lakes, picturesque bridges and picnic perfect pastures, Forest Lawn embodied everything I had been raised to appreciate about the circle of life. Some of my favorite childhood memories were of visiting Forest Lawn with my dad and listening to the stories of the people buried there, both the famous residents and the everyday people my dad had helped memorialize. To me, cemeteries were a place much more about life than about death and I couldn't wait to watch my classmates as they celebrated the stories of the cemetery for the first time. Although I wasn't sure exactly who's grave would be on the docket, we had covered a few of the residents in class and I was certain that we would be visiting former President Millard Fillmore, civil rights leader Mary Talbert and Dorothy Goetz Berlin, wife of world-famous song writer Irving Berlin. I remember always being especially touched by the story of the Berlins and would ask my dad to tell it every time we visited the cemetery. From what I remember, Dorothy was a Buffalo girl who met Irving in New York City when she auditioned for one of his shows. Although she didn't get the part, she did get a date and the couple was married not long after. Tragically, Dorothy caught typhoid on their Cuban honeymoon and died just six months later. Following her death, my dad reported that Irving had a long-standing contract with a Buffalo florist who would bring a single white rose to her grave every other day. I think all I wanted out of life was for someone to love me like Irving did Dorothy. It was just like Buddy Holly promised. Not fade away.

It was a beautiful May morning when our school bus drove through the iconic stone arch and entered Forest Lawn Cemetery. Descending the bus stairs, I admired the cherry trees, already in bloom, and followed my classmates to the Red Jacket Monument, our first stop on the tour. Red Jack was a famous Seneca orator and chief of the Wolf clan, who was awarded the silver medal by George Washington himself! Although he had run messages for the British during the Revolutionary War, Red Jacket's allegiance quickly shifted to the colonies, and he fought alongside the Americans during the War of 1812. With the entire junior class standing in front of Red Jacket's imposing bronze figure, I was too preoccupied with one singular thing to pay any sort of attention to what our teacher was talking about. Red Jacket was inspiring and all, but I was one hundred percent consumed with finding out exactly who would be in my group for the scavenger hunt portion of our trip. For this assignment, we would be split into teams and given a list of noteworthy residents. Using a list of clues, our mission was to find them in the cemetery and document the section where their plot was located. I wasn't even ashamed to admit that all I wanted from this field trip was to be able to spend this beautiful spring day strolling around one of my favorite places in Buffalo with Jack on my team. Holding my breath, I listened as the teacher listed group after group. No mention of either one of us yet. Then, like a dream, it happened. I heard Jack's name and two people later, miraculously heard my own. As if that wasn't great enough, this particular list had one other inconceivably perfect thing working for me. Most of the kids in this group were from the same honors class and had very little interest in working with mediocre brains like mine and Jack's. Before we knew it, we were given a small list by Harvard bound Lavinia Cole and told to be on our way. I swear to God, you just can't make this stuff up! To be honest, though, I shouldn't have been surprised. That's just how things worked for Jack and me. Fate was on our side. I had seen it countless times. Even if the real world was against us, I always took incredible solace in trusting that the universe knew better. Our invisible string was pretty sturdy.

I figured out the first person on our list in no time. I probably could have done it from the first clue: "This resident is noteworthy for providing speedy transport of goods between California and the Atlantic coast," but the second clue really sealed it; "Winning five Tony Awards last month, a new musical features towns people eagerly awaiting items from this man's business." Obviously, we were searching for William Fargo, head of the American Express and Wells Fargo companies. Always being a big fan of Broadway, I had already bought the record album and memorized the entire score of *The Music Man* and "The Wells Fargo Wagon" was one of my favorite songs.

"Here we are. He's in Section AA!" I shouted with way too much gusto.

Jack just smiled and documented our conquest on the sheet of paper. Good lord, why did I have to be such a geek about things like this? Between my love of cemeteries and my adoration for Jack, I was in some serious state of nirvana right now. Luckily, I knew Jack's mannerisms very well, and I was certain he found my irrational excitement adorable.

"What's next," I asked Jack, hoping to avoid a conversation about my behavior.

"Ummm, let me look," Jack said, smiling at the unbridled enthusiasm I still couldn't control, "This designer of the Hotel Lafayette was the first woman member of the American Institute of Architects. Ironically, this woman's ashes are buried in the grave of her husband, and she doesn't even have her own stone. A historical marker has been erected in her honor instead."

"Louise Blanchard Bethune!" I shouted. "She's this way," I said, dragging Jack by the arm. "Sheesh. They aren't even making this hard!"

Having found Louise's marker, Jack and I took a left and set off down the road toward our last famous resident. I knew exactly where the plot was and felt incredibly honored that I was the one assigned to find this particular monument. Although the clues made it obvious to me, I was a little annoyed that they didn't contain any information about the real magic of this memorial. The clues merely talked about the extravagant Italian marble mausoleum and how the Civil War veteran buried here was one of the wealthiest figures in Buffalo, having made his millions selling boots and shoes to the military. The resident we were looking for was John Blocher, and the sight of his family monument will never cease to take my breath away. Standing at the Blocher Monument is the single most vivid memory I have of visiting Forest Lawn with my dad and being in its presence covers my body in goosebumps every time.

Architecturally, the Blocher Monument is probably my favorite piece of art in the entire world. The elaborate stone mausoleum is a bell-shaped structure with five pillars set on top of a circular stone base. A large, decorated ball sits atop the peak of the bell, drawing your eyes toward the heavens. Four panes of one-inch-thick glass extend between each of the pilasters while a final hinged pane serves as a discrete door. Inside of the mausoleum's pillars, life size figures of the Blocher family tell a tragic tale of forbidden love and parental grief. Carved from angel white marble, the haunting character of each figure is simply mesmerizing, and the story behind them, unimaginably tragic. The Victorian figures depict John and Elizabeth Blocher standing on either side of their adult son, Nelson, who lay on his death bed, a Bible clutched to his chest. An angel floats above Nelson's head, her naked body discreetly covered in a garland of wildflowers.

"Is that it?" Jack yelled, pointing down one of the three sidewalks leading up to the monument.

"Yes," I said. "The parents and the son are each buried here. There is a separate sidewalk and stone bench for each of them."

While Jack ran toward the tomb, my body was frozen. No matter how many times I came here, I would always be equally in awe of the tragedy and the magic. Standing here with Jack, however, was bringing this iconic tale to a whole new level for me and I was perilously frozen.

"This is AMAZING, Josie!" Jack said respectfully, standing on the ledge of the mausoleum and peering at the figures inside the windows. "So, tell me the real story."

Sitting on the stone bench dedicated to the Blocher's son, Nelson, I looked at Jack and took a deep breath.

"Well," I said "I guess it all started in the spring of 1881 when the Blocher family hired a twenty-year-old housemaid named Katherine. By all accounts, Katherine was as sweet as she was beautiful and immediately hit it off with the Blocher's son Nelson. I guess Nelson made no effort to hide how he felt about Katherine and spent his days finding ways to be near her."

Wow. As the words left my lips, I felt extremely exposed. Over the last four months all I had done was try and find ways to be near Jack. Until this moment, I had never really wondered whether Jack was astute enough to notice.

"By summer," I continued, "Katherine began to return his feelings and it was obvious to everyone that the two were madly in love. There is even a rumor that Nelson had bought her an engagement ring. Well, I'm sure you can guess how his multi-millionaire parents felt about the prospect of Nelson marrying their maid and ultimately decided that the two needed to be separated."

At that moment, Jack stepped down from the monument's ledge and walked sullenly toward one of the other benches. From the looks of it, Jack was also feeling this story on a whole other level. I just wished I could know which level that was.

"Go on…" he said softly.

"That fall, Nelson was told that there was urgent business that needed to be attended to with one of their international contacts and he should plan for an extended stay in Europe. While Nelson was gone, the Blochers fired Katherine, who was ominously told to never return. Unable to even write Nelson a note, Katherine found a way to leave her Bible in Nelson's room. Two weeks later, the Blochers told Nelson that Katherine had run away in the middle of the night, leaving nothing behind but her Bible. Obviously, Nelson was devastated."

I peered over at Jack. He was staring at the cold marble figures, unable to even look at me. I really wondered what he was feeling. Was this the look of a boy who was realizing he was sitting with his own Katherine or just the sadness of a boy who was sick of living under his parents' oppression? A bit shaken, I forced myself to finish the story.

"When he returned to America the following spring, he began an exhaustive search for Katherine, neglecting his business and his health for nearly a year and a half. Eventually, Nelson retuned to Buffalo, exhausted and sick with fever. A short time later, Nelson Blocher died with Katherine's Bible clutched to his chest. A broken heart was named as his cause of death."

I looked at Jack. He was eerily silent. I knew we both felt the weight of this story, but also knew that neither of us was going to point it out. The kinship I felt with Katherine in that moment was overwhelming and watching Jack stare at the lifeless image of Nelson Blocher was more than a little heartbreaking. I had always known that our love story was hopeless, but I hadn't expected the benefits I would be able to take away from it anyway. Even at this moment, sitting here with Jack was making me stronger. Not knowing what else to do, I continued.

"The Blochers felt so guilty about their snobbery killing their only child that they built this monument in tribute. It is a depiction of their last moments with Nelson. Oh – and see that angel floating above Nelson's head?"

Jack cocked his head to get a better look and nodded.

"That angel is supposed to be Katherine. Apparently, it looks just like her. I guess they felt so guilty about keeping them apart in life that they decided to unite them in death."

With that, Jack jumped from the bench and ran toward the tomb.

"And what good does that do?" he almost shouted. "So, they built him a guilt tomb. Big deal. Look at them standing there, hovering over his dead body. Maybe if they had given him a little more space when he was alive none of this would have happened!"

The sight of Jack losing his cool left me stunned. I thought I was the only one who was angry about our situation. I mean I didn't know for sure that Jack's breakdown was about me, but let's face it, the similarities were undeniable!

"So, this is their apology? Those idiots were more concerned with their social status than their only son's happiness. That's just crap! Nelson's death served no purpose. Here we are almost seventy five years later, and things are no better."

With that, Jack turned his back to the marble figures and walked away. I'm pretty sure I saw him spit on John Blocher's bench as he walked past.

Strolling back to the bus, I saw Jack studying the blooming cherry trees that lined our path and they seemed to provide him with some level of comfort. As we carried on, I couldn't help but notice that Jack seemed much more taken with the fallen blossoms, haplessly scatted at the base of the trees, than he did with the full pink bouquets that adorned them. As I watched him bend down and sneak a few of the fallen blossoms into his pocket, I somehow knew exactly what he was feeling. Our existence was just as fragile and as fleeting as those blossoms. Although in the landscape of Olmsted's design, the beauty of the blooming cherry tree was unparalleled, its transience made its brief reign all the more poignant. Like Katherine and Nelson...like me and Jack...those blossoms were destined to disappear as quickly as they arrived, victims of a lifecycle that didn't provide them nearly enough time to live.

That night I couldn't stop thinking about what had transpired with Jack. Despite his anger, or maybe because of it, I felt closer to him than ever. I may not have known exactly how things would turn out for us - heck I wasn't even sure of what Jack's feelings for me were. There was one thing I did know though. We were never going to be Nelson and Kathrine. I simply wouldn't let us. Whatever this was between us, it was not a tragedy. We were worth more than that. Even if it couldn't be what we wanted it to be, we had to find a way to make it all worthwhile. I felt like we owed Nelson that much.

June

"So often, below the word spoken, is the thing known and unspoken"
Harold Pinter, playwright

* * *

The Hidden Language

Sometimes I wonder if this adventure with Jack would have been better or worse if we had been able to talk about it. To this day I don't truly know what Jack was thinking about most of our issues or how he felt about the bulk of our adventures. I have no proof of what things meant to him or his perspective on how things turned out. The most tangible things I have from Jack are a few notes, this key around my neck and, of course my valentine. But for all the tangible things that I don't have, I will always hold complete faith in the one thing I don't need a memento to remember – and it connects Jack and me to this day.

Although I still firmly believe that most things concerning Jack and I were laced with magic, there is one particular talent Jack and I possessed that I have never experienced with anyone before or since. For whatever reason, of the many gifts Jack and I received, the most unique was the ability to communicate without words. Whether it was a look, a feeling or something said between the lines, we understood each other on a level I can't even begin to explain. It was like the supernatural connection of biological twins, except it was between two people who had absolutely no business having it.

At first, I didn't know what to make of this connection and I honestly can't even tell you how long it had been going on. The more these oddities happened though, the more I started to make sense of them and the more I started to think that Jack and I had some sort of superpower. You know how there are times in life when people say something cliché but, for some reason, you feel it on a much deeper level? Or times when someone silently looks at you and you can hear an entire soliloquy bleeding from that one look? That seemed to happen a lot with Jack and as the school year progressed, I started to realize that it wasn't a coincidence. There was something deeper going on between Jack and me, some connection that we were just starting to make use of. Although I had no idea why or how, Jack and I had instinctively begun to use what I can only call a "hidden language."

To me, the existence of this hidden layer was very ironic. At my core, I loved my verbal conversations with Jack. I appreciated everything from his perfect word choices to the melodic way his voice would string them together. For as much as I hung on his every spoken word, however, I also accepted that there was a layer of subtext based entirely on glances and emotions. As he spoke, not only could I hear Jack with his words, but I could silently see his message and feel his meaning, even if it didn't align what his words were saying. At first, I wasn't sure if he did it on purpose, like a hidden truth or something, or if it really was just another layer of this bizarre connection we had. More and more frequently there were things that left Jack's mouth that I swore he meant differently for me. Almost like a secret love note, hiding in plain sight. Regardless of the words Jack's lips were pronouncing, I seemed to be able to feel what Jack's soul was trying to say, like his heart had a direct teleport to mine. What's weirder is that I started to believe that Jack could interpret the truth beneath my words just as accurately. Without trying, I would make some socially acceptable comment and the way Jack looked at me would make me feel like he knew all the things I wasn't saying out loud. Regardless of the words that left my mouth, I could tell that Jack knew what my heart was saying, however socially unacceptable that may be.

I'm not going to lie; having this deep of a connection was a little intimidating – if not downright inconvenient. There were certainly things about me that I wasn't ready for Jack to know. It was all part of the package though. I guess it's only logical that these very real but very wrong feelings we had for each other would exist the same way in our conversations that they did in our lives…lurking below our reality, but never far from the surface. Let's face it, when something is such a fundamental part of you, it is bound to escape in any way it can.

As if our hidden language wasn't enough, over time I started to realize that our superpower ran a lot deeper. Once I accepted the way our souls could communicate with each other, I began to make sense of another phenomenon we shared. I know it's going to sound insane (which is exactly why I have never told anyone before), but I am one hundred percent certain that I could actually FEEL what Jack was feeling and judging from the way he always knew the right thing to say or would pop up at times when I needed him most, I fully believe that Jack was able to feel me too. It was nothing we tried to do and, for a long time, nothing we actually understood. Over time though, it became clear that our feelings, both emotional and tangible, were physically connected. I could wake in the middle of the night and know that something had upset Jack at home and Jack could wake in the morning and feel my anxiety as I tried to balance my family responsibilities. Without making it weird, we would always find a way to check on the other, offering our silent support in the wake of our silent warning signal. I know it sounds crazy but knowing that Jack and I shared this connection was one of the most comforting things I have ever felt. No matter what life threw at me, and no matter how trying a situation could be, I knew I wasn't alone. Jack was always there, standing with me, healing me from the inside out.

Now, I know telling you that we had a superpower sounds ridiculous, but you're just going to have to trust me on this one. It was real and it was accurate. So, by the beginning of June, at any given time there were two simultaneous conversations going on. There was the one our words were having and then there was the "other" one…. the hidden one.

Take yesterday, for example. My mom was staring down an incredibly busy day in her basement salon and had given me the car so I could drive my siblings to and from school and then run errands for her in my extra time. I had a forty-five-minute window between when Bennett got out and when I had to get my sisters from the elementary school, so I had decided to run to the market around the corner and pick up some things on my shopping list. Already respecting the strength of our invisible string, I wasn't surprised when I turned down the cookie aisle and ran straight into Jack. Laughing, he explained that he and the guys had popped over to grab a few snacks before their Varsity Club meeting. Knowing I would be passing Bennett on my way to the elementary school, I immediately offered to drop them off so they wouldn't need to sprint just to make it back in time.

"I think that's what Max was hoping for," Jack joked, "but I'll drive. You look like you need a breather."

He was right. I did need a breather, but probably not for the reason he thought. Yes, my day was hectic, but I was pretty sure my flushed face and increased heart rate was presently due to the cologne Jack was wearing and the way his shirt was making his eyes look even more blue than usual. Not figuring that was something I should share, I simply said thank you.

Jack pulled up to the school and parked in a space by the door. They had exactly six minutes to make it to their meeting, so the guys hopped out and immediately ran into the building. Jack, on the other hand, opened his door and stood next to the car as I scooted over from the passenger seat. Bending down to look at me through the open window, Jack held on to the side of the car and said, with an intoxicatingly crooked smile,

"Don't forget your seatbelt."

Now to most people, this sentence sounds simple and insignificant, but to me it was anything but. Due to the powers of our hidden language, the message I heard was twofold. Yes, there have been a few times where I have neglected to fasten my seatbelt (it wasn't a law back then, you know) and yes, I may have joked with Jack about this very thing. To me, the fact that he remembered this tiny indiscretion showed his genuine commitment to the details of my life. More than that, something about his reminder immediately felt like a secret love note.... like he couldn't say what he wanted to as we parted, so he said it in code. Although I have no proof beyond my own feelings and the tone of his voice as he said it, I was certain that Jack did not say that sentence just because he was concerned for my safety; he was letting me know how much he cared about me. The way it felt to me, "don't forget your seatbelt" actually meant "I'm really glad I ran into you today and wish you didn't have to leave so soon."

On one hand, I found the fact that our true feelings had to lay between the lines pretty frustrating. On the other, there was no denying that having something that was completely untarnished by the outside world had a pure and beautiful quality to it. There was no denying the security I found in our cocoon of secrets. I felt so close to Jack in those moments - the ones where I knew the outside world couldn't possibly be processing things the same way we were. No one would ever understand how we could physically feel what was going on inside the other – no matter how great the distance between us. No one else would ever hear the words the same way we did or interpret the smiles in the right context. In these moments, I didn't mind wearing the white gloves when I handled our relationship. Being the only ones who could see what was invisible gave our everyday encounters an extra layer of intimacy and wonder. Sure, not being able to share things with others could be frustrating - but that frustration didn't stand a chance of dulling the glow our hidden conversations lit inside of me.

I looked at Jack through my open window and became hopelessly lost in the sunshine dancing in his eyes. Now, as I said before, on my end, the use of our hidden language was completely involuntarily. While I would occasionally throw things out there just to see if Jack would pick up on them, most of the time, I genuinely had no intention of speaking in riddles or sending SOS signals. I also had no intentions of accidentally flirting with him. It wasn't until the words rolled out of my mouth and I saw his smirking reaction that I would grasp the other side.

"So, what is on Josie's afternoon calendar?' he asked, still not going inside.

"Well," I said, "my mom is slammed with work, so after I get my sisters, I need to cook dinner and then help them with their Sunday School project.

It's pretty exciting stuff."

Now I knew that bringing up religion was tricky, and I think I kind of did it to see what his reaction would be. Besides the differences in our socioeconomic status, the differences in our religion were also a subject we never talked about.

"Please tell me it involves arts and crafts," Jack said with a snarky reference to my lack of artistic ability.

The fact that Jack was joking about this and not getting weird was huge for me. Maybe it's because of that, or maybe simply because I'm a complete idiot that I just kept talking about it.

"Oh, it sure does," I said laughing. "The class is constructing the Garden of Eden and we are in charge of the Tree of Knowledge. I get to spend the evening making fruit."

"You sound pretty excited about it," Jack replied, and the look on his face made me feel like he found me adorable.

Apparently, this was all too much for me and I followed it up with the most embarrassing (yet accurate) sentence I may have ever said,

"Heck, yes," I all but shouted, "we all know how much I like my forbidden fruit!"

I know you probably think I'm kidding right now, but this is the God's honest truth. I said those exact words – out loud – to Jack. And I didn't say them to be flirty or clever; I have absolutely no idea why I said them. It was like word vomit, and I had no control over it. What's worse, Jack didn't even flinch. Instead, he looked right at me and calmly replied,

"Oh, I know you do!"

The way Jack smirked at me in that moment sent me straight to pieces. Good God. In the history of forever, there has never been anyone who could make me laugh at myself the way that Jack could. Granted, this was largely due to the fact that nobody could make me behave as stupidly as Jack could, but it was an impressive skill, nonetheless.

Despite the comfort of our hidden language, by the following week I really began to struggle with the fact that it was June and the school year was almost over. Just go ahead and add that to the list of things that made me angry these days. My problem was that I had no idea what the summer would bring, and I feared for my sanity once I didn't see Jack in school every day. Even though my sense of self had grown by leaps and bounds since January, I still struggled with my natural insecurities and not having anything tangible to prove our feelings existed could absolutely torture me. Despite how clear and easy things were when Jack and I were together, when we weren't together, I could be an absolute mess. I would begin to doubt things I usually held as true and would somehow convince myself that I had imagined the entire affair. I would relive our encounters in my head over and over and dissect every tiny thing Jack said, trying to figure out exactly how he might have meant it. Looking back, I'm sure that my issues were largely due to my fear that I didn't deserve Jack. But come on, this whole thing was so preposterous that doubting it was only inevitable sometimes.

Regardless of my insecurities, I'm pretty sure my dread for the summer was rooted in a severe problem I had developed. One of the more annoying burdens I carried these days was this persistent craving to know where Jack was at all times. To be honest, I don't even know if calling it a craving is strong enough. It's more like I felt this psychotic and unbearable NEED to know where Jack was and what he was doing. In the days before social media, any time you weren't in school was like a social blackout. The minute the school doors closed your whole world went dark. For me, the uncertainty of what Jack was up to was unbearable. The irony, of course, is that any time I did actually know of his plans, it usually made me angrier and more uncomfortable than when I had no clue. When I had no idea where he was, I could at least find comfort in my oblivion. When I had a little information though - that's when my mind would run away from me. The weekends were always more annoying than school nights and don't even get me started on school vacations. Knowing that the Riley's were bowling with the Carson's on a Saturday night was hard enough (they had a daughter you know...what if she liked him? Okay so she was twenty, but in my head, no one was immune to Jack's charms. Anything with a uterus was a threat!!). Long breaks from school, though, those were absolute torture. I always imagined Jack living some Great Gatsby kind of life and felt left out of things that probably didn't even exist. Jack's parents kept a very tight social calendar, and I never even knew what city Jack would be in during breaks. Being naturally insecure I would immediately mistake his busyness for indifference and wind up crushed when I didn't hear from him. Of course, I had no actual reason to be hearing from him over a break but hey - a girl can dream. If I couldn't be with Jack, I at least wanted the opportunity to watch his life like a movie. My need to be in Jack's orbit was like a drug and the thought of being without it all summer was starting to give me the jitters. It's truly a good thing that modern technology didn't exist back then, because we all know I would have been using my phone to track Jack Riley 24/7!

You Jump, I Jump, Jack!

As the school year drew to a close, the buzzing about Jack and I was palpable. Each of our personal friend groups seemed to be okay with us hanging out and because of Rosie's unique situation they had even managed to merge on occasion. The people on the outside though, were much less accepting. Even at our age, some people in Buffalo took the social divide very seriously. The upper class was bred to feel superior and the middle and lower classes were conditioned to feel bitter about it. So, even though our friend groups knew that Jack and I had never done anything wrong (except possibly in my daydreams...) certain people seemed to have an issue with us. Some of the rich kids at school would make snarky comments to Jack about me,

"Hey Jack, I didn't realize you had hired your own maid. What else does she do? Do you think she will work for me too?"

Some of working-class kids took offense to what they perceived as my disloyalty to my circle,

"I don't know who you think you are lately, Princess Josie, but everyone knows where you came from."

And even Rosie was starting to have concerns,

"I know you and Jack are just friends, but I hope you know what you are doing. This isn't a game you know, and things could turn into a "Kelly Mulligan" any minute."

With those words, my stomach sank. Oh, poor Kelly Mulligan. Her tragic story of forbidden love was so iconic in our parts that her name had been universally accepted as part of our local dictionary.

Kelly Mulligan – verb. To be ostracized from your family and your community as a result of falling in love with someone deemed to be of the wrong religion

I guess the whole thing happened before I was born, but the gist of Kelly Mulligan's legend was really starting to hit home. Despite being raised a devout South Buffalo Irish Catholic, Kelly fell hopelessly in love with Dewey Donovan, son of Pastor Donovan, one of North Buffalo's Methodist ministers. When their affair was discovered, both congregations rallied in opposition, each fearing that any "cross-breeding" would pollute the purity of their bloodlines. Poor Kelly was eventually run out of town - disowned by her family and shunned by the community at large. Although Dewey initially followed her, I guess he cracked at some point and came running home to daddy and the security of his small world. Kelly, on the other hand, was never welcomed back and no one seems to know what happened to her. I'd like to think that she went out into the real world and found something better. Obviously, her soul was too big for our community's small mindedness and Dewey, well, clearly Dewey was a dick.

Despite the Kelly Mulligans and the very real obstacles of our economic divide, Jack and I never talked about the drama. I'm sure we both realized that it was out there but addressing it would have opened a can of worms that neither one of us was ready for. Obviously, their jabs were cause for concern, if for nothing more than the fact that they were associating us with each other. I don't think anyone had the gall to see the connection we were fighting but they were astute enough to know that something unusual was afoot.

Between my annoyance with the gossip and my often-suffocating rage at our tragic love story, I knew that I was empty and needed replenishing fast…and that's when it happened…just like it always did. Like clockwork, the moment I plunged into some shadowy canyon of doubt and disgust – the moment I reevaluated this insane attachment and non-existent future – the moment I considered moving on for my own good (and the safety of those around me)…THAT was the moment that it always happened. At that exact moment, fate would take our invisible string and reel me back in like a helpless, flopping fish.

Let's start with a little backstory. About twenty miles from the heart of Buffalo lay Akron Falls Park, a two hundred forty-acre refuge frequented by all of Western New York. Akron Falls Park seemed as old as time and was well known for its lush green moss and cliffs full of exaggerated folklore. The crowned jewel of the park was Akron Falls, a forty-foot waterfall located along the infamous Murder Creek which was originally known to the natives as See-un-gut (roar of distant waters). As macabre as the name implies, the legend of Murer Creek dates back to the early 1800s and revolves around the tragic love triangle of a young native woman, her fiancé and a white officer who became obsessed with her. Aware but unconcerned that the woman was in love with another, the white officer proposed marriage. Fearful of rejection, he then vowed to murder both her and her family if she refused him. His proposal ignored, the officer waited until the girl was away and then followed through on his threat to kill her parents. Irate and unwavering, he set off in search of his obsession - determined to either marry her or murder her too. Terrified and unwilling to marry anyone but her true love, the young woman ran toward Akron Falls and hid in a cave near the creek. Although she found help from a local pioneer, she was soon discovered by both the white man and her fiancé, Gray Wolf, who had come to rescue her. Refusing to abandon his true love, Gray Wolf fought and killed the white man, but succumb to his own wounds soon after, leaving his bride-to-be heartbroken and alone. To be honest, I was always a little annoyed that the name only highlighted the murders that took place there and not the love story behind them. I feel like Gray Wolf deserved better.

Fast forward to 1957 and although the falls and park were always a popular spot for the area teenagers to party or go hiking, every few years something called the "Death Fall Challenge" was resurrected and the whole vibe changed.

The "Death Fall," you see, involved daring each other to climb to a plateau on the cliffs and jump from its absurd height, landing in Murder Creek. Per tradition, the next participant would be challenged when the jumper yelled their name during the free-fall. Without fail, onlookers would hold their breath in fear of hearing their own name echo through the canyon. Once the challenge was issued, the recipient had to complete the jump within a week or be "murdered" socially.

As you might have guessed, challenges were plentiful this year. Ever since the weather turned, I had watched throngs of idiots jump off those rocks, scream out names and smack the water below. It was always great fun and although I had fully planned on going to Akron Falls this weekend, I was even more certain of it after Jack asked if I would be there.

"You bet," I said with a creepy amount of enthusiasm. "Rosie and I should be there about 3pm."

"Prefect," Jack said with just a little bit of mischief, "I'll see you there."

When Rosie and I arrived we all know that my first instinct was to look for Jack and I was more than a little disappointed when I didn't see him or his friends anywhere. Dejected, I meandered around the rocks for what felt like an eternity before I heard some commotion. Looking up, I saw a group of people gathered on the protruding cliffs and in the center of them, highlighted by his personal ray of sunshine, was a shirtless (yes shirtless) Jack Riley. He looked to be standing a few yards from the edge and was wearing the most adorable plaid swim trunks I had ever seen. Believe it or not, how he looked (did I mention shirtless??) was not my biggest concern at this moment. All I could focus on was that Jack was about to be the next challenger.

"Holy cow," I said to Rosie, "Jack must have known he was jumping today, and he wanted to make sure we would be here to see it."

As Rosie and I scurried up the rocks to watch the show, the notion that Jack was concerned about my attendance made me fuzzy all over and I couldn't help but smile. Standing on those rocks, with the sun shining on him like a spotlight, Jack encompassed all the majesty of DaVinci's Statue of David. Dear God, just being in his presence filled me up like nothing I had ever known. Not that I had ever tried, but at that moment, I was certain that no drug or alcoholic beverage could possibly make me feel as good as I did just being allowed to walk the same planet as Jack Freaking Riley.

And then, all at once, I started to connect the dots. The revelation hit me like a bullet, and I immediately spiraled into a dignified fit of panic. Oh, holy hell, was Jack about to jump off of those rocks and call out my name? Is that why he wanted to make sure I would be here? My thoughts were spinning. He might have just invited me so I could see it, I told myself. Yeah, maybe I'm not the next victim - maybe he just wanted me in the audience so I could tell the kids at the center about it.

Quite honestly, this whole situation left me conflicted. Was I off the hook? I loved heights but feared water. This contradiction made jumping a daunting proposition. As I mulled this over, I quickly realized that there was really no contest here. Any fear I had of that water was nothing compared to my feelings for Jack. Let's face it. I WANTED to be the one on his mind. I WANTED to be his first choice. I WANTED to hear him say my name as he tumbled through the air. I NEEDED to feel that connection again. I was already drowning. No icy body of water was going to make that feeling any worse.

Holding my breath, I looked directly at Jack. The sun was shining, Jack was smiling and...I'm not sure if I mentioned this...but he was shirtless. Jack playfully asked the crowd if they were listening and when he got their full attention, he started some sort of shtick about not being able to swim. With Jack's words floating in the air above him, my thoughts nervously raced around in my head.

"I wonder who nominated him."

"He's a really good public speaker."

"I wonder if he is thinking about me."

Predictably, my thoughts were interrupted when I heard someone talking about Jack's six pack...or lack thereof. Obviously, this was a topic that demanded my full attention! As I refocused, Jack was being teased about the disparity between his current workout schedule and the current state of his abs. What followed was a prime example of the subtext that characterized our hidden language. Dodging barbs like a ninja, my leading man decided to take control of the situation in a way only Quarterback Jack could. Wryly, Jack turned and addressed the crowd directly, looking as adorable as ever while doing it. Even though Jack was using his serious voice, the smirk on his face betrayed him in an instant. That boy oozed of pure mischief and something about the tone of his voice made me feel as if he was talking directly to me. And then, with a twinkle in his eye, and a quick glance to make sure I was listening, Jack proceeded to offer the following explanation as to his missing six-pack:

"It's like love," he declared, "you can't see it, but you know it's there."

My whole body went numb. What the holy hell WAS THAT? Those words invaded my bloodstream as if he had whispered them directly into my ear. Through the powers of our hidden language, my soul felt each syllable that left his mouth, and I was certain that sentence was all about me. As my thoughts spun, I could see Jack animatedly running toward the ledge and I held my breath as if I were the one falling. Then, in one magical instant my latest funk was broken. As Jack fell, he clearly, enthusiastically, and irresistibly called out my name. I accidentally squealed so loudly that my head nearly flew off and spun around on the ground.

And there you have it. Of all the people in Jack's life, he chose ME. Once again, this pesky demon had weaseled its way into my everyday life and made things complicated. Don't get me wrong...they were complicated in the most beautiful and satisfying way...but they were irrefutably and undeniably complicated, nonetheless. I was Jack's first choice for this challenge. I couldn't help wondering what else I might be his first choice for...

As I collected myself, I realized that all eyes on that cliff were suddenly on me. What must they be thinking? Besides the obvious conversations about whether I would chicken out, there were bound to be raised eyebrows as to why Jack chose me. Some, undoubtedly, would look at the black and white versions of our pedigrees and assume that Jack was bullying me, although anyone who truly knew Jack knew there was not a malicious bone in his body. It wasn't those idiots I was worried about; it was the intuitive ones that had me nervous.

Luckily, after the initial buzz of the jump had died down, the crowds scattered like pebbles, quietly off to their next adventure. Even Rosie, having a country club party to get ready for, politely asked if she could leave me in my "hour of need" and catch a ride with Monica. Rosie knew I was probably going to nervously stare off the ledge of the cliff for a good twenty minutes still and, to be honest; the whole situation was probably making her uncomfortable. I'm sure the last thing she wanted to talk about was why, exactly, Jack had just chosen me.

So, alone with my thoughts, I sat at the literal edge of reason and surveyed the pure majesty of Akron Falls Park – the place where I would forevermore hear Jack call out my name. I tried to tell myself that I was hanging around strictly to revel in my triumph, but my ulterior motive was pretty clear. I knew that the last obligation of the Death Fall Challenge was to clean up from the party in the gorge and, judging from the bottles and trash I could see below me, Jack still had to be down there somewhere. He was no more likely to be someone who would shirk his duties than he was to be a litterer. After everything that had just happened, we all know there was no way I was leaving if Jack was still around.

After what seemed like an eternity, Jack finally meandered into the gorge, seemingly unaware that I was still on the ledge. Too much in love to be discrete, I spied on Jack from up above and contemplated what my next move should be. I guess I must have taken a little too long to figure that out, because the next thing I knew, I heard Jack's voice, startled but somehow still happy, yell out,

"Holy cow Josie, you just scared me to death! What are you still doing here?"

"Oh – sorry," I shouted with some pretty hearty laughter. "Thanks to you I was just sitting up here trying to find the nerve to jump someday."

"Well, you don't need to worry about that right now," Jack said with adorable reassurance. "So… you creepy stalker…are you just going to sit up there all night or are you going to come down and help me?"

I'd like to say I planned what happened next, but to be honest, I really didn't. The effect Jack had on me was indescribable and occasionally the decisions I made because of it were a little...oh ...what's the word? ...Irrational! To this day I don't know if I did it for the symbolism, out of fear, out of obligation, or simply because I thought it was the quickest way to get to him. Regardless of the reason, upon hearing Jack call out to me, I stood up, looked directly at Jack, and jumped!

And then, like a dream, I was falling - literally falling for Jack Riley all over again. As the smack of cold water rushed through my body and I frantically peddled myself toward the surface, I saw a hand come below the waves to grab me. Pulling me quickly toward the rocks, Jack was laughing and shaking his head as I emerged.

"You are simultaneously the worst and the greatest, Josie Johnson," Jack said between fits of laughter, "but I am seriously concerned that no one will believe that this happened. What if you don't get credit for your jump? What are you going to do then?"

Regardless of whether anyone believed that I jumped or not, I knew this day was a turning point for us. By choosing me, Jack had publicly acknowledged our friendship and all but dared society to be okay with it. The nonchalance with which he did it and the way he made our unusual situation look perfectly pedestrian was immeasurably comforting. A stunt like this could have left me and my scandalous emotions feeling exposed, but I felt nothing but security. Regardless of the gossip and the drama, Jack was choosing me. Maybe not in the way I wished for, but like I've said, living within our limits was always going to be better than living without him. All that mattered was that on this day, on that cliff, in front of those people (and did I mention, shirtless) Jack Riley chose ME and that was all I needed.

So, looking at Jack, I answered his question by saying exactly what was on my mind, even if that answer was going to make our blurry line a little fuzzier.

"I don't care if anyone believes it or not," I said proudly, "I didn't do it for them."

Although I was starting to shiver, I smiled just enough to let Jack know I wasn't sorry.

"You didn't?" Jack said with a smirk.

"Of course not," I said, as he handed me his towel. "I did it for you."

And there you have it. Obviously, I knew that Jack and I had no future, but by plummeting into Murder Creek that day, I was making a statement. Even knowing our time together was fleeting, there was no reason I couldn't live in every minute of it. Regardless of how hopeless it was, I was fighting for him – and I really wanted to believe that Gray Wolf was smiling somewhere.

Stage III - Bargaining

Without a doubt, bargaining can be the most enjoyable of all the stages of your forbidden crush. After surviving some very trying periods of denial and anger, during bargaining your emotions finally stumble into to a place of clarity. You start to see your situation in a different light and attempt to regain control of your feelings by looking for alternate threads of hope. Basically, your energy becomes focused on finding a way to make your desire more manageable and you desperately try to squeeze moments of "normal" out of a situation that is anything but. I don't mean to imply that you pretend that your limits don't exist, but the bargaining stage is where you try to redefine where those limits are. During bargaining, you and your crush may begin to spend more time together. Both of you may even convince yourselves that if you behave in a certain way and stay a respectable distance from the invisible line that no one will get hurt. You think that maybe if you run fast enough or wish hard enough that time or society will never catch up with you. You hope that if you can prove to the universe that you can live in the same world as your crush and not turn to stone, that you will be able to stay there - with him – like this - forever.

In the case of the forbidden crush, there are two fundamental problems with this line of thinking. First, no matter how close you and your crush get without crossing the line, you are never going to change the powers that keep you apart. You are always going to be too young, too poor, or share too many genetics. Whatever your original obstacle was, bargaining is not going to change it. No matter how much you discuss, deny, or pretend otherwise, time never changes the distance between parallel lines.

That brings us to the second and possibly more painful problem with the bargaining phase: you will be flying pretty close to the sun. In the bargaining phase, you may let your guard down and find yourself more emotionally connected to your crush than you ever dreamed possible. Regardless of how it looks on the outside, love affairs are not defined by physical contact, so when you and your crush "bargain" together you can quickly find yourself in over your head. Even though you have never physically crossed the line, the struggle of coming within inches of it might be too much for your heart to handle.

At the very least, no matter how long it lasts ~ and no matter how amazing it is ~ your bargaining phase will ultimately leave you incomplete. The fact remains that you will never be a couple and both of you will eventually admit that your pretending is only causing heartache. I'm not saying that the closeness you discover during bargaining won't be beautiful, but until you accept that bargaining has a ceiling, it will never be enough.

July & August

"Stars, hide your fires; let not light see my black and deep desires"
William Shakespeare

* * *

In Search of Danny and Sandy

For the rest of the summer, Jack and I remained inseparable. Safe within the anonymity of moonlight, we found our rhythm beneath the stars. We went for slushies, ate M&Ms, and we even spent my birthday together, laughing around the campfire with our closest friends. Jack acted like going to his house that night was just a casual summer get together, but time would reveal that he had bailed on a few obligations to make himself free that night…obligations he really had no business bailing on. The hard truth was that Jack wanted to spend the final hours of my birthday with me…at his house…as close to an old married couple as we were ever going to get. In true Jack fashion, he simply wanted to give me a memorable birthday and he absolutely knocked it out of the park.

Jack had been hinting to his friends all week that he might want to have a fire Friday night. For Mother's Day, Jack had conveniently gotten his mom tickets to see *Guys and Dolls* at Shea's Buffalo Theatre (his mom was a sucker for that Sky Masterson). Jack claimed that this Friday night show was the only one with "good seats," even though I had heard a few people say things that seemed to prove otherwise. I was certain that Jack knew Friday was my birthday, but he remained successfully nonchalant about the entire series of events. Jack was not throwing me a party; he was simply having a few people over on a night that happened to coincide with the day of my birth. Nothing suspicious about that at all! There was also nothing suspicious about the fact that this was exactly…I mean EXACTLY how I wanted to spend my birthday. There was no better combination of elements than Jack and moonlight.

With seemingly little fanfare, it was just past 9 pm when I picked up Rosie. If anyone could have seen the cosmetic gymnastics I had gone through during the previous six hours they would have immediately known how important this night was to me. Playing things very close to the vest, however, I hoped that my perfectly wavy hair, on point make-up and "just the right amount of sexy" birthday outfit would pass by most eyes unnoticed. There was only one set of eyes I was hoping to catch anyway. By the time we arrived, a collection of chairs had been pulled into the yard and the fire was beautifully ablaze. Jack was rocking a tattered red tee-shirt and was predictably barefoot. In the summer, whether he was walking down the street or riding in the car, Jack's shoes were more often found in his hands than on his feet. I loved that carefree part of him. Spotting Rosie and me through the darkness, Jack immediately rushed toward us and wished me a Happy Birthday. He then proceeded to smother me in a full body hug before offering me a chair by the fire - and the fact that this chair was directly next to Jack's did not pass by my eyes unnoticed! Already having the best birthday of my young life, I happily slid back into that Adirondack chair, put my feet up on the side table and surveyed the scene. Yeah. There was no doubt about it; I loved looking at Jack though the smoke of the campfire. The firelight seemed to make his complexion even more irresistible and the way the flames danced in his eyes was positively mesmerizing.

True to his word, Jack's guest list was small, and true to our "thing" it involved M&Ms. Yes, Jack seemed to be employing his full bag of tricks to entertain me tonight and I was flabbergasted at how well he could play on my weaknesses. He knew exactly which songs to put on the record player, how to perfectly toast a marshmallow and how to steer the conversation away from anything that might make things awkward. Looking back, that night was probably the first time I truly understood the strength of our connection and depths of Jack's perfection. It was like he could see into the deepest parts of my brain and spot every secret I was hiding. Jack knew exactly what I wanted and exactly how I wanted it. He said all the right things, suggested all of the right activities, and systematically fulfilled scads of my hidden desires. To be honest, I found it all a little bit creepy. It was a kind of witchcraft I had never before experienced and unquestionably knew I would never encounter again.

As if that wasn't great enough, as the night wore on, I became absolutely enamored with the way Jack seemed tethered to my side. Even when he was engrossed in conversation with someone else, he managed to throw me reassuring looks...like he was letting me know that I was still his main priority. And don't even get me started on how he "lost" his cup of ice-water and decided that he and I would be sharing for the rest of the night. As soon as he picked up my glass, I couldn't help myself from watching as his perfectly rosy lips brushed against the rim. Smirking, he handed it back to me and I felt our fingers touch. Looking up into Jack's eyes, I saw him watch just as intently as I put my lips on that exact same spot – a secret kiss from our common cup. That was a high I can't even describe.

Settling back into my chair, I pulled my knees up to my chest and looked up at the stars. It's funny. At times like this, the elephant in the room barely seemed to matter. Jack and I were just two people, drifting through the darkness and enjoying each other's company. What I wasn't enjoying, was the incriminating giggling that was taking place behind my back. Oh, my wicked friends. They were plotting something – I was sure of it – and I only hoped that I had the fortitude to survive it.

It was just past 11 pm when it happened.

"In case you didn't know, it's my best friend's birthday tonight," Rosie proclaimed while walking toward the side of the driveway, "and a few of us have put a little something together - Happy Birthday Josie!"

As I slunk in my chair, Sean proudly whispered to me,

"I think this was Jack's idea!"

With those words, I was equal parts excited and terrified and as the scene unfolded, I quietly gasped at what I was seeing. Oh no! Rosie was preparing to serenade me, and it appeared that Jack and our friend Monica were going to be her back-up dancers. As Max began strumming his guitar, I couldn't help but shake my head. The song they were about to perform was one that I had been listening to a lot lately. It reminded me of Jack...of me and Jack... and Jack would have to be blind, deaf, and dumb if he didn't feel it too. I could sense that it was no fluke they were doing this song. Even if the choice was Rosie's, I knew that Jack understood the significance and it was just one more way that the universe was pulling on that invisible string. Even all these years later, I don't know whether it was Jack or Rosie that chose the song...and I kind of prefer it that way.

Looking at the inevitable train wreck in front of me, there was no doubt in my mind that this was going to be hilarious... horribly embarrassing ... but hilarious. And so, already laughing hysterically, I watched in wonder as Rosie skillfully began belting out an almost punk version of "Why Do Fools Fall in Love," and Jack and Monica stood behind her, proudly performing the cheesiest synchronized back-up chorography since the 1920s. Swaying from side to side, Jack and Monica executed their steps brilliantly and no one in the yard could hold back their laughter. Smiling with my whole soul, I looked directly at Jack and as our eyes met, he began to blush just a little and smiled with all the charm and embarrassment of a schoolboy caught mooning over his teacher. This crack in Jack's armor was noteworthy and I was more than a little surprised that he wasn't better able to hold it together. Jack was usually so cool and razor sharp. Seeing him a little rattled was both adorable and unnerving. I'm not sure if it could be considered a birthday gift, but it was it was this incident...on my birthday...that finally gave me the clarity to see the power I had over Jack.

As the lyrics professed love to be a losing game, Jack continued to unravel, and I didn't quite know what to do with that. Regardless of who chose this song, Jack was embracing it like an anthem and truth was beginning to ooze from his cracks. Sure, they were all singing to me (it was my serenade after all), but the force that came out of Jack's eyes as he looked at me was different...polarizing. Like they were trying to hide that Jack was the fool everyone was singing about. In a way, Jack looked as surprised as I was about what was unfolding, as if he too had expected to handle it better.

I struggled to catch my breath and quickly tried to survey the crowd. I wondered if anyone else could see what was happening between us and if they were reading his eyes as clearly as I was. In truth, while everyone else may have been seeing a hilarious and innocent birthday tribute, I knew that Jack and our secrets were dancing dangerously close to the line. By the time the song got to the part about the heart being defeated, I was done for. That lyric tore through me like a bullet and the word "defeat" seemed to dangle in the smoke in front of me. At that same moment, Jack was looking right at me, and his smirk was filled with a unique blend of defiance and pain. Oh yeah. This was a song Jack sang with purpose...I could see that much. Even though this might look like a spoof to everyone else, I knew that for us, this was more...so much more. This song was Jack's confession... his admission...and my real gift.

Immediately following the performance, I ran up to Rosie, Monica, Max and Jack to thank them for their awesome, albeit unusual birthday tribute. Still hiding behind my laughter, I turned to Jack and simply shook my head. I had no words. Jack on the other hand had plenty. With that devilish look I had come to know all too well, he looked directly into my eyes and said,

"I was actually going to dress up like a clown for the party, but then I thought better of it."

Whether that was a joke or a fact was irrelevant. I knew exactly what he was doing and exactly what those words meant. He didn't have to be dressed like a clown or a jester for me to see it. Jack was a fool- we both were – fools who were falling in love.

Oh, those summer nights...

Cruising into "The Middle"

Without ever admitting it, by August Jack and I seemed to be living in some imaginary version of a relationship. Almost as if our impossibility didn't exist, we happily settled into a comfort zone where nothing was as it seemed and everything was subject to interpretation. We saw each other often and seemed to be avoiding any suspicion of impropriety. I had gotten pretty good at "playing it cool" in public and was learning to control my emotions to a satisfactory degree. I still knew that people were displeased with our alliance, but we somehow managed to keep things in a gray zone that kept their disapproval at bay. Now I feel like it's important to point out that Jack and I had still NEVER talked about any of this. We never discussed our feelings, our parent's fears or the inquisitive eyes of the community. I know it sounds strange, but our connection was so transparent that I don't think either of us felt like we needed to – or more importantly – SHOULD be talking about it. It was almost like we didn't want to risk speaking of it and having that act break the spell. We also never discussed a bizarre issue that had come to light this summer. At the core of it, I think our connection had become so strong that our unspoken bond had literally begun to burst from the seams. Crazy as it sounds, Jack and I had involuntarily begun dressing alike. One day, our yellow shirts and navy-blue shorts made this phenomenon impossible to ignore and once I thought back about it, I realized that it had been happening for quite some time. From head to toe, Jack and I would sport the same style and the same color scheme, accidentally coordinated as we set forth on our adventures. Always in perfect syncopation, Jack and I found our true colors that summer, and then watched them slowly seep through every crack in our illusion. I never would have through it possible, but everyone who looked at us was suddenly witness to the chemistry between us. Like a billboard, there it was …involuntarily on display for the world…leaving absolutely no doubt that what we had together was real and deep and true - visual evidence of our silent truth.

So, like I said, by August, Jack and I seemed to be living in some imaginary version of a relationship. I was beginning to know Jack so well, on levels I never dreamed possible, and the way we fit together blew my mind day after day. Sometimes I wished other people could know Jack the way that I did. He was so much more than "Quarterback Jack" and so much deeper than the persona he had around town. And while I felt bad that others didn't appreciate him the way that I did, I also secretly liked having that connection all to myself.

If we are being honest, one of the things I loved most about Jack was his car. Let me be clear though, I don't mean I loved the actual car (although it was pretty cool). I loved the relationship Jack had with his car. Even though the Riley's had plenty of money and could have afforded to buy Jack any new toy he wanted, last summer Jack insisted on buying his own car with money he had earned himself. So, while all of Jack's friends drove around in shiny new cars their parents picked out, Jack spent his days in a faded blue 1946 Chrysler Windsor convertible. The interior upholstery had a few tatters in it and the body was rusting in a couple key places. Even though it may not have had the latest gadgets or shiniest paint job, Jack's car had one intangible thing that all the others did not – character! I can't really explain it, but Jack just fit in that car, like it was made for him. I noticed it the minute I saw him in it and even though all of his friends gave him crap about it, I knew that Jack didn't mind. Jack was no idiot and I think he was astute enough to know that his friends weren't deep enough to get it – but he did – so that's all he ever cared about. I secretly wanted to let him know that I got it too, but we weren't exactly friends last summer so that obviously didn't happen.

By this summer, I was on the inner circle, and I had no trouble letting Jack know how much I respected his car choice and how much I too was beginning to care about that amazing piece of machinery. It didn't take long before I could see that Jack felt very smug about my kinship to his car. He could tell I was sincere in my attachment and I'm sure he could feel that I wasn't sucking up. What I liked the most though, was the way Jack was so willing to share the connection with me. He loved that I loved his car and we both loved any time we spent together in it. Before I knew it there was one particular sentence Jack could say, and the minute I heard it my entire world would stop,

"Do you want to cruise?"

Hearing those words come out of Jack's mouth was like nirvana. In a blur I was out the door, buckled up and practically senseless with anticipation. I loved being in that convertible and sitting next to Jack as he drove had to be one of my favorite things on the planet.

Nothing compared to Jack's silhouette on a hot summer day....one arm out the window and the other dangling on the top of the steering wheel. His seat was reclined to optimum cruising position and the wind ran through his hair in a way I desperately wished my fingers could. Almost as if rocked to sleep by the road, my problems instantly faded the minute those doors slammed. Music up and sunglasses on, we could have been the only two people in the world. Jack called me his co-pilot and I embraced that role far beyond the boundaries of that car. Sure, there were obstacles, and the way we were looking at each other probably broke about three different rules of society, but right here, on this road and under this sky, we were both comfortably numb to all of it. We didn't need to talk about it. We both knew how it felt and we both knew that days like these didn't come around much. Days like these were a gift.

It was inside the car that Jack and I developed a syncopation that would come to characterize our relationship. I would toss the keys and Jack would catch them without looking. He would reach over me to adjust my visor and I would lean back past him to turn on the lights. Jack and I functioned as a well-oiled machine, anticipating each other's needs, and solidifying our poetically unspoken bond. When Jack let me drive, he would use funny voices to read to me from our favorite books and when Jack drove, I would put my feet on the dashboard and let the summer air wash over me like a new beginning. Whether we were gossiping about our deepest secrets or Jack was singing Frank Sinatra at the top of his lungs, the connection between us was unmistakable. We were just a couple of pirates, sailing the world in our pirate ship and answering to our own rules. I suppose we both knew that we were dancing pretty close to the line, but in those magical moments inside that car, the purity of what passed between us seemed to make that blurry line okay. Nothing that felt like this should be considered wrong. And so - under our cloak of awesomeness - this charade continued. Whether we were making promises, sharing secrets, or eating an entire batch of cookie dough, whatever occurred inside that car was laced in magic. I never felt more authentic, and Jack never looked more at ease. On any given day our connection was undeniable, but inside that car, well that may have been the one place where we both felt comfortable enough to completely give in to it. Of course, we never spoke of it, and of course we never acted on it, but it didn't take a genius to connect the dots. In the sanctuary of that car, Jack and I were a couple.

And never did we feel more like a couple than during one of our mythical midnight cruises. Call it any politically correct thing you want, but when the midnight cruise was scheduled in advance, it was a date...a black and white, pick me up at 10:00 pm in our time machine kind of date. When the air was warm, the breeze was light and the moon was three quarters full, we could talk and drive for hours and never feel the realities of the time and place we were living in. Cloaked in summer's darkness, we were on our own clock and played by our own rules. The stars offered us the acceptance the real world couldn't and in the wee hours of the morning, the stillness of the outside world presented us a blank canvas to write one night's worth of fiction.

Unlike our daytime adventures, the midnight cruise had some unique traditions, not all of which came naturally to me. First and foremost, the instant Jack turned on the car, the radio was turned off. Jack felt strongly about becoming one with the sounds of the darkness and he tried to help me become a connoisseur of midnight's silence. At first, this concept was extremely difficult for me. Having the radio on was almost like having a chaperone, and there was a nakedness without it that initially made me very uncomfortable. Like anything else though, it didn't take long for Jack's magic to find its way to me. By the end of the summer, that lack of radio was probably the thing I appreciated most. You see, it wasn't until these nights with Jack that I understood the intimacy of silence. Parked on the overpass to Glen Falls and listening to nothing but the rush of the water, I had never felt so connected to someone else's essence. Without the distraction of music, you are forced to focus on each other and your place in the world around you. Even separated by six inches and an armrest, I had never felt Jack as vividly as I did in that silence. No matter how many times we visited the falls, we knew what awaited us and neither of us could resist getting lost in the oblivion of our connection. And soon, that connection wasn't limited to the falls. We could find it parked in Forest Lawn Cemetery or turning off the car in the middle of a deserted backstreet. Whether we were hitting 60mph on Jack's favorite stretch of road or inadvertently driving toward some leftover July fireworks, the silence of the midnight cruise became the thing that I would most remember about our year together. Truth be told, for the rest of my life I have never been able to replicate the way I felt whenever we were cocooned inside that car. On those nights with Jack, I experienced a kind of contentment that can't be given justice by ordinary words. The stars that shone above always guided us to a perfect nowhere and I knew that tiny tin box was truly our Neverland.

For as timeless as we felt inside that car, no day ever proved endless, and all open roads eventually led home. As bittersweet as it was, I loved the way Jack lingered long after the car was in park. Sitting straight and frozen I could almost see him fighting off the thoughts inside his own head. Sometimes he struggled for new conversation and sometimes just sat - silent and reflective. Yes, in those peculiar moments after the car became still, there always seemed to be a beautiful awkwardness between the two of us. It was one of those Pinter Moments where the things you didn't say spoke louder than all the things that you did. In the stillness and the silence that followed our adventures, Jack and I both seemed to wrestle with the finality of what was about to occur...we were leaving Neverland. The minute those doors opened, our real lives would grab us by the throat and suffocate any delusions that car ride might have given us.

Oh, if only our whole world could exist inside that car...that magical place where complications didn't matter, and everyone was without age, color, faith or social status. Within that car there were no rules, no judgements, and no crippling limitations. In that car we were equals. "Oh my God," I thought to myself, "that car is *The Middle*!"

The middle was something I had dreamt about almost my whole life. It was a vision I had when I was little and I had never shaken it. The middle was a place where anyone in history could simultaneously exist in their true form. We would live in a timeline with the people we were meant to be aligned with and be of the age, gender, or gene pool that we felt destined for. Unlike heaven, the middle was a place I envisioned existing between the layers of our present reality. It was a place where hearts and destinies could truly "meet in the middle" and carry on in a way their real worlds didn't allow. It was a physical and a metaphorical middle and I secretly dreamt that one day…one magical day…I would find it.

That night I shut the door to my room, curled up by the open window and breathed in that intangible romance that only the summer air can generate. Consumed with thoughts of The Middle, I pulled out a sheet of paper and sat like a bystander as the words flowed effortlessly from my fingertips. The result was a poem I would keep with me for the rest of my life. I knew I probably couldn't let anyone read it, but that was okay. Just putting those words on paper was a sort of freedom. Plus, now that those words existed, I hoped the fates would find me…find both of us…and take us for a walk in the haze. And so, it read…

A Walk in the Haze

There is a place
stuck in the strands of time,
that waits breathlessly for those lucky enough to find it
~ a place that is neither here nor there
and is neither past nor present~
It exists like a Brigadoon
suspended in the mist and immune to the rules of tradition.
Layered, yet mixed in perfect harmony,
the best pieces of each age meet to form something invincible...
something extraordinary.
It is in this place that chronological miscues can be righted
and star-crossed casualties can find their forever.
Woven together by destiny,
the pages of the calendar create a tapestry of time
and the players find their way through the chapters of their story
...rewritten with absolute certainty...

the way fate intended
but their worlds would not allow.
Magical and impossible
Scenes unfold and lives are scrambled.
Before your eyes, the impractical merges with the ridiculous
And the hopeless are reborn indestructible
Yes, in this place
...outside of time...and inside of fortune
Dreams are realized, holes are filled and impulses are validated
While many have tried, most have yet to find their way
So, she waits...tied to the invisible string.
Of what lies on the other end, she is certain.
Determined and undaunted, she will keep searching
lost in the blue eyes of temptation
and dreaming of the day she meets them face to face
when they both arrive safely
in the mist
of The Middle

Two Thirty A.M.

Saying that I loved our bargaining phase is an understatement. Without a doubt, that summer with Jack stands out as one of the greatest periods of my life. What I have always found peculiar though, is that my affection for it can't be attributed to any singular or series of events. Our summer wasn't magical because of what he said or what we did, it was iconic because of the way being with Jack made me feel. Before Jack I observed life from a respectable distance, never wanting to stand out and never wanting to get hurt. I was organized and calculated and enjoyed being predictable. And then along came Jack. Falling for him wasn't a choice; it was a whole-body revolution. For the first time in my life my emotions were running around unsupervised, and I had little to no control over them. Being with Jack changed the way I looked at the world and, more importantly, at myself. Just waking up in the morning and knowing Jack was in my life was enough to make me feel complete. But more than anything, having Jack in my life filled it with that one particular thing that I had never felt before – possibility.

So, by late August, when the days were just a little shorter and the air was just a little cooler, change was on the horizon and I was determined to soak in every bit of magic this summer had left. Knowing my mother would be out half the night at one of her card parties, I decided to go out on a limb and invite some people over for one last night under the stars. When I called Jack, he jumped at the chance to get some of the guys together and Rosie was already spreading the word to some of the girls in our crowd. What ensued was a night of music and memories that defined the essence of being young. Rosie strung lights across the patio, Monica roasted marshmallows, Max played the guitar and Jack tried his best to play the (wait for it….) harmonica. I'm still not sure why. Even though I can't remember what songs we sang, what we talked about or who exactly came and went, I vividly remember Jack staying with me after everyone had gone. Almost invisible in the darkness, Jack sat on my lawn and quietly continued to sing to me as I cleaned up. Pop songs… church hymns… his repertoire was wide and his voice surprisingly angelic. It was amazing how beautiful he sounded when he wasn't goofing around.

With the backyard clean, Jack and I walked down the driveway toward his car. Even though it was past midnight, my evening still felt unfinished and looking at Jack it became clear that neither of us were ready for this night to end. The next thing I knew we were nestled into two Adirondack chairs, simply content with the opportunity to be together. If I close my eyes, it still feels like yesterday.

It was one of those nights you dream about - the kind that haunts you in the thick of winter when the magic of summer seems like more of a fable than inevitability. It was a night where goodness dripped from him like starlight and the world was powerless not to get lost inside his perfection. I knew nights like this were as fleeting as the moonlight and I cherished every minute, every second that I spent lost inside his charm. Being with Jack would never cease to amaze me. His ability to hold my heart in the low whisper of his voice, the way he could wrap me up in his essence without even trying, his knack for making me feel so calm and so alive all in the same instant, these were the things that defined him, and these were the things no other man on earth possessed.

Sitting next to Jack, I treasured both the weight and the privilege of the spot I was occupying, and I could feel my own lungs hanging on every breath he took. I had longed for this so many times...to sit together beneath my bedroom window and get lost adrift the magnitude of our connection. The cocoon we had created was so real and so effortless. I wanted to live in it forever - wrapped in the darkness and serenaded by the silence. Jack looked at me and smiled and although his eyes were concealed behind the shadows of summer, I could feel the electricity shooting from them and I sighed as our bond traveled through my bloodstream. It's amazing how the simple act of sitting with him could make me feel so content and so secure. As he spoke, sentences melodically flowing from him like a symphony, I knew that he was letting me into places few others would ever see, and I responded by inviting him into corners I usually saved for myself. The intimacy we were able to create with our words was one of the most powerful things I had ever felt, and I wanted to put it in my pocket and save it for the day he would be gone.

I knew summer couldn't last forever. Winds would blow, leaves would change and the knowledge of existing beneath the same sky would be my only comfort. Looking past an unbroken web of stars, I glanced at him and contemplated my place in infinity. I knew that his friendship was a gift, and it was better to appreciate it for what it was than to regret what it could never be. So, for tonight, I sat...aware of the future but blissfully entangled in the present. The key to a great love affair is in recognizing it for what it is, and there was no doubt that ours was magic. As inconceivable as the colors in the dark sky and as unattainable as summer nights in winter, what we had been given remained defiantly genuine and beautifully simple. In the end, there are truths that matter and truths that don't. The secret is in knowing the difference.

With that, I sat back and soaked in the final drops of summer's pixie dust. My soul was full and my smile genuine. As Jack looked down at me from the corner of his eye, my heart melted into him, and his smirk told me he was keeping it. And with that, I knew. Destiny is fickle, forever is a state of mind, and father time is often wrong. Tonight had proven that if this was the closest we were to ever get, it could be enough. Our intentions were true, our words were infinite, and even within its boundaries our connection seemed limitless. Although I had always suspected it, that night with Jack left no doubts in my mind. Jack Riley was my miracle and even if I was the only one who ever knew it, I would be thankful for him forever.

September

"Affection is a coal that must be cooled: else, suffered, it will set the heart on fire"
William Shakespeare

* * *

Your Own Personal Animal House

A few weeks before school started, Jack's parents dropped the bomb. He would be spending his senior year at Canisus High School. To be honest, I had been worried about this since last April when it was announced that Canisus was demolishing two buildings on West Ferry Street and dedicating $30,000 to the construction of a state of the art playing field and athletic complex, grand enough to "rival any facility in town." Additionally, the school was also tearing down the old Milburn Mansion at 1168 Delaware Avenue and spending another $325,000 on the construction of a new faulty residence. Apparently, the departure of families like the Rileys had created the desired ripple effect. Considering that the Milburn Mansion was such a prominent part of our local history, to be tearing it down in the midst of the 125th Anniversary Celebration was quite noteworthy. The Milburns, you see, were the family who played host to President McKinley when he arrived in Buffalo for the Pan American Exposition of 1901. Consequently, it was the home where the president was brought after being mortally shot in the Expo's Temple of Music. He died there eight days later. Although there was push back from the local preservationists, the school was too powerful for them and the 100-year-old historical site was torn down in the spring of 1957. The irony was not lost on me that the demolition of McKinley's death house was bringing death to my school days with Jack. Fate is funny that way.

Nevertheless, the improvements at Canisus must have been deemed satisfactory by the Rileys and the decision to remove Jack from Bennett had officially been made. I always secretly wondered if part of their objective was to get Jack away from me, but I never quite found the nerve to ask. At the very least, I'm sure the Riley's saw the chance to put some distance between Jack and me as a big perk. Hence, regardless of my despair, our senior year began with Jack at Canisus and me at Bennett. Our schools may have only been 10 minutes apart, but to me, it was enough to feel like we were living in different worlds. Even though I knew the distance was probably a good thing, (let's face it, this affair was complicated enough), I still couldn't help obsessing over the next time I might see him. The ghosts of our summer haunted my thoughts, and I could feel that hole in my soul growing with every leaf that fell. If I was being honest, I knew that this separation was only the beginning of the end. I had always known that we couldn't be together, and I had always known that each day we pretended otherwise would eventually catch up with me. That rational part of my brain could hibernate a little longer though - I just wasn't ready to give this up yet.

The good news is, regardless of how I felt about the distance, our present school situation did have a couple of perks. Due to the ongoing construction at Canisus, students were not allowed to drive their own cars and park on campus. Everyone either had to take the bus or be picked up in the front of the school. I don't think those construction workers will ever understand the favor they were doing me. The combination of getting out earlier and being the one with access to a car, you see, opened a world of opportunities for me. When I nonchalantly told Jack that I could be his backup taxi, I didn't expect him to actually take me up on it, but we hadn't even been back in school a week the first time I got his call. I knew it was ridiculous, but there was no denying it - just the possibility of driving Jack home after school was enough to get me through my entire day. I was all too aware of Jack's schedule and every day I savagely held my breath as the minutes ticked closer to his dismissal. As time approached, I diligently sat by the phone, praying for Jack's call. I convinced myself that I wouldn't be disappointed if it didn't come (which, of course, I was) and that I wouldn't overreact if it did (which, of course, was impossible). On those magical days when Jack did call, my heart would sink to my toes solely at the sound of his voice (oh heck...who are we kidding...it did that all the time anyway). Invariably, I would try to play it cool - but I wasn't even fooling myself. That call was everything!! I laughed at how Jack always treated his ride request as an inconvenience - not my entire reason for getting out of bed in the morning! More than anything, I loved that on that particular day, and under those particular circumstances, Jack once again was choosing ME. Even with a school full of friends, Jack Riley would still occasionally choose me!

Turning into the lot of Jack's school always made me a little anxious. I worried that people could sense the impropriety of our fake relationship and I felt tremendously conspicuous as I passed through their tunnel of judgement. I could feel them scrutinizing what I was driving, what I was up to and why seven out of eight times Jack and I would be dressed alike. I knew they wondered why I was there and what exactly that relationship was between the two of us. The jokes were inevitable. The jury of our peers was very unforgiving - and regrettably intuitive!

Once I navigated the driveway, pulling up to the front of the school was always a crapshoot. Sometimes I was met with comedy...like the day Jack was wearing all gray sweats and laid completely flat on the gray stone benches by the door. I didn't even notice him until he dramatically rose from the bench like a gargoyle. It was hilarious. Sometimes I found him downright ragged after a session in the weight room. Even at his worst, he still managed to drip perfection. But other times...well, let's face it...there were those mythical times when the simple sight of Jack left me completely undone. Beyond the rays of sunshine that I swore radiated from his body, beyond the lightening that shot from his eyes as they spotted me, beyond the electricity that sizzled from his smile on a daily basis...yes beyond all of those things...I also had to deal with the occasional x-factor.... like Toga Day. Dear God... like freaking Toga Day.

Having been given advanced notice, I really thought that I had sufficiently prepared for the occasion. Jack had happily filled me in on the tradition, so I knew the Toga Day basics: the seniors wore togas and, despite the administration's disapproval, used markers to sign each other's skin like some sort of living yearbook. Trying to picture the scene in my head, I thought it seemed somewhat ridiculous and I had diligently worked on desensitizing myself to the many possibilities surrounding seeing Jack in some silly toga. I had imagined everything from cuddly cute to absolute cringeworthy...and I pulled up to that curb with confidence in my ability to hold myself together. What I found that day, however, was the one thing I hadn't had the foresight to prepare for. What I saw emerge from that crowd was like nothing I had ever imagined... like no place I had ever allowed my mind to go. What stood before me was the one possibility that I hadn't dared to believe could even exist. That boy that walked toward me...was drop dead SEXY!

Jack stood before me like biblical temptation... a striped bed sheet draped around him like he was some sort of Greek god. The way he was wrapped left just as much to the imagination as it did NOT and the combination immediately unleashed a firestorm of chemicals inside my body. In an act of self-preservation, I instinctively looked away. Realistically, if I could just keep my eyes on the road and off of that nipple, I would probably be okay. Damn!! My core temperature was easily two thousand and three degrees. I didn't even turn my head as Jack got in the car. As he buckled in, that strap cascading against his bare skin paralyzed my peripheral vision. Oh crap - there's that nipple. Damn!! I wasn't even out of the parking lot and sweat was already pouring form me like a faucet. Of all the things I had prepared for, raging sexual chemistry was not one of them. Our issues had always stemmed from our deep emotional connection - forbidden but sophisticated. This - on the other hand - was anything but sophisticated. Every bit of decorum I had flew out of my head the minute I laid eyes on that chest. It's not like I hadn't seen it before, but I clearly hadn't seen it since he committed to his summer workouts. Sweet Jesus!!

Naturally, Jack dawdled tremendously as I dropped him off. Standing next to the car, his chest seemed to glisten in the sunshine... keeping my full attention on it at all times. As he spoke to me, I prayed that I didn't look like a deer in headlights, although I was positively certain that I did. Even with the homecoming graffiti strewn across it, that chest was still the smoothest and most inviting thing I may have ever seen. I got lost in Shakespearean thoughts of that pen someone must have used to write on it.

"Oh, that I were a pen in that hand that I might touch that.... DAMN!!"

I tried to raise my eyes back up to his face. He was still talking...about what is anybody's guess. My thoughts were literally the consistency of Jell-O.

As I looked up at him, that one magical wave of hair dangling mockingly in front of his right eye, it took everything I had not to cross that line. As if Jack's eyes weren't paralyzing enough, seeing those baby blues peek out from behind that lock of hair was just about the sexiest thing I had ever seen. Although I wouldn't even have thought it possible, in that moment those eyes beguiled me in a way they had never managed before. Maybe it was because I was already defenseless, or maybe because he spoke with the mocking confidence of a guy who sensed what I was feeling. All I knew was that the longer he spoke the more that lock of hair danced in my vision like a serpent...tempting me to taste the forbidden fruit. I promised myself that if I made it out of his driveway intact, I would immediately go to church and pray that our next encounter involved a tee-shirt and a haircut!!

Mercifully, Jack eventually stopped talking and turned to go inside. I remember saying something to him as he walked up the driveway, although I wasn't exactly sure what it was. It wasn't my fault though. I couldn't seem to hear my own voice over the whooshing of my spinning thoughts. Damn! If Jack's smirk was any indication, it must have been pretty incriminating though. Still frozen, I watched him walk up the driveway and clung to the small hope that my behavior wasn't nearly as frazzled I feared. What happened next, unfortunately, confirmed my every concern. Crossing directly in front of the car, Jack impishly raised his water bottle - and with a mischievous glint in his eye – seductively squeezed one devilish surge of water onto my windshield. Oh yeah. It didn't take a Freudian scholar to explain that one. His smug smile said it all. I was busted.

It wasn't until years later that I was able to put that whole fiasco into words. Fast forward to July 4th, 2004, when I was at Darien Lake to see a Goo Goo Dolls concert with my teenage granddaughter (yeah – I appreciate good homegrown Buffalo music and yeah - I'm a cool grandma about stuff like that). It was at this concert that I had the most vivid flashback to Jack and his toga, proving that 1957 never rests far from my surface. As I stood in the pouring rain listening to our hometown rock-stars, I heard the opening lyrics to "Iris" and was suddenly 17 years old, struggling in Jack's driveway. There were so many things I would have "given up" for that one magical moment with Jack. I knew he could feel it too and knowing that made it so much harder. Yep. It took forty-seven years, but Johnny Rzeznic finally did it. In two poignant lines, he perfectly explained to the world the burden I felt keeping my hands to myself while walking the same earth as Jack Freaking Riley. Leave it to some Buffalo boys to have my back!

Sun-Kissed

If I could only pick one thing that this whole charade with Jack had taught me, it would unquestionably be this: *Without a doubt, the universe puts me in situations just so it can sit back, gawk and laugh uncontrollably at me.* On this particular day, I was sitting in Delaware Park, another piece of Fredrick Law Olmsted's elaborate park system, waiting to pick up a little girl that I occasionally watched afterschool. I was early (I was admittedly neurotic like that) so I was happily waiting…enjoying the fall sunshine and eavesdropping on the music blaring from some soccer player's transistor radio. To be honest, Delaware Park had some historical significance for me, and I couldn't seem to pass through without reflecting on it. Although it probably wasn't the first place I had actually seen Jack Riley…odds are that we had crossed paths numerous times before…it was, however, the first place I REMEMBERED interacting with Jack Riley. We were just kids, and he was there playing football with his friends. Rosie's family's "new money" was even newer at that point, but she had gotten to know Jack and his friends enough for a polite conversation in the park. It might seem insignificant, but this place was where I first heard Jack's voice and first appreciated his humor. It was where we were formally introduced. Although our encounter was brief and insignificant, something clicked in me that day. I didn't understand it of course, but if I was being honest with myself, I would have accepted that from that very moment, my heart never quite beat the same.

Contently, there I sat, soaking in the sunshine and basking in the cozy memories of yesterday. Like clockwork, "Why Do Fools Fall in Love" began to ooze from the tiny radio and I smiled. At this point, I didn't even pretend to be surprised by these things. I had kind of accepted the fact that my life literally had a soundtrack. What I didn't bank on was what would happen next…or that it would happen in the cheesiest movie-like way imaginable.

Still humming along I looked up and saw a figure walking toward me from across the grass. Like Mr. Darcy emerging from the mist of the countryside, his figure was simply mesmerizing. The sun was radiantly glaring overhead and he literally looked like he was walking straight out of the sunbeams. In an instant, I knew it was Jack. The vision of him walking toward me was like some epic daydream and I couldn't take my eyes off him. He was wearing a faded green tee-shirt and his jeans were shredded in all the right places. The tips of his summer-bleached hair glistened in the sunshine and rainbows radiated from his mirrored sunglasses. We saw each other simultaneously. Feeling dazed, I instinctively tilted my head back in disbelief and laughed. Jack responded with his impish grin and a nod of the head. I don't think either one of us were surprised by our invisible string anymore. As his hand slowly rose from his side I prepared for an innocent wave. What happened instead was the stuff of teenage legend. Never breaking stride and with his smirking eyes clearly locked with mine, Jack grabbed the bottom of his tee-shirt and in one mesmerizing motion, pulled that faded green piece of perfection up to wipe his face. As he removed his sunglasses to dry the sweat from his forehead my entire existence became lost in the sight of his stomach. Still walking, his new six-pack glistened with tiny beads of sweat and the tanned muscles rippled with every stride. If there was one thing in this world that begged to be licked like a Popsicle, it was that stomach.

Thank the good Lord that someone else in the park called him over before he reached me. I was still powerless against this new dynamic, and I REALLY needed a few moments to compose myself. Head in my hands, I was frozen in my seat. Sure, I appreciated the pure ridiculousness of this entire episode... but COME ON! How much was I seriously expected to take? Why on earth would he think that was okay? He had literally just flashed me. Magnificently clueless my ass...Jack was the world's most maniacal evil genius.

By the time Jack reached me, I could barely look at him. I was sitting, he was standing, and I was keenly aware that I was eye level with that stomach. I tried to get my eyes high enough to meet his face, but that was little help. Good God he looked amazing in this sunshine. Leaning on a tree Jack proceeded to talk about...oh heck...we all know that I had NO IDEA what he was talking about. I was just trying to get out of this alive! I was visibly frazzled and even the biggest of morons would be able to see it. Not to mention, at this point, I was pretty certain that Jack was playing with me. First the flashing and now even the most harmless of topics began to blow up in my face. Case in point – I made a joke about the pizza delivery tee-shirt he was wearing. Usually, if all else failed, I could make fun of him about something, and all order would be restored. Unfortunately, I should have already known that today was not an ordinary day. My tee-shirt joke unleashed one of Jack's best (and most painfully accurate) observations of all time,

"...but this shirt makes me the perfect combination of awesome and delicious!"

AWESOME AND DELICIOUS??.... Had two truer adjectives ever been used in the same sentence? That was it. I exploded into some purely psychotic fit of laughter...we all know the kind...the over-the-top kind of laughter that completely implicates the person doing it...the kind of laughter that says,

"Holy cow! I was just thinking the exact same thing about YOU! Awesome and delicious..."

Unfortunately, my laughter was followed by the exchange of some excruciatingly awkward glances. For the next few moments, every time our eyes met things felt different. Jack almost looked at me as if he was waiting for me to say something, and it was making me terribly uncomfortable. Luckily, the tension was broken by a loose dog that playfully ran past us. In typical superhero fashion, I watched Jack instinctively run after the dog, scoop it up and return it to its owners.

"Gee," I said to him as he walked back over, "picking up strange dogs with your bare hands? That's impressive work Spider Man!"

"Yeah," he replied sarcastically, "I'm just a rebel like that."

"Yep, rebel is definitely the first word that comes to my mind when I think of you!" I said mockingly.

With my words still floating in the air, a suffocating silence was suddenly born between us. It was almost like that eerie calm that drifts through the breeze just before a big storm. Something was happening; I didn't know what, but I could feel it. Freakishly uncomfortable, I looked at the ground and Jack did the same. With all four of our eyes sturdily fixed on those tiny blades of grass, Jack broke the silence.

"Rebel is the first word huh?"

I smiled sheepishly at him. What happened next, I will remember with complete and utter clarity for as long as I live. Boldly, Jack used his serious voice to pose one of the most dangerous and intriguing questions he had ever asked me:

"So, what's the second word?"

"Oh my God," I thought, more in love with him than ever, "he KNOWS!!!!!"

Mercifully, my instantaneous panic was interrupted by a squeaky voice.

"What are you guys talking about, Josie?" my little friend said.

Whew - a stay of execution. I would not have to answer Jack's question today!

That night I tried (rather unsuccessfully) to wrap my head around what had just happened. "So, what's the second word?" The sentence looped though my thoughts unapologetically. Jack was baiting me. I knew him and our hidden language well enough to know exactly what those words meant. Jack was calling me out. It was a rhetorical question from someone who knew he had me against the ropes. What kind of an answer was he hoping for? Had he really wanted me to say it out loud? Preposterous! Even though I was very clear about how I felt about Jack, and even though I was pretty certain of the way Jack felt about me, I was also very certain that those things could never be addressed out loud. Crossing that line was never an option and the prospect of Jack pushing me toward it was positively terrifying. We had been pretending for months and I was starting to feel the sting of it. Although I wasn't entirely sure if we had been pretending that our feelings didn't exist or pretending that our limits didn't exist, either way, I knew this fairytale was quickly coming toward its end. Jack was done pretending.

Indian Summer

Waking up Saturday morning, I could immediately tell this day was going to be special. I remember having no idea why, but there are those days in your life where you just wake up and KNOW that something is about to change. Even feeling that warning, I honestly had no idea I was beginning a day I would never forget. During the night the thermometer had climbed to near record highs and as I opened my curtains, I immediately smiled when I felt the warm sunshine hit my face. Plus, thanks to the city's General Mills Plant, as I opened my window, the smells in the morning air were a peculiar combination of Cheerios and possibility. Looking at the forecast, I knew what awaited me, and I took an extra deep cleansing breath as I prepared to start my day. Indian summer, you see, is a bittersweet thing. While the sensation of it helps to ease the transition back to fall's responsibilities, it regrettably comes with the stigma of knowing this taste of summer's magic is only temporary. While these deceivingly warm fall days may give your heart one last chance to relive the glory of your summer, they are also a painful reminder of what you are losing once the bitterness of winter buries your memories beneath the snow. Let's face it; I had never spent a summer as magical as the one I just spent with Jack. We had only been back in school for a few weeks, but I was already feeling the sting of our separation and our awkward exchange in Delaware Park last week gave me the impression that Jack was wrestling with it too. I wasn't an idiot. I knew we would never again be as close as we were that summer, and I was still struggling to be okay with that. I mean, I knew that our summer was nothing more than a grand illusion, but dear God, I loved that illusion. What I didn't anticipate was how learning to live in its aftermath was going to be such a long process. Then again, when you love something in such an irrational way, I guess it's hard to face the rational side of the situation. Regardless, I knew that in order to carry on I would have to learn to appreciate Jack for what he was, not for what he could never be. Real life wasn't the fairytale we created last summer. Real life was a villain.

Despite our obstacles though, I could feel things between us changing. I don't think we had passed the point of no return, but we were dangerously close to a place we wouldn't be able to turn back from. I know I'm not describing this well, but I guess that's because my relationship with Jack was never rooted in logic, it was entirely defined by how it felt – and I knew that things FELT different. Our bargaining phase had brought us so close to what we wanted that sometimes it actually felt real. It felt like Jack was going to walk through my door, scoop me up in his arms and kiss me like it was no big deal. God, I wanted that, and what's worse, it felt like he wanted it too. He was definitely proposing the idea of talking about our feelings when we were in the park, but in no way could we allow those thoughts to enter the universe. No matter how much I longed to hear the words, we couldn't let things become real. Jack and I needed to live in a world of nuances. It might have been ridiculous, but I firmly believed that those things we never said were the only things keeping us safe.

So, when Jack called me later that morning, my reaction was a little unexpected. Jack knew I was scheduled to work until 8pm and he called to let me know he was planning a visit. Getting those adorable kids out of your system was a pretty tall order, so I wasn't surprised that he wanted to meet me at the community center and have some quality time with them. Our director loved visitors and given Jack's impact last winter, he was high on her list of approved guests. Although I happily accepted Jack's invitation (I wasn't crazy after all) I couldn't help struggling with some major apprehension after I hung up. While Jack's request might have seemed harmless on any other day, given the weather forecast, I knew we both realized his visit would be followed by one of the most perfect convertible nights any September could hope to provide. Although spending the evening with Jack was always my first choice, the weight of this one felt different. First, it was a Saturday during the school year and tradition would lean toward Jack spending it partying with school friends, not alone with me. Second, with the desperation of our ending in my blood, I wasn't entirely secure in my ability to control my mouth or my actions. Jack had been pretty bold in the park. What if he asked about "the second word" again – and what if I said something crazy in a desperate attempt to hang on to our fairytale? And then there was number three: the nagging fact that Jack's parents were out of town. I wasn't exactly sure why that bothered me so much, but I couldn't help thinking that it was a variable I wasn't prepared to handle. I mean good God, what if that overpowering sexual chemistry came back into play? Ugh. Unlike all the other times, this "date" with Jack left me feeling very uneasy.

And if all of that wasn't enough, I also think a major part of my uneasiness stemmed from Jack's mother. Although she had never acted anything but cordial toward me (that was the "County Club way" after all), I was beginning to feel her increased disgust with Jack and me spending time together. I mean Jack wasn't crazy, so I couldn't imagine that she had any idea how often we actually spoke or how much we had been hanging out, but she obviously knew that our friend groups were mixing – and she was not a fan. I could see the reprimanding looks she would give him whenever we crossed paths in at a 125th Anniversary event and I swear once I even heard his dad say something about not sacrificing his future. That was a real eye opener for me. I guess up until this point I had been entirely focused on how an indiscretion or a scandal would affect ME, how it would ruin MY family. I hadn't really considered how it would affect Jack. In a lot of ways, he had just as much to lose as I did. At the end of the day, Jack was dependent on his family and their money if he wanted to keep pursuing his dreams. He couldn't risk a fallout either.

So, with a crazy blend of trepidation and anticipation, I watched the clock all through my shift and it wasn't until about 45 minutes before it ended that

Jack appeared at the classroom door. Predictably, the kids went berserk at the sight of him, and I spent the remainder of that night placidly enjoying the pure love that passed between him and these beautiful children. Good grief, there was no end to the depths of his perfection. As if I wasn't crazy about him enough already, seeing the goodness that spilled from him as he played blocks and drew cartoon animals was irresistible. Even as he said goodbye to each one, promising to visit again soon, I could see the genuine goodness and sincerity that defined him. It was almost sexier than his toga.

As I began to clean up, Jack dug into his backpack with a smirk on his face.

"I brought you something," he said proudly. Handing me a paper bag and keeping an identical one himself, Jack coyly added "I figured you would be hungry."

With a deep breath, I prepared to open the bag, but I was already pretty certain of what I was holding. Not that long ago, Jack and I had become completely engrossed in a conversation about our favorite childhood foods and I embarrassingly admitted that I still hadn't outgrown my deep love for peanut butter and Marshmallow Fluff sandwiches.

"Are you kidding me?" I squealed, already turning several shades of red. "Peter Pan Peanut Butter I assume," (referencing the in-depth peanut butter conversation that had also occurred that evening.)

Jack just smirked with extreme satisfaction and motioned to open the bag. Looking inside, not only did I see my perfectly gooey sandwich, but sitting atop was a handwritten note from Jack on which he had scrawled three simple – and appropriate – words,

NEVER grow up

My heart immediately melted. With one clever reference to Peter Pan's peanut butter, Jack had not only reassured me that he had made the perfect sandwich, but also pinpointed just how great it would be if we could find some pixie dust, fly to Neverland and stay forever young.

"I love this SOOOOO much," I blurted out with inappropriate enthusiasm.

"Oh! That's not all," Jack said as I tucked his note in the left breast pocket of my shirt. Pulling a transistor radio out of his bag of tricks, Jack followed up one surprise with another, "I brought us some music."

"ARE YOU KIDDING ME?" I screamed.

Everyone knew there was no quicker way to my heart than with music. As if the sandwich wasn't enough of a challenge, now I had to endure this? If anyone ever wondered if it was possible to be in heaven and hell at the same time, I was officially able to comment.

What ensued was a dinner date complete with perfect food, perfect conversation, and perfect music. The way Jack knew me was comforting on a level I couldn't describe or comprehend. In all my life I had never known anyone who knew me so well and took care of me so completely. Given our restrictions, there was no suspicion of ulterior motives or of being manipulated by a teenage boy with one thing on his mind. The things Jack did were genuine... wholesome. Jack took care of me for no other reason than because he wanted to. I had never been loved like that before and was pretty certain that I never would again.

When we finished, Jack didn't even have to suggest dropping my car at his house and going cruising. I think we both knew that's how this date was supposed to end. Settling into the passenger seat, I let all my anxieties fly out the window as soon as Jack started driving. There was no place we fit together better than in this car and I had every intention of soaking it in one last time. The way Jack and I glided through the nighttime was like dancing to music only we could hear. Even knowing we would soon be separated; I couldn't help crawling back into that place we had discovered last summer. Lying back and looking up at the moon, it felt like the car wasn't even moving. The stars stayed steady in the fall sky and the eternity of the darkness above them made it feel like we were standing still. It was a beautiful illusion and even as the warm air rushed through my hair, I felt the stillness of our infinity.

"I love watching the sky as we drive," I sighed out loud.

"I wouldn't know," Jack joked, his eyes on the road.

With my seat fully reclined, I looked up at Jack's silhouette and said with complete sincerity,

"That's why I love when you drive."

Turning his head just a smidge, he gazed down at me and smiled. If I live to be 100, I will never forget the look he gave me or the way it felt as that look traveled through my bloodstream.

"And that's why I love to drive," he reassured me with a tenderness that came within inches of crossing the line.

At that moment, looking up at Jack's face, beaming amidst a backdrop of stars, I knew I was experiencing something epic. This realm that Jack and I had discovered…tucked away in the darkness and mystically detached from the outside world, well that place was nothing short of spiritual. Being here with Jack, lounging as he drove and listening to nothing but the quiet of the world around us, I had never felt more loved or more at peace. And it was then that I realized something. Even as Jack was driving at a carefully calculated 35mph and even as the world rushed by us in one iridescent stream of flashing light, at that moment I discovered the secret. Being with Jack made time stand still.

Parked in the driveway of Jack's empty house, I lay back on the hood of the car and rested my head on the windshield. Frank Sinatra's "Fly Me to the Moon" hummed from Jack's transistor radio and, even in the dark, Jack's eyes were as iconic as Ol' Blue Eyes himself.

"Look," I gushed while pointing at the sky, "I found the big dipper!"

Jack just smiled at me from his spot on the lawn. I wondered if Sinatra's lyrics were getting to him. Did he want to dance among those stars with me?

"How come the stars are always so much brighter in your yard?" I continued with a smirk.

"I don't know" he said, walking closer, "but it always seems to be like that when you're here."

Jack looked at me sheepishly but was careful to keep a respectable distance. Regardless of how things felt right now, Jack knew that lying next to me on the hood of that car would unleash feelings we weren't prepared to defend. Instead, he stood next to me, his hand gently tracing the contours of the car.

"Don't worry," I said as he caressed the hood, "I'm not denting it."

"Oh, I know," Jack said with a laugh, "I just really love this car."

In my life, there have only been a few moments that made me want to crawl directly out of my skin, and this was definitely one of them. I knew the car was a metaphor and I really couldn't believe what Jack had just said. What's worse, the power of our connection let me hear the truth hidden behind everything Jack was about to say, and I knew he was struggling too.

"I'm sure my friends don't understand why I love this car so much," he said quietly, "and honestly, before I drove this car, I never would have understood it either. It's funny because it's not about how it looks or how old it is. It's not about any of those regular things."

With that, Jack looked at me and I knew for certain that he was no longer talking about the car.

"I don't care about any of those things because it's not about that. It's only about one thing. It's about how it *feels*."

How it feels. If I didn't know it already, the minute I heard Jack say those words I knew we were soulmates. If there was one singular thing our relationship was about, it was about how it feels. It was about the way my stomach felt every time he looked at me with those kryptonite eyes and how silently sitting next to him made me feel complete. It was about the way I could feel what Jack was saying even when he wasn't saying it and how I knew Jack was feeling all of the same things I was, even if neither one of us ever admitted them out loud. More than any of those things though, it really boiled down to one thing that I never imagined I would be able to feel, and it was something I could feel more vividly than anything else in my life. It was like Jack said about the car. I don't think my friends would understand it and before this, I don't think I would have understood it either, but now it was just a fact. No matter where he seemed to be on this planet, I could always ***feel*** Jack Riley.

In that moment, although my soul felt so at home that it could have crawled up inside of Jack's essence and lived there; my blood was racing with panic. I knew things were getting real and the magnitude of that reality was suffocating. The elephant we were running from was so big and so terrifying, there was just no way to process it. The fact that I didn't want to run at all…well that was also a pretty big roadblock. I had never experienced feelings like this before and I certainly had no practice at fighting them off. Jack must have noticed the panic in my face because he immediately backed off and started practicing football drills in his driveway. As I watched him bend down to take the invisible snap, I couldn't help but smile. Jack responded with a quip about learning to do his footwork like a ballet dancer and the tension was broken. As he pirouetted about the driveway I both appreciated and cringed at his ability to make the moves look halfway decent. Before I knew it, we were back in our sweet spot, deep in conversation and oblivious to the outside world. As we talked about life and careers and how playing football made him feel, time ticked away with alarming speed. We could both see the elephant we were dancing around, and we both knew that calling it a night should have occurred about two hours ago. Still, as the clock approached 1:30am, Jack, our elephant and I happily coexisted on the Riley's front lawn.

When I finally mustered the strength to open my car door, Jack stood right next to me, still analyzing the mechanics of his three-step drop. I loved talking football with Jack and I knew my knowledge of the game made me his ideal sparring partner. Unlike the rest of the town, I never sugar coated anything and always told him the ugly truths. Jack was always very clear about how much he appreciated that. So, for those and an unimaginable host of other reasons, Jack made a desperate statement as I climbed into my car.

"I wish I could talk to you about this all night."

Wham. The sentence and its delivery hit me like a sledgehammer. I knew Jack's parents were out of town and in that instant, I could feel that he didn't want me to leave. In sharp contrast to his imposing size, Jack looked small and vulnerable as he stood in the driveway, and I couldn't help but feel the weight of what he just said. Even if he didn't say it with his words, he said it through the unspoken connection we had, and he said it with all of the terror and awkwardness you would expect out of a seventeen-year-old boy. By throwing that sentence into the universe, Jack was attempting to harness a piece of the fairytale we knew we couldn't have. To this day, I still don't know if Jack said it on purpose or if hearing it spoken surprised him as much as it did me. Speechless, I looked at Jack, and he nervously began throwing the invisible football to avoid my gaze. Feeling Jack more clearly than I had ever felt him before; it didn't take the visual for me to process what had just happened. No, standing helplessly in front of Jack's empty house, I knew exactly what he was doing. Quarterback Jack was throwing a Hail Mary.

Shaken, I stood with one foot inside my car and tried to catch my breath. Despite all the reasons that going in that house with him would be so easy, the fire in my stomach left no mistake of how catastrophic it would be. Temptation like this was nothing short of cruel and I couldn't believe that Jack was putting me in this position. Besides dealing with my own struggle, I could see that Jack was sinking and it was breaking my heart. It was that night that I first began to question whether the pain of this charade would cause both of us permanent damage.

I can't honestly tell you what I said or how I managed to get inside the car and out of his driveway. What I vividly remember is valiantly fighting back tears all the way home. For as magical as this night had been, it made me explore consequences of our relationship that I wasn't ready to face. At this point, being with Jack was starting to feel like standing on the wrong side of an electric fence. I could see my life through it…so close I could almost grab it…but the sheer act of ever trying to touch it would be the end of me. In some ways, seeing what you are missing is worse than never seeing it at all.

STAGE IV - DEPRESSION

For anyone enduring the stages of their own forbidden love, I hate to break it to you, but the highs of your "Bargaining" period will eventually (and quicker than you would hope) be followed by the lows of the "Depression" stage. I wish I could say that knowing it's coming will make it easier, but I fear that no amount of planning or self-awareness will prepare you for the moment you have to accept all the truths you have been running from. If a forbidden crush is authentic, if it is truly forbidden, then there is no other way your story is going to end. Sooner or later, you will accept that you will never be together, and once you do, depression is inevitable. Obviously, everyone will experience their depression differently and their reactions will be just as varied as human nature itself.

For some, Depression might entail more running. Much in the same way you have been running from the truth about your relationship, some will run from their depression with equal enthusiasm. You might even try to drown your feelings by throwing yourself into something else. Whether you choose to immerse yourself in schoolwork, go on an extended vacation or (gasp) start dating a substitute, you might desperately try to find something new to fill this void you feel in your life. The problem with running is that you can't run forever. Feelings exist to be felt and until you allow yourself to work through them, you will never be able to move on. Trying to move on with a new boy is one thing, but you must be in it for the right reasons. You can't date someone with the hope that they will make you get over someone else. Right away, that makes the relationship more about the old boy than the new one. That recipe is doomed for failure and not fair to any of you… your forbidden crush included.

For others, Depression will be a complete wipeout. Instead of substitutes and running your days will be filled with tears and wallowing. There won't be enough ice cream to stop the longing or enough cookie dough to plug your holes. You will feel hopeless and empty and wonder how you ever let yourself get to this point. What's worse, your sadness might not be limited to your complete lack of romantic options, you could also feel a certain amount of self-loathing and embarrassment for letting things get this out of hand. More than likely, you always knew that this relationship was impossible, so the day you have to admit that you had been pretending otherwise probably won't be an easy day for your self-esteem.

My hope for you is that the depression stage is something that happens naturally as you progress through the stages of your own forbidden crush. Sometimes, however, depression can be brought about by forces beyond your control. Perhaps you and your crush have been forced apart by your friends, your family, or the burden of distance. Although progression to the Depression stage is painful for anyone, I would have to believe that it is those couples who are forced into it that need the longest to work through it.

October

"If I loved you less, I might be able to talk about it more."
Jane Austen

* * *

Hello World – Goodbye Jack

Before I knew it, it was full out fall and the brightly colored leaves crinkled under my feet as I walked down Humboldt Parkway, admiring the neighborhood I barely recognized. The time had finally come for the signature event of the 125th Anniversary and World Port Celebration and the entire city was abuzz. Last Saturday, Buffalo kicked off the premier eleven-day civic celebration and the event had enticed tourists from all over the world. I could hardly believe the chaos. We were only a few days in, and strangers had overtaken every square inch of our beloved city. I suddenly felt like an outsider in my own backyard.

Apart from driving past some of the venues, I hadn't really participated in anything before today, but since it was "Young America Day," we had been given this Tuesday off from school and our history teacher expected a paper detailing the events we attended. The choices were endless: an art show at the Albright Knox Art Gallery, the historical speaker series at the Statler Hotel, a railroad equipment exhibit in LaSalle Park and practical history demonstrations at the Masten Street Armory (I really wanted to know how to make candles). I wasn't quite sure what my friends wanted to attend during the day, but by evening, I had my heart set on the Ice Capades in Memorial Auditorium and then, the signature event of the festival, "Hello World" in Civic Stadium. "Hello World" had a cast of three thousand and the advertisements called it "The story of Buffalo from arrows to atoms." You must understand, the United States and the Soviet Union were still in the midst of the arms race and fears of nuclear warfare were part of our daily existence. In addition to bomb shelters and "duck and cover" drills, schools went so far as to issue dog tags to students so authorities could identify them in the wake of a nuclear attack. Yeah. Creepy, right? I should have known that this reference to the atom bomb did not bode well for my night at the festival.

Walking toward Rosie's house, I couldn't shake an odd feeling I had about today. It was almost like the Halloween decorations I was passing seemed to be warning me that something sinister was in my future. I couldn't pretend that things had been normal lately because they most certainly had not. I knew Jack was avoiding me; he had been doing it ever since the night of our last cruise. For some reason, the unfinished business of that night, coupled with those words that were never said in the park…those confessions that were never made…it was all suddenly weighing him down like an anchor. He would still call, but those calls would seem rushed, and when it came to the next time we would see each other, things always got complicated. He was always "overscheduled" or out of town on a recruiting visit. He would reassure me that we would see each other soon, but as time dragged on, it became clear that he had no intentions of seeing me. If I wanted to take a positive out of this, it would unquestionably be in my composure. At no point did I panic that Jack didn't care about me anymore or that I had imagined everything that had transpired between us – and this isn't something I could have said about myself a few months ago. Even though our affair had been silent, I was at a point where I had complete faith in it, and in Jack. On some level I even understood what he was doing. Jack wasn't forgetting about me; he was outrunning me. Avoiding me all together must have seemed easier than dealing with what was truly going on. Sometimes, once you get a little bit of distance, opening that wound again seems like more than you can bear. Instead, you run as fast as you can to avoid the train that is screaming toward you. The train that carries all your realities and takes you to the future that doesn't include each other. Pretending you don't see it, pretending you don't feel the fear or pretending that you can outrun it feel like your best options.

I knew where he was coming from. Our bond had been steadily growing and our summer had been nothing short of mythical. In a way I kind of think we peeked. I mean let's be real- there wasn't much closer we could get without crossing the invisible line - and no matter how much I dreamt about it - we both knew it was never going to happen. Heck, we came dangerously close on Toga Day. Sure, we may not have said or done anything inappropriate, but my thoughts crossed every line out there and Jack's borderline obscene gesture with that water bottle told me that he didn't mind. And I still haven't recovered from that beautiful Indian summer night in Jack's driveway. It honestly haunts me with regret and emptiness every time I think about it. Still, in no reenactment was I ever going into Jack's empty house and in no universe were our silent desires ever going to be fulfilled.

So that leaves both of us with the hard truth that there is nowhere to go but down. Even I knew that we couldn't keep going like we were. We defiantly pushed the limits all summer - and while it was crazy ass awesome - it was also crazy ass reckless...for a lot of reasons. It wasn't just my mother's trust and my family's livelihood that I was risking. I was playing with the very foundations of my character and my heart. More than that, I was playing with Jack's. For as much as I loved him and wanted him for myself, I also wanted him to have everything out of this life that he deserved, and in no rewrite was I ever going to be able to give him that. Somehow, I had to find a place within myself where I would be able to watch Jack live the life he was destined for and still hold on to what we were to each other. I had to be prepared to test the limits of our invisible string and believe that no matter where we were or who we were with; our connection would always be there. I wished I could talk to Jack about it. When it came to pouring out my soul, he was my closest confidant and my voice of reason. Not being able to have his perspective on this was unbearable. I felt alone and hopeless. The voice inside my head always tried to reassure me that the mere knowledge of our unfathomable connection would be enough…that its mere existence was the only gift I needed. That voice was a liar.

While my brain wrestled itself, I could see that, for Jack, it all seemed to be too much. In my analysis, Jack, quite simply, was empty. He was exhausted from struggling with things we couldn't control and feeling defeated from fighting an unwinnable war. I think Jack knew he was in over his head and, having no one to talk with, was silently floundering. Although I hated to admit it, in my heart, I knew what he was doing. Jack was desperately trying to find a balance between acceptance and moving on.

Staring at a particularly extravagant Halloween lawn display, I couldn't seem to take my eyes off of a life size figurine of Death. His black cape flowing in the wind, Death was holding a sickle; his face, lost in the oblivion of his hood. I don't know if I would have called it a premonition, but, at that moment, I probably should have listened a little closer to the nagging fear floundering behind my brain. Ever since that last night in Jack's driveway, I had been fighting off a most disturbing sensation. I had always been incredibly in tune with Jack and had a pretty decent finger on the pulse of our relationship. Right now, though, I didn't want to believe in that connection. I didn't like the things these feelings were telling me. I didn't like that they were begging me to move on…or that they were telling me I was flying too close to the sun. Sush – I told them! I can't worry about any of that today. Today was about me, my friends and the biggest festival of my lifetime!

Seeing this many tourists in Buffalo was crazy! Eyewitness News had reported that it expected millions of visitors to pass through the festival, and I felt like I had seen every single one of them today. After a full morning of historical art and antique trains, my friends and I tried our hand at blacksmithing and butter churning in the early afternoon, before heading home to regroup. I had promised to go to the Ice Capades with my mom and little sisters later this afternoon and then had plans to meet Rosie and

Monica at "Hello World" tonight. Hello World was advertised as the "must see" event of the 125th Anniversary and it played at 8:30pm each evening in Civic Stadium. The "brilliant and colorful" program was based on a historical outline, beginning with the Iroquois, and tracing the events of our city all the way to present. The promotions, however, warned that some events had been changed to "meet the demands of staging and for dramatic effect," whatever that meant! All I knew was that it was the signature event of the festival, and I was not missing it!!

Dropping my mom and sisters at home after the Ice Capades, I took the car and headed back toward "The Rockpile." The stadium had gone through a few name changes over the years, Roesch Memorial Stadium, Grover Cleveland Stadium and now, Civic Stadium (in fact, in 1960 the name would change again to War Memorial Stadium.) Through it all, The Rockpile, as it was affectionately known, served our sports community well and had even hosted a NASCAR event last year! This, however, was the biggest event The Rockpile had ever hosted, and I was more than ready!

Rosie, Monica, and I settled into our seats just as the spectacle was kicking off. I had cut the timing pretty close, but I had fit in everything I wanted to do today and as the show started, I was feeling pretty pleased with myself. This mood, however, was perilously short lived.

According to the official Hello World program, what we were about to see was a "dramatic historic spectacle" split into 13 episodes. To kick it off, the Celebration Queens were welcoming our visitors from all over the globe. Simultaneously, the Trumpeters, Cadets, Sailorettes, Antebellum Ladies, Boy Scouts, Girl Scouts, Majorettes, and the Princesses of the Royal Court assembled to pay homage to Miss Niagara Frontier and Miss Greater Buffalo. Wow. What a spectacle!

And then it happened. As *Episode 1 – Land of the Iroquois* commenced, I saw it - the scene Death had been trying to warn me about. Looking out over the sold-out crowd, my attention was suddenly drawn to one specific section of the stadium. And it was there, halfway down the bowl and off to the right, that I spotted Jack, seated with a group of people, completely unaware of my presence.

"With a sweep of his mighty hand," the narrator's booming voice began, "the Great Spirit created the Heavens above the Heavens and the world below"

The stadium lights flashed, and I shuddered. I had no idea Jack was going to be at the show tonight, but I guess I shouldn't have been surprised. Even with things as awkward as they were, our invisible string was still unbreakable. For some reason though, Jack's presence didn't fill me with the same awe and wonder it usually did. This was no Elvis concert encounter. This felt different...like I was seeing something I wasn't supposed to.

"...but this tranquility will soon be at an end – a new era is on its way," the voice warned.

Like a trainwreck, I couldn't take my eyes off Jack's group. I spotted a few of Jack's typical guy friends, some girl I probably should have recognized but did not and a girl that I did recognize but wish I had not. That girl got under my skin. That girl brought my claws out. That girl was a groupie.

I stared at that odd collection of teenagers all through *Episode 2 – Surveyin' an' Settlin.'* I knew my positioning in the stadium left me hidden from Jack's view and that there was no way he was spotting me unless he actively turned around and looked. So, I sat there, secretly watching everything that unfolded, consumed with feelings of terror and foreboding. The boy goofing around with his friends down there almost looked like a stranger and I couldn't seem to digest what I was feeling.

"Episode 3 – The Burring of Buffalo," the voice announced.

I looked again to Jack. For as connected as we usually felt, at this moment I felt nothing but fear. As the voice talked about the impending War of 1812 and the hostile conditions in our city, I could tell my world was crumbling.

"No one would be the victor. Everyone would lose," the voice ominously said.

As the stadium music began to crescendo, I sat frozen in my seat, still hidden in the crowd. It was here, with all the terror of a deer in headlights, that I sat in the shadows and silently watched as my world fell apart. Yes, what I witnessed over the course of the next five minutes would traumatize me in a way I never even dreamt possible. I would feel pain like I had never imagined and helplessness in a way no one person should ever have to endure. For weeks afterward, every time I closed my eyes, I saw it. I saw his hands - his baby soft hands - make the one move capable of shattering my entire existence. Yes, with horror, I watched one of those hands slowly reach over and seductively lock fingers with that groupie of a girl. I was shattered. As Buffalo burned on the stage before me, my heart burned inside of my chest.

"Everyone would lose," the narrator's voice echoed.

Despite the lights and music carrying on around me, my world had gone black. Time passed in a dusky haze and reality seemed to spin about me in a blur. Before I knew it, it was *"Episode 12 – The Atomic Age."* Ominously, the once booming voice became sullen as he despairingly sent a desperate and heartbreaking warning cry out into the audience,

"Is this what man will do with his discovery?" the voice asked? "In one blaze, will all things be gone? The Empire State – The Parthenon? And must the sudden atom's flash turn cities, statues, poems to ash? Only tomorrow can answer."

With that, I saw the one thing capable of bringing that atomic fire and brimstone down upon my entire world. I saw that girl grab Jack by the face and enthusiastically smack him right on the lips – and from the looks of it - it wasn't the first time. This, ladies and gentlemen, was my worst nightmare and my own atomic bomb. Unable to look away, with the sight of that one kiss, a part of me instantaneously and excruciatingly turned to ash.

"Episode 13 – To the Future," the voice proclaimed. "Ahead, people of Buffalo, lie New Horizons. Stand here today and see tomorrow – multitudes of ships sailing into port flying the flags of the world. And when they arrive – reach out your hand and say – Hello World – We are Americans!"

As applause roared and the crowd rose to their feet, I remained frozen in my seat. I didn't want new horizons. I didn't want to see tomorrow. I wanted my summer back. More than that, I wanted that girl to be trampled by the stampede of people beginning to leave the stadium.

Somehow, I managed to get out of the stadium and back to my car without my friends noticing that I was acting more bizarre than usual. Closing the car door, I sat for a few minutes and waited for traffic to clear. Alone. Reflective.

Heartbroken. I didn't know how to process what I was feeling. It all seemed so surreal. And then, out of nowhere, it happened, just like always. From across the parking lot, Jack spotted my car and instinctively followed our invisible string all the way to the door. Opening the passenger side, he tried to talk to me as if nothing was amiss, but we both knew it was. Over his shoulder I could see that girl, that stupidly bitchy girl, smiling dreamily at Jack, waiting to regain his attention. In that moment, I almost felt like I needed to be selfless...like keeping Jack for my own, regardless of how poor his other choice, was not fair to either of us. It was then that I knew I had to let him go. Jack was still talking when I looked at him and shook my head. He seemed confused as I used my eyes to motion to that stupid groupie standing behind him. My eyes told him to go...to move on...to try and be normal. Silent and stoic, Jack just looked at me with confusion.

"Shut the door," I said coldly. Those were my poignant last words: *shut the door.*

By contrast, Jack's last words absolutely shredded me.

"I'm sorry."

He had mumbled it as he turned, and the words stung almost as much as watching him walk away. God, I didn't want his pity - if that's even what it was. Pity sucked. In a less emotional state I might have considered that this was probably more of a comprehensive "sorry." Sorry about the impossibilities; sorry about the pretending; sorry about the tremendous lack of judgement in the space-time continuum. Yeah, I was universally sorry as well.

It felt like dying on your birthday. Letting him go at this event – on this monumental day in history...well, the Shakespearean tragedy of it was almost too much to handle. Sitting in the car, covered with tears and regret, I couldn't believe I had actually done it. Sending him to be with her... pretending my heart wasn't breaking... watching him walk out of my life and into his future...MAN THAT SUCKED. Loving someone hard enough to let them go was way worse than it looked on paper. The worst part was, of all the endings I had pictured in my head, this was certainly not one of them. I suppose I expected the ending to be much more glamorous...or at the very least, more expected. This was neither of those things. I was completely blindsided and then as quickly as it began, it was over. Ten months of my life literally came to a screeching halt in 30 seconds. Yeah – I wasn't a complete idiot. Of course, I knew this whole affair had to end, I just didn't know that it had to end today. Talk about ripping off the Band-Aid! Jack didn't even take one last look as he walked away. That was a dagger.

Pass the Cookie Dough

As the days progressed, I would like to think that I could have handled Jack's attempt to move on a little more gracefully if his choice in partners hadn't been so God-awful. My mother always taught me to start with a compliment, so I will acknowledge that this girl was pretty… very pretty. That, unfortunately, is where it ends. For as pretty as she was on the outside, I knew this groupie was a complete black hole on the inside. You can call her pretentious, judgmental, entitled, possessive, or any of the other things that she unquestionably was. Believe it or not though, those weren't my biggest issues. I mean at first they probably were. They were all I knew. Well, that and the fact that she dressed in that conflicting style of sophisticated slut. You know the look I'm talking about - that trampy style that only the aristocracy can pass off as glamorous. Anyone who would try that look with the Woolworth's brand would look like a whore, but because it came from 5th Avenue it was somehow chic. Gross.

Anyway, as their relationship progressed, I moved on to bigger fish. Ultimately, my raging issue was centered on the way that she treated Jack… like he was some sort of possession. I didn't like the way she looked at him with ownership, the way she stared down anyone she didn't deem worthy of talking to him and I especially didn't like the way Jack didn't seem to mind! Good God, did he think that was what he deserved? To be just another sheep in this white-collar flock? He was so much better than that. Jack was born to push the limits and blaze his own trail, not show up at the country club in the tie she picked for him and chat up her real estate baron father just to earn her approval. Gross. In all honesty, the longer they were together the less I was able to recognize Jack and all the things that I knew defined him.

Thus, began what one can only refer to as "The Dark Ages." Horrifically, this was no fleeting impulse and no ordinary girlfriend debacle. Instead of being hidden and trivialized, this relationship was flaunted, touted and otherwise paraded in front of me. Jack seemed to use it as a defense... holding it like a shield...and methodically deflecting any unwanted feeling or situation that came his way. Even when she wasn't around, Jack acted like our summer had never existed and he treated me one step better than a casual acquaintance. He talked with me like I was one of the guys and tried to tell me stories about how he and this girl got together. Jesus. He must have known. On some level, he MUST have known that my heart was breaking. Why was he acting like this had no reason to affect me? He was being a total ass. On the surface, though, he seemed happy. Maybe it was just wishful thinking, but I didn't buy it. Regardless of his performance, I knew something was off. Even he wasn't that good of an actor.

If there was one thing that was clear, it was that I needed a break. In addition to being fed up with Jack's passive aggressive behavior, I found myself absolutely incapable of dealing with his groupie (see, I still can't even bring myself to say her name). I found the pair of them impossible to be around and continuously fought back the impulse to tie that guard dog to a post. Not only did that girl drape herself on him like a hooker, but she was also controlling, possessive and, worst of all, annoyingly intuitive. Yes, that groupie seemed to see what everyone else on the planet had missed. Her X-ray vision spotted our invisible string immediately and dedicated her days to finding a pair of scissors strong enough to snip it. She resisted no opportunity to point out my inferior social stature and seemed genuinely pleased with herself every time she put me in my place. If it wasn't so infuriating, her behavior might have been comical, or at the very least pathetic. Given the circumstances, however, I found it just plain annoying. Plus, it was as if Jack was never "allowed" to go places anymore...especially places where I would be and the girlfriend would not. Although he never admitted that it was the girlfriend keeping him away, he would make glib comments about how she "had her issues" or "he would hear about this later." Our relationship became so annoyingly convoluted that eventually, I decided to stop trying. Watching

Jack with that girl was absolute torture and I honestly didn't think my heart could take any more of it. As inconceivable as it was, I had lost him and getting over that looked like it was going to be a twenty-four hour a day job. With that, I made the only decision I thought I could live with - I decided to cut him off. Forget altruism. Commence depression.

I couldn't put my finger on how I was feeling but as soon as I cut him off, it became clear that getting over him was not even an option. In the beginning, each day was a struggle not to go backwards, and I held very little interest in ever going forwards. I missed him in ways I didn't understand and at times I didn't expect. I was unpredictably emotional and became that person who randomly cried at insignificant moments. The problem was, to me, nothing was actually insignificant. The song on the radio, the street I just passed, and the cookies I was eating.... they all brought back some memory, some moment with Jack that I knew I would never get again. I suffered a million tiny deaths every day and sometimes I didn't know if I would ever again find meaning in my completely empty life.

For me, learning to coexist with this memory was not going to be easy. Obviously, I was sad because I missed him, but it was more than that. I could handle regular "missing" but this hole was different. This felt like being in mourning. Like I was mourning what we were never going to be. So, learning how to live a new life - one that was somewhere in the pocket between holding on and moving on - well that was a magic trick that I hadn't quite mastered yet. I knew I needed to pull it together, but I had absolutely no idea how accomplish that. I couldn't quite put my finger on it but I did know that finding my peace was more a state of mind than a series of steps. Sure, for the last ten months I had been pretty good at appreciating this for what it was and trying not to focus on what it could never be. Right now, though - that was an impossible task. Out of nowhere I seemed to have this canyon of emptiness and while I could usually fill those voids with the simple knowledge that Jack existed, this hole seemed to be filled with nothing but hopelessness. This - I suppose - was the danger of getting too close. The summer had opened parts of my soul I had never seen and while I know that's amazing in its own right, I soon realized that some of those places only functioned when Jack was within my circle. His absence had me feeling empty and our situation left me hopeless.

Unfortunately, trying to put some distance between me and Jack did little to make my life drama- free. Despite the girlfriend, I knew rumors still circulated about Jack and me and their existence always left me a little conflicted. On one hand, knowing the fire and brimstone they could rain down upon my family was rightfully terrifying, but on the other, I couldn't help feeling a little smug that, even in its silence, our connection was deep enough for people to see. I knew it was impossible, but I sincerely wished that the people in this city could just mind their business. Never was I more terrified of the speculation, however, than the day of "the phone call.

From the outside, it was a normal Wednesday evening. The grandfather clock had just struck 5:30pm and I was puttering in the kitchen, helping my mother prepare a pasta salad. From down the hallway, I could hear the ringing of our telephone and noticing my mother intimately involved in the stuffing of a chicken, I ran down the hall to answer it.

"Hello, Johnson residence."

"Good evening," a voice said, "is this Josephine?"

Josephine? Good God no one besides my dead grandmother ever called me Josephine.

"Um yes," I mumbled, with significant trepidation.

"Splendid! I was calling your mother, but it's nice to get this chance to speak with you, Josephine. This is Mrs. Riley...you know...Jack's mom."

I think I would have been less horrified if it was, in fact, my dead grandmother.

"Oh, yes, of course. Hello, Mrs. Riley," I said with complete and utter panic. "Let me get my mother for you."

Before I could put the receiver down, however, Mrs. Riley all but shouted, "Wait, dear. Let's have us a little chat first."

Oh my God, I thought while instinctively putting my hand over my chest, this is how it ends. I was all too familiar with the cattiness of Mrs. Riley's world, you see, and I knew that people like that had the ability to rip your heart straight from your chest, all the while smiling politely and talking about how pretty your hair looked despite the blood spurting into it.

As I stood in the hallway, I silently hoped that my mom's "mothering instincts" would be standing on end and she would soon come charging out of the kitchen to save me. Having no such luck, I listened as Mrs. Riley prattled on about the new memorial bricks in the Canisus courtyard (she had donated some) and the upcoming school concert (she was in charge of beverages) and I inserted the appropriate "I agree," and "yes ma'am's" when necessary. She was clearly taking this opportunity to gloat that Jack was back at Canisus and away from me. Obnoxious? Yes, but I could handle obnoxious. Then, just as I thought I might escape this conversation unscathed, she said it,

"So, Jack left for Indiana today on a recruiting trip. Did you know that? Did he mention it?"

Now if she had just said "Did you know that?" I would have been fine but adding "Did he mention it?" brought this to a whole other level. She was fishing…trying to find out if Jack and I were still close enough to talk about such things.

"No, I had no idea," I said, thanking the lord that I could say that with complete honesty.

"Interesting," she all but mumbled to herself. "Well, I'm holding high hopes for this one. Notre Dame would be a dream-come-true. I just hope Jacky keeps his eyes where they belong. It sure would be a shame if he did anything to mess this one up."

What in the holy hell was that supposed to mean? The way she said it was so sinister that I couldn't help feeling like she had just issued some sort of threat. As I stood there bewildered, Mrs. Riley continued,

"But enough about Jack," she said in a way that sounded more like a demand than a statement, "I'm sure you don't find all of this very interesting anyway. It's been so nice chatting with you Josephine. Could you be a dear and find your mother for me? I have an event this weekend and couldn't possibly go without a full treatment from your mother. Gosh, I can't imagine what would become of me if I ever had to lose her…"

And there it was - the actual threat. What I had just heard was high society code for "stay away from Jack or your mother will never work in this city again."

Who Uses the Word "Weaning?"

Despite his time in Indiana, Jack had to know that I was ghosting him. All those places that I used to run into him, all of the little things that I usually called to tell him, all of those things stopped, and I didn't see him chasing after me. I wondered if he missed me as much as I missed him and if he understood why I had disappeared. I avoided any situation where we might see each other and cocooned myself inside my schoolwork and the unconditional love that I received from the children at the center. Thank God for them.

The next few weeks passed slower than any period of time in my entire life. It was the longest I had gone without talking to him since the world of "Josie and Jack" had been created and I was still unfathomably lost. I don't know how I expected this affair to play out, but I can assure you that THIS was not it. Not talking to him was torture. At the very least, I missed my best friend.

In the end, Jack was the one to break the silence,

"I feel like I have not talked to you in forever," he said when I picked up the phone.

"Well," I thought to myself, "at least he noticed!"

Remaining silent for an awkwardly long time, I realized I had no idea how to respond. Regardless of what etiquette or even girl code called for, I simply had to protect myself. Jack was obviously still in my system. I dreamt about him almost every night. To make matters worse, they weren't even interesting dreams. I'm serious. Most nights literally nothing happened. We would just be sitting on the couch or driving in the car. Much like our whole relationship, the dreams weren't significant because of what happened they were significant because of how I felt: content. I felt flawlessly and unwaveringly content. I woke up with a brand-new hole every time.

"So.... will I see you later?" he finally said.

Ugh. I couldn't avoid him forever. Regardless of how I felt about it, life was going on around me, and he, regrettably, was still part of it. I had managed it for a couple weeks, but today appeared to be the day that I could no longer avoid seeing him. It was Sean's eighteenth birthday and his parents had rented the ballroom at The Statler for an absurdly large party. Sean was tremendously popular, and it felt like half the city had been invited. I had no good reason to skip the party and no good reason to run from Jack once I got there. Like it or not, I knew it was time to fight this dragon.

"Yes," I said coolly, "I'll be there."

After the pep talk of a lifetime in my bathroom mirror, I was determined to arrive at Sean's party with optimism. I was raised with class, this was a public place, and regardless of the tsunami going on inside of me, I was way too conservative to make a scene in front of strangers. In a strategic move, I made sure to arrive first. That way I could get comfortable, practice breathing and have some sense of inner peace when Jack ultimately appeared. I'm not sure who I thought I was fooling, but that plan didn't even hold me through the first fifteen seconds after he rounded the corner. The minute I laid eyes on him each of my limbs went numb and all hell broke loose inside my head. My initial reaction was predictable. Despite the fact that we still tragically wore the same colors, Jack looked different. He had gotten a haircut; he had new shoes. I hated both of them. His girlfriend's influence obviously sucked, and I genuinely wasn't sure if that was comforting or not. Sure, I wanted her to suck but I didn't want her to ruin him! At least I had been spared having to see her. I had learned earlier that day that her family had to rush out of town on a family emergency. Her sick Aunt had no idea how much I loved her right now.

All of that aside, I instantaneously knew that something much more severe was going on. As hard as it was for me to admit, the damage spread even deeper than the surface. Yes, Jack's style choices were disturbing, but this travesty went way beyond fashion. I spotted the difference immediately and I was dumbfounded. As I looked at him there was no denying that Jack…the brightest ray of sunshine that I had ever seen…was no longer glowing….and I really hadn't expected that. The sparks in his eyes…gone. The glimmer in his smile…gone. The sunshine that seemed to radiate from his very core…

GONE! I realize that you're probably thinking the same thing I was: how is this possible and whose fault was it? Did he truly stop glowing or did I suddenly lose the ability to see it? Your guess is as good as mine. All I knew was that Broadway was dark and I was heartbroken all over again.

Determined to push through the pain, I met Jack with a smile and some typically lame teasing. Thank God the other people in the room were too caught up in their own lives to notice how weird I was acting. I felt like I was in the middle of drowning...an arms flailing... frantically splashing and gasping for air kind of drowning. I had absolutely no idea how to behave. Jack was clearly trying to make things as normal as possible, but his "pick up where we left off" attitude was leaving me a little conflicted. Sure, I wanted our old selves back more than anything - we all know I was not ready for this to be it for us - but had he not felt the same ending that I had felt? I really had no idea what to do with this.

After a few minutes of excruciating awkwardness, Sean's dad mercifully summoned Jack to the other side of the room. Realizing I was temporarily off the hook, I committed the next few minutes to trying to compose myself. Jack's lack of internal sunshine had me rattled. I just couldn't fathom how the most magical thing about him could have been snuffed out. Seeing him without it made me sadder than I already was, and I didn't know how to process any of it.

What happened next, I will always remember. Not because it shed light on my situation and not because it was so crucial to the end of this story. I will remember it because it was the first time in my life that I experienced the contradiction of painful happiness.

"Can I have everyone's attention?" Sean's Dad bellowed across the room. "I have some news to share with you."

For the next few minutes, I felt like I was watching the scene unfold from outside of my body. Almost as if perched on the ceiling, I seemed to be looking down and experiencing the series of events in slow motion. I could see myself standing there, listening to Sean's dad. I looked small and uncomfortable. Powerless, I watched my face as I heard the news Mr. Harrigan was delivering and saw my body slump as I digested the consequences. Almost immediately after, however, I saw myself look directly at Jack, my unconditional love dripping from my eyeballs.

"This young man here...my second son, if you will...has just shared some amazing news."

With his arm around Jack, Sean's dad proceeded to tell the eager crowd what Jack had been keeping a secret. He was going to Europe. Jack had been offered the chance to play football in a very prestigious spring league and the agents had worked it so his last few high school classes could be finished abroad. Jack was leaving right after New Year's and would only be coming back to pack for college.

And there you have it. Jack's days in Buffalo were numbered and somehow, I was overcome with the most painful happiness. Obviously, I was proud. Obviously, I was sad. Obviously, this news was a tremendous wrinkle to the current storyline.

Within minutes Jack was standing next to me, and his demeanor let me know that he had most certainly seen the way I just looked at him.

"... I take it this means you no longer despise me," he asked softly.

Oh my freaking God. I couldn't believe what was happening. Everything suddenly made sense and I didn't like it. For one thing, with those words I realized that Jack's darkness was entirely my fault. Jack's light had been snuffed out because he was in pain. Jack was in pain, and I was responsible. "Good Lord it was me" I gasped. I was the snuffer.

Realizing I had that sort of impact on him was a little bit empowering and a little bit daunting. I had never actually considered that Jack might have been going through the same sort of withdrawal I was, and I really hasn't considered that he would assign himself blame. As irrational as I was, even I could concede that this was not a situation where anyone could be considered at fault. In fact, if there was any fault to go around it would be in our crazy situation itself, not in his attempt to lead a normal life. Still, Jack was feeling something - something valid - and I probably needed to address it. I did kind of despise him. I wasn't ready to let this go, and his premature departure had made me more than a little angry. Not to mention that his choice of girlfriends was absolutely unacceptable. Like it or not, he really knew me, and our connection obviously transcended the gap this had put between us. At the very least, Jack was feeling my pain and I couldn't even let my heart question whether he was experiencing his own. It was in that moment that I first considered something. Maybe Jack's light was gone because that light was a mutual flame. It shined when our eyes met, and it continued to glow whenever I was on his mind. I always knew that we would eventually be separated, but I had never questioned whether Jack's light would stay with me.

I looked up from the ground and saw Jack smiling at me. Crap. He was so annoyingly charming. There was no possible way I was hanging on to this grudge. Within seconds I was impulsively giggling, and Jack was hugging me. Well doesn't that figure, I thought. Instead of fighting the dragon I just invited him in for cocktails.

Unlike our bizarre exchange five minutes earlier, this meeting felt like starting over.

"So, what's new?" I said sarcastically. "I really haven't seen you in forever… and apparently, I have missed some things."

"I know." Jack replied, "I guess we were doing that thing…what's it called… that thing where you practice not being together?"

"Weaning?" I gasped.

"Yeah, weaning…I thought maybe we might need to start weaning."

"Well that idea sucked." I said with a little more anger than I should have, and Jack immediately looked at the ground.

"I already have so much regret from that mistake… please… I don't need any more."

Although he said it with an air of whimsy, I could tell that it was rooted in absolute truth. Jack knew that he was leaving, and I suppose he panicked. In his own way, he had orchestrated all of this to try and make our ending less tragic. Looking back, I think Jack decided to have a girlfriend as a way to test drive a future that was approaching a little quicker than he had imagined. Whether he did it to push me away or to outrun me will probably always be a mystery. It doesn't really matter though. Either way, I think that girlfriend was like Silly Putty. Something he used to try and fill the hole he knew I never could.

Jack stood there and looked at me with one eyebrow in the air. As I tried my best to process everything that had just happened, I couldn't deny that I sympathized with where Jack was coming from. I guess he thought if we took a step back right now, it might be easier when we ultimately had to walk away. At that moment though, both of us could feel that a gracious separation wasn't in the cards for us. It was clear that this magic between us wasn't over, and our pirate ship still had a few good trips left in it.

"So...," Jack said smugly, "you never answered my question."

Already completely smitten, I couldn't even pause for dramatic effect.

"Yes, I no longer despise you," I said with unusually sassy confidence.

And like flicking a switch, lightning once again danced in his eyes.

November

"We have woven a web, you and I, attached to this world
but a separate world of our own invention

John Keates

* * *

Life in the Bubble

And just like that, the dark ages were behind us. Following a brief mourning period, I decided to ignore the girlfriend to the best of my ability and committed to finishing our year with respect and dignity. If nothing else, Jack's girlfriend did provide good cover and immediately threw off anyone who may have suspected the impropriety of our true feelings. I would have been naive to think that people still weren't disgusted by our friendship, but the existence of his girlfriend certainly helped to extinguish any outright panic that we were more than friends. Besides, I had convinced myself that learning to coexist with the she-devil was going to be good practice for our future. No amount of denial was going to change the fact that Jack was leaving, and our fairytale was leaving with him. Somehow, I would need to accept that Jack's other life would move on and that all the happiness and heartache of that other life would have absolutely nothing to do with this one. I would have to trust in my place - in my role in the bigger story. I would have to accept that our life together couldn't be packed inside a box and forgotten. I would have to accept that our life was untouchable, intangible and completely separate from all other things. I would need to accept that even though what we had was invisible – what we had was forever.

As for Jack, he slowly rediscovered himself and flawlessly returned to his goofily charming ways. Almost as if the dark ages had never existed, he slid back into our daily soap opera with amazingly uncomplicated ease. Jack and I had a level of communication that I had never experienced with any other person and we both silently understood that the subject of "us" was fundamentally off limits. When you consider that we had spent the most amazing summer of my entire life together, yet never discussed how either of us felt about it, it didn't take a genius to see that we were never going to discuss the girlfriend, our previously strained relationship or any other dynamic pertinent to this charade we were living. Obviously, we had a pretty good idea of what we had been though, but I was pretty sure we were never going to allow those feelings to be spoken into the universe. Besides, I was starting to be able to distinguish the things that mattered from the things that didn't, and I had decided that the girlfriend didn't matter. I could feel that our story still had a few good chapters in it, and I was reconciled to living as many of them as I could in this time we had left. Luckily, our hidden language hadn't missed a beat, so life, again, was easy.

Lately, however, I started to realize that something about our boundaries was changing. Jack seemed more willing to point out those times when he knew I was special, and I found myself suddenly wanting to analyze what made us work. I had honestly been giving it a lot of thought lately and even though we couldn't do anything about it, I was still fascinated by our connection. I don't know. Maybe I was just hoping that if I understood it better, I would be able to find it again someday. Regardless, one night on the phone, Jack and I entered uncharted territory. We talked about our friendship.

The scene really couldn't have been set any better. I was home alone; he was home alone and neither of us had anywhere to be. Jack had been at football practice all evening and called me as soon as he was out of the shower. I'm not sure why he felt the need to mention that he was fresh out of the shower, but I always seemed to know more than necessary about Jack's shower schedule. Nevertheless, while I curled up under the covers, Jack managed to get dressed, do his hair and have a snack. I secretly loved being part of Jack's everyday routine. To me, it just cemented that comfort level that made our inappropriate connection seem ordinary.

I was very familiar with reading our dynamic by now and the more we talked, it was clear that it was one of those nights where we could talk about anything. He told me about some of his biggest concerns regarding his future and I did my best to offer ideas and reassurance. Jack also confessed how he was starting to feel differently about being semi-famous at school and around town. When I seemed surprised, he explained that he had never really thought about it when he was younger; that he was almost oblivious to it. Lately though, he had really begun to digest how unusual it was that everyone recognized him and that everyone was interested in his personal business. At his core, Jack was very humble and a genuine fan of the human race. He honestly never felt more talented or important than other people and never measured his success by other people's shortcomings. The idea that anyone was putting him on a pedestal made him very uncomfortable and he truly didn't understand why he was there. And that was when he said it,

"Thanks for listening. I had been thinking about this all week and I knew it was something I could only tell you."

That was it. I knew Jack had just left me an open door and if I was ever going to unleash everything I had been thinking about, this was my chance. There was no way I was going to squander it.

"It's funny you say that, because I have been sort of analyzing my life lately and I've been thinking about why you and I are such good friends."

"Really!" he said with enthusiasm, "so what did you come up with?"

I have to admit, the way he reacted left me really relieved. He could have brushed me off with a joke, ignored it entirely or worse yet, said something horrifying like,

"Wait...why would you ever consider us good friends?"

Good God. If any one of those things had happened, we all know I would have immediately hung up and hidden in my room for a month. Instead, being rightfully encouraged, I continued,

"I think it's because we know we can tell each other anything and it won't get any farther than the two of us. We can say anything, do anything, go anywhere and it won't matter. You and I live in two different worlds and "you and I" don't exist beyond you and I. I think that freedom lets you be a different kind of person with me than you are with everyone else. There's no pressure to be Quarterback Jack or to say what you think you're supposed to. I think we are so close because I'm the only person you have allowed to know the real Jack Riley."

I am not exaggerating when I tell you that my monologue was followed by one of the longest and most excruciating silences of my entire life. At one point I actually wondered if Jack was still alive. I honest to Jesus feared that hearing me speak those thoughts might have just killed him.

"Yes," a faint voice finally said.

Unfortunately, by the time Jack decided to speak, my entire body was already consumed by debilitating panic. My thoughts were racing and all I could hear was my own deafening silence. I actually lost the ability to speak for such a humiliatingly long time that Jack seriously said,

"Are you still there?"

"Oh. Yes. I'm here." I finally spit out. And trying to look less ridiculous, continued with a lie, "I thought I heard your mom and that you were talking to her."

"No," Jack replied with impressive honestly, "I was just digesting what you said and yes, you are absolutely right."

Having that out in the universe was unbelievably liberating. Sure, it didn't address any of our romantic issues, but it did validate our friendship, and that wasn't nothing. To be honest, I would have been fine if that's where the conversation ended, but Jack had the last word that night, and it was tremendous.

"It's like a bubble," he said, "It's like you and I live in our own bubble."

DAMN! Leave it to Jack to make the world's most perfect analogy. Not only did it capture exactly how things felt when we were in the sweet spot, but it also encompassed how incredibly fragile our existence was. While we blissfully drifted through the air, simply content to be together, at any point something sharp could fly by and burst our entire world. Yes, Jack and I indeed lived in a bubble, and I was prepared to hide-away in it and float with him anywhere.

Pin Up Problems...

Now, if I am being honest, I will admit that despite our reconciliation, the burgeoning winter air smelled of change. Jack, I assume, was too polite to mention it and I, not quite willing to take that bullet yet, stubbornly refused to address it. Instead, I went about my daily routine, repressing anything that hinted at our impending separation.

On this particular day I was running errands for my mother when it happened - a moment that came out of nowhere and, for the first time in a long time, knocked me straight on my ass. It's a moment I still feel as plainly as if it happened yesterday and, stupid as it sounds, all stemmed from one unfortunate run-in with a bulletin board. Yes, you read that right, a bulletin board. Okay, so I'm sure you are confused, but, believe me, as things started to unravel, so was I! I guess that's the funny thing about emotional breakdowns – a lot of the time you never see them coming! At this point in my life, the things that set me off were unpredictable, almost irrational, and I never knew when they would strike. The fact was, for as solid as I wanted to believe I was inside my fairytale with Jack, in reality, my composure was always one step away from falling off the edge.

Thus - with a completely false sense of confidence - I walked into the market on Wednesday afternoon and instinctively stopped to look at the bulletin board. In my neighborhood, you see, the market bulletin board was a well know community hub and no one could pass through Loblaws doors without examining it for new content. If you wanted to know what was going on in town, look at the bulletin board. If you wanted to know if anyone was hiring, look at the bulletin board. If you wanted to suddenly spot a giant picture of Quarterback Jack, just look at the…

"Holy mother of…" I squealed out loud.

Yes, in the dead center of that board, valiantly gazing out upon the patrons of the Loblaws Grocery Store was a giant Jack Riley, poster boy for the Regional All Star Football Game. Don't get me wrong, it's not like I didn't know that the all-star game was coming up and it's not like I was surprised that Jack, the brightest star of them all, should be their poster boy. The existence of this advertisement was perfectly ordinary, but let me tell you, the effect it was having on me was NOT! First of all, Jack was beyond beautiful on this poster. Sporting his white football jersey and a pair of jeans, Jack was clutching his football with both hands and looking almost inquisitively at the camera. The look on his face was half smirk half innocence and I could feel his true character bleeding from the ink it took to print it. For one of the first times in public, the boy on that poster looked like MY Jack – the real Jack. Even though it was a promo for one of the most anticipated games of the year, the boy on the poster didn't look like your ordinary Quarterback Jack. There was no swagger, no game face, and no super-human confidence. Staring at me from that poster was just Jack and the instant I saw it, it ripped me straight to shreds.

Not caring that I must have looked insane, I immediately turned around and bolted straight out of the store. Rushing to my car I was already muttering to myself, and I didn't seem to care if anyone could hear me.

"You have got to be kidding me. I just can't. What on earth am I supposed to do with this? Come ON, universe - I just can't. I can't. Good God, did you SEE that? What the hell? How am I supposed to carry on with my day? Jesus…"

Sitting in my car with the windows up and the radio blaring, I spent a good 10 minutes screaming irrational sentence fragments at the top of my lungs - and I wasn't even sure why! For some reason, that picture of Jack had ripped my heart straight from my chest and here I was, alone in the Loblaws parking lot, having an absolute meltdown.

Putting my finger on why I was so angry was tricky. At my core, knew I had no right to feel like this. Things between us were solid… better than I ever even dared to hope for. I wasn't insecure and I wouldn't even say that I was feeling needy. Plus, I had every intention of going to the all-star game, so it's not like this was my typical anger at events I was going to miss. That wasn't the problem here. I was just angry. Sure, the storyline we were living was beyond any of my expectations, but those expectations were grown from the reality that we were living in - and I was starting to realize that reality was my problem. Why were we stuck with this one? Why was the boy on that poster NOT my boyfriend?

Out of nowhere, I began yelling at Jack as I sat in my car. (I realize that might sound a little strange to some of you, but I guarantee that the majority of you have had conversations with invisible people more than once…just admit it.)

"Is it just me Jack? Am I the only one feeling like this? I don't think I'm going out on a limb when I say that in any other reality we would be 'more together' than we are in this one."

I paused for a second, like I could almost hear Jack in my head, trying to make me feel better.

"Yes, we are close - but we could be closer! Yes, we spend time together - but we could be making better use of it! And yes, obviously I know that there is nothing wrong with what we have - but we shouldn't kid ourselves by thinking it couldn't be better."

Suddenly, I was overcome with an all-new kind of anger – one bred from a carnal kind of honesty I usually didn't allow myself to feel.

"I don't want to say goodbye in your driveway, and I don't want to hide our connection from the people that matter to us. I don't want to wonder which day will be our last day and I don't want to know that our best days are probably behind us. I want to say all the things that I'm thinking, and I want to hear all the things that you can't admit out loud. I guess I just want it to be real, and I know it's never going to be. Let's face it, no matter how many mini-adventures we have and no matter how many words we say, we are always going to end unfinished – and right now – living unfinished seems really unfair."

It all seemed too much. Even though I thought I had been fine with everything these last few weeks, when I saw that poster, something snapped. I felt empty and victimized and downright irate at the universe. In hindsight, it's easy to see that not all my anger stemmed from resenting reality, but at the time, I think it was too painful for me to admit the rest. Now of course I can see the other reason and know that my melt down had less to do with who was on the poster that with what that poster represented. Hanging on the bulletin board that Wednesday was the embodiment of the one thing I was trying to run from - our future. Sadly, that poster was just one more reminder that things were changing, and I couldn't stop them. Jack was graduating and I'm sure this poster was just the first of many advertisements he would be featured on. Even though I was so proud of him for the career he was building, I also knew that as that career escalated, he would be taken father and farther from me. Someday, these posters would be the only thing I had left.

Love, it is a Razor

After a few days of feeling sorry for myself (and avoiding any reason to step foot in Loblaws) I was able to let go of my anger enough to function. My poor family had no idea why I was so cranky, and Rosie just endured my moods the best way she knew how – with distraction. Sometimes I really wondered how much she suspected about my saga with Jack. I felt terribly guilty not confiding in her about this, but besides being a little afraid of her opinions, I also didn't want to burden her with having to keep my secrets. If this whole relationship were to ever blow up in our faces, the last thing I wanted was for Rosie to get dragged down with the ship.

So instead of talking to anyone about what was really bothering me, I continued to shove those fears and longings down as deeply as I could. Heck, by this point I had an entire cemetery of secrets buried down there. One more couldn't hurt. Plus, I was staring down one of my favorite times of the year and simply didn't have room in my brain for anything that would interrupt my impending joy. I couldn't change the future, but I could sure as heck try to enjoy Jack the best I could for as long as I could. And this night was something I knew I was going to enjoy.

Of all of the things Jack did well, you see...sports...academics...general beautifulness ...there were actually a few things at which he was not perfect. Despite his hectic schedule, Jack managed to find time for those activities that he enjoyed, but admittedly wasn't the best at...like band. Yes, although Jack loved music, his natural talents definitely lay elsewhere. Affable as always, he did not let this "technicality" prevent him from staying with the school's music program and enjoying his merger role in the percussion section. Yes, there was never a soul that played the triangle with more enthusiasm than our carefree leading man. As you would imagine, Jack took a lot of flak about it, but remained completely unaffected by the scrutiny of his peers. If nothing else, Jack was always his own man, and this I respected tremendously. Maybe it was because he could see my respect that he chose to share his reasoning with me one day, and it was pretty deep.

"In sports," he explained "not everyone is rooting for the same team. Whether we win or lose, I always look into the stands and find faces filled with disappointment."

I smiled. I loved this vulnerable and sentimental side of him.

"With music," he continued, "everyone is on the same team, and when the night is over, no one leaves with regret." He paused and looked at me sheepishly. "I guess I just like the way it feels...when the music stops and the applause begins....and the entire auditorium is filled with pure love"

Jack's confession could not have captured my feelings more completely. If there was anything I was good at, it was looking at him and being filled with "pure love." Much like sporting events, I looked forward to his school music concerts with unwavering enthusiasm. Jack's talents - or lack thereof - were irrelevant. The opportunity to watch him from afar...not to mention the opportunity to see him in a tuxedo...was nothing short of heroin in my world. Add in the fact that concerts took place in a DARK auditorium, where the truth that bled from my face anytime I watched him would finally be hidden, well that was just about as good as it gets.

For these reasons, on a crisp November night just after Thanksgiving, I found myself settling into a fuzzy blue auditorium seat with a smile full of optimism. Jack was about to be back in Bennett High, and I was more than a little excited. Three times a year, a few of the high schools in Buffalo combined to give a master concert and Bennett, having the biggest auditorium in the area, always served as host. For as much as I loved all these concerts, I had to admit that I loved the holiday concert most of all. Not only was it the perfect kick-off to a magical season, in a lot of ways it was another anniversary celebration for me. I couldn't help remembering that it was at a holiday concert years ago that this crazy adventure of ours sort-of began. It was 8th grade, and I had attended a similar holiday concert with Rosie and her parents. Although I knew of his existence and had run into him one or two times in my life, I feel like I had never really seen Jack prior to that concert. Even though I wouldn't truly admit it to myself until years later, THAT was the night that changed everything. I couldn't really put my finger on how…or why…it happened. All I could remember was Jack, standing on the stage in his red bow tie. For no logical reason, looking at him made me feel complete and I suddenly knew my life would never be the same. Sitting at that concert, this virtual stranger…completely irrelevant an hour ago… was suddenly the center of my attention – like the spotlight was shining directly on him. While everyone else on stage seemed to embody the twirpy tween years, Jack was simply flawless. Sure, he was lanky and a little bit clumsy, but even back then the look that twinkled from his eyes was absolute magic. Wow. Little did I know how quickly that magic would turn to kryptonite.

Fast forward a few years and here I was again, sitting in a dark auditorium, waiting to lose myself in those eyes. Since Rosie had a last-minute babysitting job fall in her lap, I came to the concert alone, and I wasn't even ashamed of it. Who I was watching was much more important than who I was watching with. Besides, I was starting to be an expert at sliding into places and burying myself in the shadows.

As the show began, it was amazing to me how much Jack always stood out, even when he was buried in the back. Sure, there was probably a lot of amazing musicianship on display in those first few rows, but I was oblivious to all of it. Fact - Wherever he was, this boy had an internal glow that lit him up like sunshine. Yes, regardless of what he was doing, I could watch the

Jack Riley show all day.

As the music began to drift through the auditorium, I closed my eyes and breathed him in. Perfection. Mesmerized, I snuggled into my seat and checked the program, which left me absolutely giddy. Yes, for their second number the band was embarking on a "Sleigh Ride" and I was more than ready for the journey. This, I gushed, was always my favorite part. They played it every year and the sight of Jack jamming on those sleigh bells was joy in its purest form. Good God he was so cute up there. Unashamed, I stared at him with genuine happiness and was instantly filled with his internal sunshine. And so I was, at that particular moment, content.

Catharsis is a funny thing. By its very nature, you don't know when it's coming and regardless of your constitution, it invariably knocks you on your ass. One minute you are bopping along merrily to the sound of sleigh bells and the next you are weeping uncontrollably in a dark corner of the auditorium. Catharsis – and reality – sucks!

Ironically, I was really looking forward to the third piece. I had heard amazing things about this new Broadway show called *West Side Story* and the combined ensembles were about to perform its smash hit, "Somewhere." I was a pretty big geek when it came to musicals, and I knew that things like this were as close to Broadway as I was getting. As the song began, things were absolutely as I had expected. Jack's perfectly gelled hair, his kryptonite blue eyes and his adorable red bow tie were all on point. I could feel myself being transported and I held my breath, ready to experience another "moment." As the strings played the melody, the song was as beautiful and as magical as I had expected. What I didn't expect was the truth that was about to hit me like a freight train with the onset of the lyrics. Innocently sitting in my fuzzy blue seat, I had no idea that I was about to be crushed by the weight of those words – those painfully true and poignant words. What no one could have expected was that on this night, beneath that melody and in front of those eyes, I was about to experience my defining moment. That moment where I loved Jack with such intensity that I literally *BROKE*.

The instant I heard the very first stanza I was frozen - like I had been shot with a Taser - and all I could do was sit there and watch all of my insecurities and longings slowly bleed out of me. Until that moment, I don't think I appreciated how much I truly wanted to live in a place where Jack and I fit together. Although Tony sang this song to give Maria hope, the hopelessness behind his words was painfully evident, and that hopelessness was gushing from me like a hemorrhage.

Paralyzed, the lyrics washed over me like an epiphany, like the truth I had always known was suddenly the truth that I could no longer deny. As I listened to Tony tell Maria there would be a place for them somewhere, all the while knowing it was untrue, I just about melted in my chair. Even though we had been living like it could be, no amount of pretending was ever going to make it true. There was no place for Jack and me and we were never going to be together. Without warning, tears began streaming down my face in a most shocking and uncontrolled manner.

Time. That's what the song was really about. It was about finding a future that didn't care about nationality, didn't care about differences. When Tony reassured Maria there would be a time for them, the words cut me wide open. As I looked at Jack's face, I felt those lyrics screaming directly from my soul. I felt like I was standing right there on stage with him, begging for a place in time where we could... but all the while knowing that we never would... be together. We had no "someday" and we had no more time. Romeo and Juliet...Tony and Maria...Jack and Josie, a hopeless collection of star-crossed lovers never finding a way to be together.

Paralyzed in my seat I was confused, shocked, and horrified by my own behavior. I was sobbing uncontrollably, completely unable to pull it together. Through the tears my gaze remained fixed on Jack's eyes. He couldn't see me...thank God...but I wondered if he felt it too. I wondered if he wanted to find our "somewhere" as desperately as I did and if the thought of holding my hand and running away tore his insides out like it did mine. Even though the song was about searching for your "somewhere" I was smart enough to know that Jack and I were never going to have one. Regardless of how much I loved him – or how much I believed he loved me – there was no place for us. Just like Tony and Maria, we were never going to find our "somewhere" and we were never going to be together.

Catharsis – I loved Jack... really, truly and desperately loved Jack. Maybe I had never actually accepted this before. Looking back, the epiphany I had that night wasn't that we were never going to be together. I had honestly always known that. My epiphany was that this was no game... no adolescent crush. I didn't just love him – I was completely and with my whole heart – one hundred percent IN LOVE with him. Oh my God. **I was in love with him** – and we were never going to be together.

As the concert ended and people began to file out into the lobby, I stumbled up the aisle and calculated my next move. I knew Jack would come out to find me and I knew that running off would make me look like a bigger lunatic than trying to face him. Walking through the crowds of people, it was clear I couldn't wait for him inside. I felt like every person was looking at me... judging me...seeing straight through my façade. Who was I kidding? I didn't even have a façade anymore. Every inappropriate feeling I had for Jack was right out there for everyone to see, highlighted by the runny mascara and puffy channels my unrelenting tears had carved in my face.

Feeling claustrophobic and overwhelmed, I burst through the doors and into the teacher's parking lot. Luckily the lot was almost empty, and I just stood in the middle of it, looking up at the stars. On nights like this, I could almost see our summer in those stars...those same stars that guided our convertible through the blackened streets and let us escape our reality long enough to really breathe. Glancing toward the school, I could see Jack through the window, and I knew our invisible string wouldn't let me down. Trapped by a group of dads (who unquestionably wanted to grill him about the big game coming up) Jack looked out the window and spotted me. I knew he would come out to meet me as soon as he could, and I was truly thankful for the few extra minutes to compose myself. Facing him after this epiphany was daunting and I truly had no idea what to say. I was broken, I was terrified, and I was more in love with him than I had ever been. What was I supposed to do with that? Pacing in circles and looking up at the stars, I decided that my only objective was to try and not say anything stupid. I already knew I wasn't going to be able to control what my face looked like, but I sure as hell hoped I could control what came out of it.

I can still see Jack walk down the stairs and take a few steps in my direction. The funny thing is, I have absolutely no idea what he was wearing. My mind was spinning so fast that I honestly don't think I ever processed it. I knew he always changed clothes after a concert (the tux's had to stay in school) and I usually couldn't wait to see what he would wear on his way out. This time though, I can't tell you if it was pants, shorts, button shirt, tee-shirt, formal shoes, or sneakers. Heck it could have been a dress for all I knew! I do, however, vividly recall Jack walking silently toward me and hugging me immediately. Not even having the strength to raise my arms, I buried my face in his chest and he grabbed me around my entire body, restraining me like a I was in a strait jacket. Yeah, I thought, that was fitting. I can still tell you what it felt like to stand there with Jack under the stars, and I can also tell you that I don't remember buttons pressing into my face – so to answer my previous question, I'm guessing he was wearing a tee-shirt or sweater. As Jack let me go, I took a few steps backward, looked up into his face and tried to say something...but absolutely NOTHING came out. The next thing I knew I was just smiling, shaking my head and waving my arms around like some sort of mime. Poor Jack just looked at me and undoubtedly wondered what the heck was wrong with me. I pleaded with my brain to form words – to just say something...anything! Well, I guess I should have set my expectations a little higher, because the first thing I remember actually spitting out was the profound and intelligent,

"...I got nothin'!"

I knew I was making an ass of myself, but I was completely unable to stop it. I was beyond rattled. Knowing I was in distress, Jack pulled me into his arms again. This time I was able to get mine around his neck and my face brushed his cheek before I rested it on his shoulder. Thankfully, as we let go, I looked up at the sky and said something that at least made sense,

"I found the big dipper."

Genius, right? I was really making quite an impression.

Probably just happy that I had formed an actual sentence, Jack jumped right in,

"Yeah, it was really bright in my yard again last night."

The way he looked at me, I think he was starting to understand what I was going through. I think he understood that I was struggling – struggling like he was that Indian summer night when we sat beneath the big dipper in his driveway. Not knowing what else to do, Jack hugged me for a third time and looked up at the stars. Suddenly remembering how soft his face felt as my cheek brushed it, I inexplicably put both hands on his face and looked into his eyes. I have absolutely no idea why I did it or what I thought I would do next; I was on autopilot.

"You were really good tonight," I heard myself saying.

"Aw shucks," Jack said impishly.

Finding the control to let go of his head, I stood there, once again mute, and silently looked at Jack. I was completely unraveled and at a total loss as how to decipher the dozens of feelings running through my body.

"I'm so glad I came."

"Me too"

I don't know if it was the sweetness or the sincerity in Jack's voice, but whatever it was proved too much for me.

"And your face is really smooth," I said like a total freak.

Hearing his name called in the distance, we both knew it was time for Jack to go, and for the first time in my life, I think I was thankful.

"My ride is ready," Jack said with a sigh, "and don't forget I have that college visit this week, so I won't be around for a while."

Hugging me a fourth and final time, Jack pulled me so close that I had to fight back the urge to tell him why I was so broken. Every part of me wanted to tell him how much I loved him, how foolish I felt for letting things get this far and how hopeless I felt knowing I had to get over it. Instead, I simply heard myself say three words – but not the three I wanted.

"I'll miss you."

Jack took a deep breath and I immediately felt stupid. Even though those were the wrong three words, Jack knew our hidden language pretty well and I was terrified that he had seen through them. And that's when the inexplicable happened. I head Jack's voice, smooth like butter and ever so sincere, whisper into my ear,

"I'll miss YOU."

Oh Yeah – I knew what that meant.

Looking back, I can't begin to express what a turning-point this night was for me. Recovering from an epiphany, you see, is no easy task. Suddenly your world spins differently and the very ground that you have built your life on seems shaken. Even though things might look the same on the outside, the inside of everything feels different. YOU feel different. You experience a kind of hopelessness that is impossible to put into words - a kind of hopelessness that can seemingly only end in complete emotional defeat. Face it, reality is a burden…and my place in that reality had never felt more cemented.

At the core of it, my epiphany had made me feel ridiculous. I was embarrassed by the pretending, ashamed of the secrets and self-conscious about my actions. I had crossed so many lines and let this get so out of control. Why hadn't I protected myself better? How had I lost my heart and my head so easily…so completely? I always knew we had no future, and yet I let myself fall in so deep that I didn't know how I would ever crawl out. Jack was eventually going to leave me behind. It was a fact and I had to prepare myself for it.

So, as I lay in bed that night, I finally began to accept all of the things I hated about this situation - and the list was extensive. First and foremost, I hated time. I hated that we never seemed to have enough of it and I hated that we were misplaced within in it. I hated that we couldn't change it and I hated that we couldn't have it back. I hated that I would never be able to freeze it and I hated that it was taking Jack farther away from me. I hated that I somehow loved him more the quicker it passed, and I especially hated that it would never change the circle of our story.

Running a close second - I hated that I loved him in a way I couldn't control. I hated that hopeless and happy were only separated by the thinnest of threads. I hated all of the things I would never be able to say, and I hated the affection I would never be able to show him. I hated that I had to walk circles under the stars just collect myself and that as we stood there, Jack seemed so close and so far at the same time. I hated that his face was so smooth that I couldn't stop touching it and I hated that he couldn't stop hugging me. I hated that those were our only options. I hated that we went home to different houses and that I would never know what it felt like to wake up next to him. I hated that I didn't know when I was going to see him again and that I still wouldn't be able to love him in the way I wanted to once I finally did.

Once again, I was crying so hard I could barely breathe. Positively irate, I looked out the window at the big dipper and began speaking directly to Jack – like that dipper was some magic portal to Jack's soul.

"I hate that when you said you'll miss me it seemed to fill me up and rip me apart all at the same time. And I hate that when I hear it replayed in my head it only makes me sadder. I hate that even when we are together, we are still too far apart. I hate that you can only tell me how you feel and not show me how you feel. I hate that words are all we have and that they are tattooed on my brain as deeply and hopelessly as they are on my heart. I hate that our story will forever be unfinished and that I have to trust that you understand me on the level I think you do. But more than anything, I hate how the universe screwed this all up. We deserved better."

And with that, I lay back down and cried myself to sleep.

Swan Song

I had been keeping my distance ever since my epiphany and with every day that passed, I missed Jack's smile, his smarmy jokes, and his uncanny ability to make me feel complete. The undertones of our everyday encounters were so real - so powerful - that this relationship was the most tangible piece of fiction I had ever felt. Sure, some might say that it's impossible to miss something you never had - but those people had clearly never met Jack or experienced THIS. To top it off, at some point, Jack had broken up with his girlfriend and never bothered to tell me. Like I said, aside from one afternoon where I may have screamed at him about how much I didn't like her, Jack and I never discussed girls.

With my self-imposed mourning period about to come to an end, I knew I needed to prepare myself to reenter our storyline. The task at hand was a complicated one, and I hoped I would find the fortitude to see my way through it. On paper it looked so simple. All I had to do was reconcile the very real future ahead of me with the very foolish present I had been living in. Sure…that sounds easy enough…said no one ever. Despite my apprehension, my first test was upon me. Today, you see, was the day I had both anticipated and dreaded with equal intensity. Although it could easily be in the running for my favorite day of every year, I was keenly aware that this year was different. This year, Jack was a senior. This year - was a swan song.

Although agony was inevitable, not going wasn't even an option. Even though I knew it was bound to rip my soul to shreds, I also knew that I needed it - like my very survival depended on it. No matter how much pain it caused, that pain could never match the pure joy I would feel from the minute I walked into that stadium. Yes, the event whose advertisement had nearly crushed me in Loblaws was upon us. Today was the day of the Regional All-Star Football game…Jack's last EVER All-Star game and watching him play in it was everything!!!

Stoically, I put on my colors, took a deep breath, and headed for the car. As I drove to All High Stadium, a poem we had just read in school kept running through my head. It was something Sir Walter Raleigh had written to Queen Elizabeth, with whom he was scandalously in love, and I was starting to digest it on a deeper level.

The Silent Lover
"Our passions are most likened to floods and streams
The shallow murmur but the deep are dumb..."

Well, that was certainly true. Just because I had never told him, didn't mean the love I had for Jack wasn't the most powerful thing in my universe, and it didn't mean I didn't think about telling him every day. Conversely, I was starting to see how that passage could be applied to Jack and his former girlfriend. Just because she was bestowed the title of "girlfriend" didn't mean she was more important to him than I was. She was just a shallow murmur.

"...Then wrong not, dearest to my heart,
My true, though secret passion;
He smarteth most that hides his smart,
And sues for no compassion"

Well, those were just about the most accurate lines of any poem I had ever read. My love for Jack was indeed true and it hurt like heck not being able to do anything about it. And now that I knew he was moving, hiding my feelings was as difficult as it was painful. I hoped he appreciated just how genuine my "secret passion" would always be. At that moment, Sir Walter Raleigh became my new soul mate.

As a side note, the following week in class our teacher informed us that Sir Walter Raleigh eventually married one of the Queen's maids in an attempt to move on. Apparently, Queen Elizabeth was so jealous that she briefly imprisoned both of them in the Tower of London. Even though I had handled Jack's girlfriend only slightly better than that, I certainly sympathized with the Queen's instincts!

Pulling up to the stadium, I was equal parts excited and apprehensive. While I knew that I was about to throw salt in an open wound, I also knew the security of that stadium would wrap both of us in a protective cocoon... one that would allow us to live our dreams for just a few hours longer. Regardless of the ramifications, I really needed that. Don't get me wrong; obviously, the complexities I was facing were daunting. There were so many pieces to today's puzzle... my pure love of the game ...my pure love of the boy...my pure heartbreak from knowing that this was Jack's last game, and my pure heartbreak from again having to confront what would never be. There was no fooling myself. For those three hours I knew that I was bound to watch all of our favorite memories flash before my eyes. I knew that every feeling and every impossible dream that we ever shared would stare me in the face and slowly eat my heart directly out of my chest. I also knew - no matter how hard I tried to ignore it - that I would see something else. The minute Jack took that field I knew that I would see the spark...that stupidly glorious and completely inappropriate spark. I would see it like I always did...and it would fill me with the most glorious adrenaline on the planet. Jack was never more alive than when he was on that field and I was never more content than when I was watching him. Beyond the complete awe with which I would observe his performance, I always knew there was something else I had to be prepared for. I was all too aware that there was at least one moment a game...one magical moment...where our eyes would meet, and time would absolutely stand still. The idea that this might be the last time I experienced that moment.... well that was a killer.

Despite my epiphany, I knew that tonight was one of those nights where I was bound to leave that stadium even more in love with Jack than when I entered. Unfortunately, knowing your demons does very little to protect you from them. A vice is a vice and this boy was the biggest vice I had ever encountered. I wasn't sorry though. Not in the slightest. I was starting to realize that no amount of pain would be able to dull the glow Jack had lit inside of me. I loved him. I couldn't have him.... but I knew that I would always love him. So right then, I decided to commit to a few rules. First, no matter what the circumstances, I vowed to have faith in everything that had passed between us over the last year. Sure, our love affair wasn't tangible or legitimate, yet somehow, it still existed. It existed in the wind that caressed my face as he drove and in the pixie dust that burst from his eyes as he looked at me. In every way that mattered, it was real - and I needed to embrace that. Next, I would try not to focus on things I couldn't control. Fate was fate and no amount of pretending was going to change it. Finally, I needed to focus on one simple fact - Jack Riley was a gift. Regardless of our limitations, Jack was a gift and if I remembered nothing else, I needed to remember that.

As it turns out, remembering my gift was easier than I gave myself credit for. That night I watched one of the most exciting football games I had ever seen. Jack's execution was brilliant, his technique was brilliant; his whole game was brilliant. Even knowing the ending this game represented, I still watched every play with the kind of awe and fulfillment that this moment deserved. When I heard others compliment him, I felt proud. It was okay that they didn't know who I was or what I meant to him. I knew. He knew. And I was starting to realize that was enough. So, for the next few hours,

I confidently entertained every emotion in my repertoire. I cheered when Jack danced into the end-zone, I laughed when he clowned on the sidelines, I sat reflective as I watched him studying plays on the bench and I teared up as I watched the clock tick down to zero. Surprisingly, what I never felt was hopeless or angry. For once, regardless of what else was happening, I simply felt content. For some reason, my post-epiphany self was able to handle all of my feelings with a newfound clarity. Yes, my perspective had certainly shifted, and I suddenly felt able to carry my baggage with an air of grace and dignity.

What I couldn't handle with grace OR dignity was the sight of Jack taking off his helmet. Yes, somehow, after all these years, I was still wildly unprepared for what happened to my body the moment Jack removed his equipment. As I watched him, triumphantly pulling the helmet from his head, I felt like I was in a Disney movie. In that moment, I was Belle, and he was the Beast, spinning in strobe lights, about to be transformed into the handsome prince. As soon as I laid eyes on his perfect face, sunshine and blue jays seemed to explode from the earth.... confetti cannons erupted and angels sang. His eyes never looked bluer, and his sweaty hair was never sexier. Without fail, that first glimpse of him always left me paralyzed. Good God he was perfect. By the time Jack victoriously pumped his fist at the crowd, I was practically catatonic.

When the game ended, I snuck away from my friends and hung around the tunnel...not right up front with the other groupies but a little more inconspicuous and off to the side. I guess epiphanies do have their good points. I had nothing to prove anymore. My sins and I could just stand back... admire the rubble... and wait to see what fate brought us. From the depths of the mob, I could see Jack trying to make his way up the crowded corridor. Skillfully bumping and jostling his way toward freedom, Jack diligently surveyed the awaiting crowd. Turning to his right, Jack spotted me, strategically set apart from the others. As our eyes met, a wry smile spread across his face and that infamous lightning once again danced in his baby blues. Walking directly past his adoring fans, Jack emerged from the tunnel and came straight to me .... once again following our invisible string.

"Hey, I know you," he quipped, before bending down to hug me.

In all honestly, I might have hugged him a little longer than socially acceptable, but I had decided not to worry about those things anymore. Jack had just walked past a hundred people to be with me. This was my moment, and I was going to take it. Sȯ, unlike the night I went full-on mime after his concert, on this night I felt immeasurably carefree. Inexplicably grabbing Jack by the cheeks (because touching his face seemed to be something I do now); I psychotically started to tell him every bizarre thought that was running through my brain.

"No matter how much I think I know what to expect from you," I said "you always manage to blow my face clean off."

Squeezing his cheeks like a grandma, I could feel his lips…his baby soft lips…brush against the palm of my hand. Much like the day back in February when I crazily wiped that frosting from his face, I could literally feel the touch of his lips on my palm for days afterward.

Naturally, my gushing and my grandma behavior made Jack laugh. He liked it when I was proud of him. Bolstered by my newfound clarity, we talked with ease and truths seemed to leap from me without reservation. Even though there was probably a line of people waiting to congratulate him, I could tell that Jack was exactly where he needed to be. So, there we stood, oblivious to the crowds around us, once again lost in our sweet spot. I don't think I will ever be able to convey how purely epic those moments together felt. Not because of what was said of course, but because of what we knew. This was our time - and we were going to embrace it.

When Jack finally turned to leave, something came over me. The funniest thing was that it happened so easily and so instinctively that I never had time to think about it.

"Okay," I said, patting Jack's back as he walked away. "I love you. See you tomorrow."

Huh. After all these months censoring myself, those three words rolled out of my mouth so naturally that I barely even realized that I had said them. Jack paused for the tiniest of moments yet never turned to face me. Even if I wasn't sure what I had just said, Jack certainly was.

"Love you too" he said as he was swallowed by the crowd.

And there you have it. Mountains didn't crumble and birds didn't fly upside down. My biggest secret was finally out there…and the world kept turning.

That night I laid down to sleep a new woman. Unlike the movies, my evening hadn't included grand gestures or epic dialogue, but it had affected me more than any of those things ever could. The way Jack had come to me, the words that we said, not to mention the fact that it had all been done so nonchalantly, well that was just everything. This night had changed me. Regardless of what came next, Jack and I had spoken the truth, and as long as I lived, I knew it could never be taken away. Take THAT, Sir Walter Raleigh!

STAGE V – ACCEPTANCE

Without a doubt, acceptance is the most challenging of all the stages. It is a cake baked in layers and constructed on the most delicate of platforms. While the completed pastry may be symbolic of a "happily ever after," the individual parts still teeter ever so delicately, each trusting the fragile layer beneath it to hold its weight.

Acceptance, likewise, is a fragile state, seemingly dependent on the success of the stages that preceded it. It is an ongoing struggle fraught with leftover baggage and crippling second guessing. Discouraging as it seems, acceptance is rarely achieved without flashbacks and memories from the previous stages, with each stage playing a crucial role in your continued success. Ironically, the true path to acceptance cannot be achieved until you no longer *deny* that you will never completely accept this. It means conceding that you will always be a little bit *angry* and a little bit *depressed*. It means admitting that you would still like to strike a *bargain* and play pretend - if only for just a few hours. Acceptance rarely means surrendering your feelings or flipping off the switch. If anything, acceptance means flipping off the universe.

I guess what it all boils down to is this: in the case of the forbidden crush, acceptance doesn't mean accepting that you can't love him - it means accepting that you already do. Acceptance teaches you how to carry that anvil and enjoy a normal life. It reinforces that you can live within your boundaries and still stay true to your conflicting priorities. It reminds you that it's okay that you're not perfect and that you don't have to know all the answers. In the end, acceptance lets you see the beauty in what you feel and the magic in what the two of you have created. Love is love. Sure, this "happily ever after" might not be the one you would have written, but it doesn't mean you can't eat the cake.

December

"...but I have promises to keep, and miles to go before I sleep
and miles to go before I sleep"

Robert Frost

The Key to his Heart

When Jack called and said he wanted to show me something, I wasn't too nervous. Things between us had been remarkably easy lately and our growing level of acceptance seemed to take the fear out of most things. I wasn't even suspicious when Jack said that I would need to pick him up because his parents weren't home, and he didn't have his car. That thing was always being fixed, so no red flags there either. Being beautifully free when Jack called, I made a few quick adjustments to my make-up, grabbed the keys, and headed to Jack's.

Looking particularly smug as he hopped in the car, Jack told me to start driving and that he would tell me when to turn. Still unclear on what adventure awaited me, I innocently followed Jack's directions toward our mystery destination. The fact that I had no idea where I was going or what I was in for didn't bother me a bit. I was with Jack for goodness sakes. I would have followed his directions anywhere. Driving further and further from our usual hangouts, it was just past 4pm when Jack instructed me to cross the Grand Island Bridge. A twenty five square mile paradise plunked in the middle of the Niagara River, Grand Island lay about six miles down the water from Niagara Falls and stood firmly between the border of the United States and Canada. I had always found Grand Island to be extremely pretty but hadn't had much chance to travel there myself. Before the Grand Island portion of the New York State Thruway opened last November, getting there could be a bit of a hassle and my mom never seemed up for it. Unfortunately, as excited as I was to be going to Grand Island, I was struggling with one major problem – a four-thousand-foot monster of a problem. Before today, you see, I had never driven across the Grand Island Bridge by myself. Staring blankly at the behemoth before me, I was more than a little intimidated. How intimidated, you ask? Let's just say that if I was David, that bridge was my Goliath, and I was woefully without my slingshot! To my five foot two inch frame, that gigantic bridge seemed incomprehensibly narrow and terrifyingly steep. If you asked me, it bore a striking resemblance to the roller coasters at Crystal Beach Park, and after a quick survey, I wasn't sure what I was more afraid of – tipping off the edge or plummeting over the other side. Not willing to ruin our day by admitting my fears, I took a deep breath and stoically ascended the ramp to the bridge. As I carefully used just enough gas to pull us up toward the arc, Jack must have noticed my white knuckles. Out of nowhere, he began softly singing his favorite Buddy Holly song, trying to distract me from the icy water on either side. Even in my panic, Jack's energy was contagious and before I knew it, I was singing some "Bop…bop…bop-bop" backup vocals. This was so much cooler than the night he sang it with Sean at the Winter Ball!

As intended, having Jack at my side gave me supernatural confidence and before I knew it, I was gliding down the opposite side of the bridge. Safely on the other side, Jack just looked at me and smiled. Perfection. To this day, I still find the Grand Island bridge a bit terrifying, but my memories of Jack faithfully guide me across every time. Clearly, Jack Riley was my slingshot. Not fade away.

A few miles after crossing onto the Island, Jack instructed me to turn down a gravely road and within minutes we pulled up to a big old warehouse, teetering at the edge of the Niagara River. I could tell from a faded logo painted on the side wall that the building belonged to the Riley's, but it didn't seem to have gotten much attention over the past few years. My guess was that it was probably a forgotten storage house for one of their many former businesses. Looking at the clunky old structure my curiosity was growing, and my mind was flooded with questions. The biggest of course, being why on earth would Jack have dragged me all the way to Grand Island and why did he look so pleased with himself about it?

"Follow me," Jack shouted as he darted out of the car like a six-year-old.

By the time I walked down to the building, Jack was already pulling open the garage size door located at the end of the gravel drive. As light poured into the dark warehouse, shapes began to appear, and I eagerly peeked inside. Not believing my eyes, I actually burst out laughing just as Jack enthusiastically yelled,

"Tah-dah!"

As I stood there, literally shaking my head at the contents of the building, I was very clear about why I had to do the driving - and I couldn't stop laughing. Jack, apparently, was getting prepared to leave for Europe and had already put his car in storage. Now I know that the growing reality of Jack leaving me was anything but funny, but the fact that he had taken me on a pilgrimage to visit his car, definitely was.

What happened next, though, was something that I was not prepared for, and it knocked the giggles right out of me. Quickly sidling up next to me, Jack pulled something from his pocket and held it in front of my face. I recognized it in an instant and while Jack was all smiles, I was speechless. Yes, dangling from Jack's hand was an object that would stay with me for the rest of my life, and until now, I have never told anyone a thing about it. So here it goes - what Jack pulled from his pocket that night was nothing less than the spare key to his Chrysler and I was about to have a moment.

Now you might think that me recognizing Jack's spare key is far-fetched, but it really wasn't. It had been a long running laugh that this particular key was full of paint. The "mishap" had happened at the children's center one day and Jack had never been able to get the paint off. The residue it left on the teeth made the key stick in the ignition just a smidge - which Jack found terribly annoying - and eventually the poor key was relegated to the status of "spare."

Already stunned at the jester, I was equally unprepared for the presentation. Instead of a keychain, the key was strung on a silver necklace, and he dangled it in front of my eyes like a hypnotist.

"I want you to keep this," he said with his usual charm. "In case you ever have an emergency, with your sisters or something, and need to get somewhere. Or even if you just need to sit in it and escape for a while, I want you to know it will always be here."

As Jack prepared to hand me the key, he just kept talking, like this moment wasn't the biggest thing that had probably ever happened to me.

"My parents never come out this way," he continued "and honestly wouldn't notice the car was gone even if they did."

Doing my darnedest not to cry, I looked up at Jack, put out my hand and smiled. The commitment this represented was staggering, but I knew Jack well enough to know that it was genuine. That car was so many things to us, and this gesture was one of the purest and most meaningful of any I could imagine. The look in Jack's eyes as he presented me that key was a look that most girls can only dream of receiving and the way his fingers pressed the key into the palm of my hand let me know that he was giving me so much more than the key to his car. Oh yes. There was no debating it. On that day, in that garage, Jack Riley was giving me the key to his heart, and I would wear it around my neck forever.

After we left the warehouse, we walked down toward the river, already frozen from the unusually harsh winter. Pulling a frozen chunk of snow from the side of the road, Jack used his youth soccer skills to launch the icy ball toward the walkway. As we passed it back and forth down the slippery sidewalk, we didn't say much. We knew we didn't have to. Our hidden language was telling us everything we needed to know. We were both feeling the sting of what was coming - Jack leaving - the bubble breaking - it was all suddenly very real - and very unfair. In the distance we could see the Mighty Niagara, sparkling against the fading afternoon sky. The river looked so smooth and gentle when covered in ice - a cunning camouflage for the raging current that ran underneath it. Even though I was trying to enjoy every last second I had with Jack, I knew I was like that river - happy and content on the surface, but raging with regret and indignation underneath.

We left the sidewalk and carried on toward the bank of the Niagara, carefully walking in the snowy footprints of those who came before us. The snow was thicker and fluffier the closer we got to the banks, but Jack and I carried on undaunted. What was a little bit of snow in your boots in the face of a moment like this? In the setting sun, the view was simply amazing. So we stood there, at the edge of the frozen river, and looked across to Canada. If only crossing into another country would make all of our issues go away. But we weren't runaway slaves or draft dodgers. We were just two kids with no way out. The ice before us was so thin - like a shimmering sheet of cellophane - and the metaphor was not lost on us. We both recognized it. We had spent the entire last year on thin ice. I bent down and broke a razor thin sheet off the slushy river's edge. The way the sun reflected from it was so beautiful and as I lifted it, a kaleidoscope of colors began to radiate from its edges. Carefully, I turned so Jack could see - it was so fragile that it almost crumbled in my hands. With just a smirk, we both knew what we had to do next. Almost like throwing a Frisbee, I flung the pane of ice on to the river and its frozen fractals skittered like a mosaic across the sheet of glass. As we watched them dance, we knew we were seeing the future. With the dawn of 1958, we too would shatter and cascade in our different directions, leaving nothing but a thousand beautiful pieces of what we once were.

* * *

Okay, let's take a break here while I try and make you feel better. At this point, I'm sure most of you are looking at this story from your twenty first century perspective and feeling inconsolably frustrated that Jack and I didn't take that key from my neck and drive off into the sunset. And while I understand how that ending might feel more satisfying, I can assure you that our story was fundamentally stronger and more beautiful. True love, you see, is unselfish and its boundaries extend far beyond the object of its affection. To love someone fully and purely you have to embrace all of the intangibles that are attached to their character and anticipate the repercussions of every slight edit you make to their storyline. Jack understood this and the only way he could keep protecting me was by keeping me at a safe distance. Sure, I can say that I tried to do the same for him, but let's be real, I had so much more to lose and he knew it. A scandal with Jack would not only vilify me and bankrupt my mother; it would compromise the future of my innocent younger sisters. Almost instantaneously, those unsuspecting kids would become social and financial paupers, doomed by a series of events they had no control over. It might seem extreme, but the truth is, to act on our feelings would not only have been selfish, but downright cruel.

So instead, Jack was fighting 1957 the only way he knew how - with the car he drove and the "friends" he was keeping. Looking back, I was naive to think there weren't consequences for Jack at home – I know his parents shared their thoughts and their warnings about me - but I am not at all shocked that Jack had too much class to tell me about them. He was so much stronger and so much deeper than anyone gave him credit for. It might not be easy for anyone else to accept, but Jack Riley was my hero - he just did it without the white horse and fanfare.

The Currier and Ives Life

Before I knew it, it was a few days before Christmas and my friends and I were on our way to a caroling party at Max's house. I knew Jack's time in Buffalo was winding down, but I had promised myself that I wasn't going to let that spoil our evening. The way I had it figured, I only had a few more weeks to collect a lifetime's worth of memories and it was completely within my power how epic those memories would be.

I had never been to Max's house before and I must admit, I was pretty excited. The Murphy's lived in a stately brick house on Nottingham Terrace, the former site of the iconic Pan American Exposition of 1901. Although all but one of the buildings from the Pan Am were made of plaster and demolished immediately after the expo, I was still looking forward to being there. In addition to admiring the lush mansions and landscaping of his neighborhood, just being in the vicinity of the place where President McKinley was assassinated was pretty cool.

When we arrived, things were just as lavish as I had expected. In typical overboard fashion, the Murphey's four car garage looked like Christmas had exploded and with the cars removed, half of Buffalo could easily have fit inside it. While Max's dad enthusiastically passed out hot "adult" beverages to the parents, I managed to find the hot chocolate just in time to stave off the chills I already felt consuming me. It was an exceptionally cold night, and I was already regretting that I dressed more for cuteness than warmth.

Huddled by the campfire, I was innocently talking with Rosie's mom when a pair of arms scooped me up and dragged me toward the snowy yard.

"Excuse us," I heard Jack yell as he whisked me into two feet of snow.

"I was cold enough, thank you," I said to Jack, who was already covered head to toe in snow.

"Well, that's too bad," he replied, "because it's time to build a snowman."

For the next few minutes, I stood with my hands buried in my pockets and talked to Jack as he enthusiastically rolled, stacked and packed each individual piece of his new friend.

"We will call him Dave," he said, for no good reason (except possibly the fact that he knew I found his antics hilarious). "We did a really good job, didn't we?"

Having participated in absolutely no way, shape, or form, I just laughed and shook my head at Jack.

"I love how you say 'we' even when I haven't done anything," I smirked.

What Jack said next might be the most epic line anyone has ever said to me, and I confess to still playing it in my head when I lie in bed at night,

"It will always be 'we'," he said in the sweetest voice ever to float across the winter air.

At that moment, even though I was feeling dangerously close to hypothermia, I was filled with the most magical internal sunshine. I had probably never heard a sentence so impossibly true. Jack was absolutely right. No matter where in the world we both ended up, it would always be "we."

The next thing I knew, I was swept up by a crowd of carolers and herded down the street to entertain anyone crazy enough to open their door on this bitter cold night. My fingers were frozen, my toes were numb, and the tips of my ears stung beneath the fur of my Santa hat. As I stood there, considering an escape back to the nicely heated house, I was suddenly faced with that very familiar feeling. Without even looking, I knew for certain that Jack had silently crept up and was standing painfully close behind me. Slyly, he peeked over my shoulder to steal a look at my caroling book and I found myself gasping for air. As "Oh Little Town of Bethlehem" perfectly cascaded from Jack's rosy-red lips my shivers were gone. I could feel his warm breath on my poor frozen ear and his cologne drifted over me like an aphrodisiac. It was a magical moment in time, and I stood motionless, trying to breathe it in and save it for later. Jack loved me. He may have only told me once, but I felt it just as certain as if he said it every day…which, in his own way… he did. He said it every time he lagged behind to wait for me, every time he chose me over something else and every time he looked at me with the loudest silence I had ever heard. He said it with his thoughtfulness, and he said it with his sarcasm. He said it by silently standing beside me no matter what the season and no matter what the consequences. Right or wrong, Jack loved me….and he loved me enough not to talk about it.

Snowflakes fell, lights twinkled, and the smell of firewood filled the street. I knew this looked like a Currier and Ives painting and I let my thoughts drift to what it would be like to live that Christmas-card kind of life together. Yep. It would be prefect. In all honesty, though, I had to admit that this - standing on the frozen street, six inches apart but connected in a way no one could ever understand - this was pretty great too.

Yes, out there in the darkness it suddenly all became clear. Somehow, through the tears, the agony, and the epiphanies, I had found my truth. This love affair was never about our past, our future or even our complete disregard for right and wrong. In every way that mattered, our true story was about the journey, and what a journey it had been. In loving Jack, I had rediscovered myself. For as black and white as my days used to be, now I woke to a world full of colors and sunshine. Just the idea of earning his love gave my days purpose. The possibility of seeing him got me out of bed in the morning and inspired me to trudge through my previously meaningless days. Jack was the reason I had this cute new wardrobe and the reason I put on mascara. Through Jack, I saw myself differently. Through Jack I had been reborn. Despite all the reasons loving him was wrong, the truth is – loving Jack made me better. Even with the hole he left in my heart, I was still more complete than I had ever been.

Happily snug inside my new perspective, I proceeded to enjoy every adventure Max's party had to offer. For maybe the first time ever, I talked with people and joined in activities I never would have had the nerve to before. I wasn't just "Josie, the hairdresser's daughter" anymore. I was Josie Freaking Johnson, the girl amazing enough to earn the love of Jack Riley. And not only did I earn it, I did it even though I wasn't supposed to. For the first time in my life, I realized that I was the hero of my own story.

Should Old Acquaintance be Forgot?

It was only fitting that Jack's going away party was planned for New Year's Eve. It was the end of one crazy year and the finale of one beyond crazy affair. January would certainly be a new beginning and I honestly had no idea how I was going to do it. I had enough clarity to know that it had to be done...that Jack's stint in Europe and then college was gracefully saving me from myself. There was no way this was ending well and the sooner we cut that invisible string the better. I knew that getting over him was impossible, but I had five entire years to learn to co-exist in this world where being together wasn't an option. I wasn't stupid. He has his six months in Europe, a year at red-shirt freshman and then four years of NCAA stardom ahead of him. If I talked to him ten times in the next five years I would be surprised. You have to remember; this was 1957 and neither technology nor society was on my side. Long distance phone calls were expensive (and conspicuous) and a young woman traveling around the world alone was not an option. Even writing letters, given our parent's disapproval and the flapping lips of our mailmen, wasn't going to work for us. I'm sure you have all seen The Notebook and know exactly where all of Jack's letters would have ended up.

Plus, in some bittersweet way, the ghost of Kelly Mulligan was also haunting my thoughts. The more I digested it; Jack and Kelly were really very similar. Sure, Jack wasn't being driven out of town on some religious witch hunt, but, just like Kelly, I knew the restrictions of our society would prevent him from ever truly returning to it. Despite the strength or length of our invisible string, this was it for us. Our fairytale was officially finished. I just hoped that all of the time and all of the distance would somehow help me live inside of its memory, but outside of its shadow.

I was totally getting ahead of myself though. First, I simply had to survive tonight. I knew it was going to be hard...really really hard...and for every second of every day since I heard the news, I had been going over our goodbye in my head. I had thought of every scenario and imagined every outcome. I had tried to prepare myself with different options – different strategies – and really hoped that I would manage not to cry.

Knowing that letting go of Jack was probably going to be one of the hardest things I had ever done, I decided to have an escape plan. Just in case I couldn't stop crying or worse yet, felt on the verge of blurting out things I should NOT be admitting in a crowd, I decided to write my official good-bye to Jack in a letter. I really liked the idea of being able to choose my words carefully and I thought it was a really fitting way to end things between us. Words, both the words we had said and the words we had not, have always been a definitive part of our relationship. So that morning I stepped into the shower and planned everything I was going to say. It was a brilliant strategy really. I was at no risk of my family hearing me crying and I liked the way the water washed my tears away like some sort of baptism. I realize this might be over-sharing, but I was (and still am) a big fan of crying in the shower.

Anyway, I started the letter by explaining that I was unsure of what tonight might bring and that the evening might end with emotions running high, resulting in me deciding to duck out early and blow him off. In anticipation, I proceeded to write everything I wished I could say in person but knew I probably wouldn't. I told him that I was proud of him, would miss him, and was so excited for his future. I also told him to soak this night in and put it in his pocket so he would always remember where he came from. Sealing the envelope with a kiss, I snuck over to Jack's warehouse and left the letter under the windshield wiper of his car. Yesterday Jack had mentioned that before going to set up the banquet center, he was stopping by the garage to store some things in the trunk of his car – things he "didn't want his parents going through" while he was gone. Leaving the letter on the car might have been a chicken move, but I knew this was not something I was equipped to hand him face to face. Besides, leaving the letter with Jack's car – our own personal Neverland – seemed oddly fitting.

Abiding by my "look better, feel better" philosophy, I went home and chose a cheery little yellow dress for Jack's party. I knew that no matter where in the world he landed, Jack would always be my sunshine and the symbolism of my color choice was not lost on me. I finished the look with my trusty saddle shoes and a string of light blue beads. As I got ready, I secretly hoped that Jack would call me to respond to my letter or better yet, sneak his own letter through my window. I don't honestly know what I expected him to say in it, but you know girls, we always hope for the grand romantic gesture. Needless to say, nothing like that actually happened, and I wasn't surprised. Grand romantic gestures weren't Jack's style.

As expected, half the town was at Jack's party and when I arrived, I immediately became lost in a crowd of Jacks' extended family and casual friends. When I spotted Jack, I shook my head in disbelief. No matter how many times in my life I saw him, I don't think I would ever stop being in awe of his perfection - or our inescapable propensity to be dressed alike! Sporting khakis, a blue blazer and yellow bow tie, Jack immediately noticed me, hanging on the end of our invisible string. From that moment on, whether I was half a yard away or half a room away, I had Jack's complete attention. Until I met Jack, I could have never fathomed feeling so physically close to someone who was physically so far away. Whether it was the way he would catch my gaze or the smile he would send from deep within the crowd, Jack always let me know he was there for me. Quite simply, Jack made me feel like a priority. I found so much power and so much comfort in our connection, and immediately felt my heart sink at the prospect of living without it. Once again confronted with the actuality of Jack's departure, I felt reality slap me in the face. I could see the tears clouding my eyes and immediately felt the walls closing in around me. From across the room Jack's twin senses were triggered and he came to me immediately. Standing there together, our feelings seemed as in sync as our outfits, and I wasn't sure how I felt about that. (Plus, how had no one noticed our consistently twinning outfits yet? I mean seriously. It bordered on ridiculous.) As I tried to hide my tears, we didn't attempt to speak. Instead, reading my thoughts, Jack simply nodded his head as if to tell me that everything was going to be okay. Then, without a word, he pulled a pack of M&Ms out of his pocket. I looked at him and smiled from behind my tears.

"Remember," he said, "there will always be M&Ms – and M&Ms make everything better."

Yep. Jack always knew how to make the complicated things simple, and the forbidden things seem innocent. He was right – the M&Ms said it all. Ours might not be your traditional love story, but it would always be there, just like that candy. Whether it was a sun-soaked September or a bitter cold December night, we could always eat M&Ms, and they would always be as "awesome and delicious" as we remembered. Jack and I were living proof that love stories don't follow a script and "happily ever after" doesn't follow a formula. Some love stories exist only in the twinkle of the stars or the beam of the spotlight. In a way it's a tragedy, but in a way it's a gift. To be loved by anyone is a blessing, but to be loved despite common sense is a miracle.

I looked at Jack with wonder. After all the years and all of the obstacles, here he was, looking at me with those eyes that still melted me from the inside out. Those eyes that told our love story every time I looked into them. Being with him was so easy and living within our limits was still better than living without him. This last year with him had been simply magical and I couldn't believe that he was leaving tomorrow.

"It's probably for the best," he said, once again knowing exactly what I was thinking.

I tried to be stoic, but I was failing. Hearing him call our separation "for the best" left me a little bit broken. He read my expression in an instant.

"Awww, don't be sad," he confessed, "it's not a lie if you believe it's true."

With that one sentence, Jack seemed to summarize our entire existence. In some bizarre way those words managed to validate our tangled past and provide me with actual comfort for my future. So with that, I decided to excuse myself and find a mirror. I knew those tears were probably wreaking havoc on the make-up I literally spent sixty minutes applying. There was no way I was forfeiting my work that easily. As I walked away, I said to Jack,

"I'll see you in a few," and his reply instantly triggered my "hidden messages" sensor.

"YEAH, you will," he replied with extremely devilish swagger.

At that moment, I knew that I was in for something, but not even my wildest movie-like fantasies could have ever anticipated what.

Emerging from the bathroom, I heard the familiar sound of my friends singing with the band. Everyone knew that this activity would eventually consume the party, and everyone universally accepted that it was the best possible ending for Jack's tenure as "big man on campus." I returned with just enough time to see Sean serenading Jack in a true testament to their "bro-mance." Perfection, I thought to myself.

As the evening wore down, everyone eagerly awaited Jack's final performance. He was the unmitigated "Cabaret King" of teenage Buffalo, and no one anticipated anything less than brilliance from his swan song. I fully expected this moment to be memorable – he was Jack Riley after all – but I don't think I could have ever expected the sheer magnitude of what was about to occur. Life defining moments are funny like that. You rarely see them coming and you unquestionably feel unprepared when they do. And so it was that I stood clueless in the audience as Jack prepared to ascend the stage. How much thought he had given this is debatable. The song was already chosen – there was no doubt about that – but how much he had thought about what he was doing – or how he was going to do it – will probably always be a mystery. All I know for certain is that once he quietly decided that it was his turn, I watched as Jack coolly climbed on stage and pulled a stool up to the microphone. This was actually a pretty surprising move for him - Jack was more than a little notorious for his dance moves and I was shocked that he was choosing to sit down for his final performance. Squirming a little bit on the stool, Jack finally leaned in toward the microphone, ran his fingers through his hair and nervously exhaled. When he finally spoke, I immediately sensed that I was in trouble….deep…deep trouble. Instead of speaking with his typical wit and swagger, Jack's voice sounded panicked and extremely high pitched. He was chattering, almost babbling as he tried to talk to his audience. Pausing, he took a deep breath and looked sternly into the ground. Again running his fingers through his hair, he finally looked up, stared directly at me and constructed his first meaningful sentence,

"This is for…. well…..this says it all"

Mere words will never describe what happened to my constitution over the next three and a half minutes. When that sentence rolled out of Jack's mouth and landed at my feet, my entire world stopped turning. He might not have finished his thought, but I knew exactly who this was for and (much to my dismay) I knew exactly what was coming. Our inconceivable connection was as strong as ever and I felt what was happening in every cell in my body. Jack was about to do the unimaginable…the unthinkable. It was the first certified "Oh Fuck" moment of my short life. As Jack looked dead at me, smug smirk on his face and the devil dripping from his essence, every nerve in my body was on end. Oooooh fuuuuuckk …. Jack Riley was about to serenade me with my death song.

Stone cold in the crowd, I was paralyzed with disbelief. The message he was sending with this song choice…the fact that he even knew the significance of "Love Me Tender" at all…well it was all perfectly inconceivable. No matter how much I hated to admit it, that boy knew me backwards and he was about to blow the roof off my circle of life.

The minute Jack began to sing, tears immediately sprung from me like a natural disaster. I listened to the lyrics in a way I never had before and knew for certain that Jack was asking me never to let him go – no matter how far apart we were. Just hearing Jack sing those words made me feel like he was committing a felony. Of course I never wanted to let him go. I loved him more than I ever thought humanly possible and finding him hadn't just made my life complete, it had made ME complete.

Jack's voice gave way just the tiniest bit as he finished the first verse and he looked to the ground to center himself. I know he had said those "three little words" once before, but that whole thing was so odd and unexpected that I don't think either one of us felt the weight of what we were saying. This time though, I heard what Jack was saying, I felt what Jack was saying and I slowly started to drown in what Jack was saying.

Listening to Jack, I knew what we had was never going to fade. That was something I knew for certain. Jack was part of me. This twin like connection that Jack and I had, well I knew it was special. I might have only been 17, but every inch of me knew that I was never getting this again. I think people search their whole lives for what Jack and I had, and I was absolutely certain that no amount of time and no amount of distance was ever going to take it away. Like a tattoo, this love was a permanent part of me.

With each verse and with each time the words asked me to be his, my heart broke just a little more. I wanted to be his. I wanted to be his just as desperately as I wanted him to be mine. And let me tell you, for as much as my common sense knew that "being his" in the Biblical sense was impossible, the way his words were wrapping around me at that moment was giving the Bible a run for its money. In that instant, I would have given up almost anything to have just five minutes in "The Middle" with Jack and that Bible. That was never going to happen though, and right now, I think Jack felt the magnitude of that just as deeply as I did. Never in his entire life had I seen Jack look this raw. He wasn't' just nervous, he was completely unhinged. As if this moment didn't feel big enough already, Jack's complete lack of composure left me reeling. He was so serious, so desperate in his delivery. Even through my tears, I couldn't take my eyes off him and verse after verse, his gaze never wavered from mine. Jesus, those eyes…those eyes that I could usually fall into and swim for days…they looked glazed, almost frozen as they burrowed into me. Never in my life had I felt someone screaming at me from their silence the way I felt Jack at that moment. He was laying it all on the table in one final and desperate confession. It was beautiful and painful, and he had never looked so vulnerable. Between the words he was saying and the words that were floating beneath them; he was letting me see into his heart in a way I had never expected. I knew what it must have taken for him to do this...to speak the unspeakable. Twelve entire months of silence were flooding from him in a tidal wave of love and pain. I felt like I should throw him a lifeline...but I was paralyzed in his performance. Two hands firmly clasped over my mouth, I sobbed unapologetically as I watched my deepest desires, and my deepest fears unfold in front of me.

Yes, for all the times I had dreamt about it, I had never imagined that my moment of truth would feel so terrifying and so tragic. It was just Jack... my Jack...and he was giving me everything I had always wanted. Why then did I find this all so overwhelming? I mean let's be honest, it's not like he was telling me anything I didn't already know. Ah, but I guess therein lies the catch. Just because I "knew" how Jack felt about me, doesn't mean that I flat out "believed" in it. I was wildly insecure and there was always that part of me that doubted and questioned and habitually panicked. So, you see, even though I "knew," that Jack loved me, it wasn't until this moment that I saw the purity and the sincerity with which Jack loved me. I had always felt it, but it wasn't until this moment that I was able to see it. THAT was my moment of truth.

Oh, how far we had come from that night in the gym. Never in my wildest dreams would I have been able to envision the journey I was embarking on that night. How would I ever have been able to imagine that a boy like Jack or a connection like this could even exist? This year with Jack was the greatest gift I had ever been given. No matter how fleeting, our love had grown into the most beautiful of cherry trees and I knew our perfectly pink blossoms would bloom in my heart forever. Jack and I were part of each other...and no social class, no religion and no distance were ever going to be able to change that. A year ago, I had stood on that dance floor, listened to these lyrics and secretly wished that Jack could love me. The funny thing is, I don't really think I loved myself before Jack came along. This experience changed everything, and twelve months later - here he was - throwing those lyrics back at me and filling me with more kinds of love than I ever knew could exist. Jack Riley was nothing if not perfect.

I'm sure there was applause as the song ended, but I never heard it. I was numb. By the time Jack left the stage I felt like everyone in the room knew our secret…and to be honest…I think most of them did. There was Max, who had handed me a pair of sunglasses to hide the torrent of tears streaming down my face, and Sean who whispered to me,

"Is this for you? I'm not even joking."

And then of course there was Rosie, who didn't even have to ask.

"Are you okay?" was all she could say.

My world was in chaos. I might even have tried to run away if all my bones hadn't just melted. As Jack walked from the mic my thoughts were swirling. What on earth had just happened? Even in my wildest dreams I never could have conjured up something like this. It was too much…too iconic. I was just plain old Josie; the same girl that thought wishing for a love letter was outrageous. Geeze, I certainly wasn't prepared for a bona fide grand romantic gesture! Luckily, Jack was swarmed by his family the instant he stepped off the stage. I was certainly in no position to face him and was both grateful and relieved that I didn't have to acknowledge what just happened. Rosie, on the other hand, had no trouble diving right in and bombarding me with truths. Grabbing me and aggressively dragging me to the side of the room, Rosie sounded almost exasperated as she began to purge everything SHE had been keeping inside for the last year.

"That was for you, you know. Don't even try to deny it. Jack just sang that about YOU."

I instinctively shook my head but even I knew Rosie wasn't going to buy it.

"I can see it, you know. That "thing" that you and Jack have and the way you can almost read each other's thoughts. I can see it. Just because I have never mentioned it, doesn't mean I haven't been able to see it. Good God you're dressed alike half the time. I get it. I'm actually kind of jealous of it. And I truly believe that you two have never done anything about it – never crossed the line - but I also believe that there are some grey areas that I probably don't want to know about. So, I guess all I'm trying to say is that I know how difficult this must be and I'm here for you."

Using every trick I knew not to cry, I just looked at Rosie and shrugged my shoulders.

"Thanks," I said. It was all I could spit out.

It was such a relief to know that Rosie wasn't angry. I think she knew me well enough to know that I hadn't been hiding this from her or shutting her out on purpose. I was simply trying to survive.

When I spotted Jack firmly engaged with a crowd of people, I knew that was my chance. I had it all figured out. I would walk over, gently tap him on the arm and say a quick goodbye. I would be out the door before he could excuse himself to follow me. It wasn't necessarily what Miss Manners would have suggested, but Miss Manners probably never had to walk a crooked line such as this! Jockeying through the crowd, I managed to get myself securely inside Jack's orbit. Although my intention was to play this out gracefully, in reality I lurked behind him, awkwardly smacked him on the bicep and robotically proclaimed,

"Tonight was great. I have to go now."

As I turned to bolt, I felt him sternly grab me by the arm.

"You're not staying?" he asked with way more shock that he should have.

"No... I warned you!" I reminded him.

"Okay," he said, while contradictorily pulling me back toward him.

What happened next, I will remember forever. I suppose it was the way things were supposed to end, assuming that any of this was supposed to have happened at all. Acceptance, you see, breeds a new sort of confidence, one that has no trouble living in the moment, especially when it knows that this moment is the beginning and the end of everything. And so it was, in the middle of a crowd of people that Jack and I lived in our first and our last moment of complete truth. Jack must have known that no words could come close to the hurricane of emotions running through our bodies, so like always, Jack chose to let me FEEL his thoughts for myself. Confidently,

Jack wrapped his arms tightly around my body and I threw mine securely around his neck. As he squeezed me, I could feel his face in my hair and I instinctively buried mine in his shoulder. Being in Jack's arms was like drifting to another world. I felt so secure and so confident when he held me. At that moment, the rules, the obstacles... heck the whole rest of the world felt irrelevant. Pulling him so close that I could feel his heart beating, I spoke with every bit of honesty and every bit of desperation that I had.

"I love you," I said breathlessly but with complete purpose this time.

Unlike before, I said it with emotion - with conviction -and I knew exactly what I was doing. I said it like a woman says it to a man and I meant it with every piece of my body and soul. I could feel the breath rush from Jack's body, and he reacted with a noise I will never quite be able to explain. All I know is that the sound he made was beautiful and tragic and immediately traveled through my bloodstream like a narcotic.

"I love you too," Jack sighed softly, his warm breath dancing on my neck.

Holding him at that moment, as those words traveled through our bodies, was beyond any hope or any expectation that I ever had. We were in the sweetest of the sweet spots and I could almost see the mist of "The Middle" creeping above the horizon. Pressed together at the base of the stage, we lived a lifetime in a single moment. Our deepest of secrets were stunningly on display for the crowds around us, with not a reservation or a judgement to be found. Pulling back, Jack impishly brushed his stubbly face across my cheek. His skin felt flushed and awesomely familiar. Just like the day I wiped frosting from that cheek I could feel it...the baby like softness of his skin. It was waiting for me behind that stubble, just like he would always be waiting for me behind our realities. Turning, I grabbed Jack's face one final time and held it before me with both hands. Looking into his eyes, knowing what this moment represented, I realized that I had no final words. And then —— finding a place inside Jack's eyes where I had never been before, I watched the impossible happen. Swirling in that ocean of blue, I could see him leaning in toward me and I watched myself stiffen as I processed what was happening. Looking deeper, I saw Jack smile just a little as his nose brushed against mine and I watched us – frozen – gazing at each other – lost deep inside the sweetest spot of all. At last, I saw his lips gently brush against mine and my world spun, every inch of me powerless in the face of true love. Closing my eyes, I could fee his warm, soft lips on mine, and I was perfectly weightless, adrift inside a kiss that had defied all reason. And so, we stood there - a thousand puzzle pieces magically swirling above us - finally on their way to finding their perfect match.

* *

"Why are they just standing there looking at each other?" I heard a voice say.

Yeah. It was true. This world that Jack and I lived in was still impermeable by anyone outside of it, and even though I knew we had both felt that kiss rearrange every cell inside our bodies, it remained invisible to everyone else in the room. Even in the wake of our parting, our connection had never been stronger, and I had never been - nor would ever be - kissed as perfectly as the one that only existed inside our gaze.

Our puzzle complete, I could feel the universe sigh with relief, and I felt whole for the first time in my life. Still unable to speak, I looked at Jack, waiting for him to break the silence, but he didn't. He couldn't. We were collectively lost.

And that's when I heard it…a single voice rising from deep within the crowd. One single voice of reason, stating the obvious and somehow making this all seem okay,

"Look," it said, "that's what true love looks like."

And with that, we both knew nothing else needed to be said. This might be the end of our story, but it wasn't the end of our legacy. With those words, the lines between upper class and middle class, Catholics and Protestants, and friendship and true love blurred just enough to let us through. Although no one would ever quite grasp the depth of our connection or the unique place our affair held in this world, we somehow felt acceptance travel through every person in that room. We were what we were, and we had finally found the conviction to face it. Jack and I had shown the world that love is love. It doesn't need a label or a piece of paper to be real and it doesn't need to be "right" to not be "wrong." Jack and I each knew that we were brought together for a reason and even from across the globe, we knew that the mere existence of the other would make us complete. In the end, we both accepted there was no harm in that.

Even all these years later, Jack's last words to me play in my head like the ending to a movie,

"I know, growing up kinda sucks," he said, "but at least there will always be M&M's."

"So, all we need are M&M's and a time machine?" I replied with a sniffle.

"No, all we need are the M&M's," he smirked. "And love. That usually helps too." ❤

With that, I looked into Jack's eyes one last time and knew that Buddy Holly was absolutely right. Our love was true. Not fade away.

Epilogue – The Afterglow

"No one you love is ever truly lost"

Earnest Hemingway

It's been sixty-four years since I walked out of that hall and away from the most iconic boy I have ever known. Although life went on and distance prevailed, a part of Jack always stayed with me, and I'm not just referring to the key that hangs around my neck. As with any great love, Jack became part of me and the person his love – and his loss – enabled me to become has fundamentally shaped my character. Through who I am and how I love, Jack is with me every day. You just have to look between the lines to see him.

And so, my friends, in parting I would like to leave you with my own kind of blessing:

I hope that you can look forward
and feel the hope and the goodness of possibility
I hope that you can look backward and see the beauty between the lines
I hope that you can look at today and know
that you are greater than the sum of your parts.

But more than anything
I hope that you can look at your own invisible strings
and find the strength and the vision to follow them anywhere
Because if loving Jack has taught me anything
it has unquestionably taught me this:

The magic isn't in how the story ends.
The magic is that there was a story at all.

Appendix – Historical Materials

Make the world of Josie and Jack come alive by visiting JuliannaWoite.com.

Dive deeper into the novel by exploring the history of Buffalo, 1957. Listen to songs from the story, investigate historical figures and find valuable community resources to assist anyone struggling with anxiety or grief.

Just look at what you can discover:

Historical Events

- Pan American Exposition of 1901
- Assassination of President McKinley
- 125th Anniversary and World Port Celebration of 1957
- "Hello World" - live dramatic tableau at Civic Stadium (aka The Rockpile)
- EC200 - Erie County Bicentennial of 2021-2022

Local Places/People

- Fredrick Law Olmsted's Park System
- Delaware Park
- Forest Lawn Cemetery
- Blocher Memorial (John, Katherine & Nelson Blocher)

- Louise Blanchard Bethune
- William Fargo
- Red Jacket
- Dorothy Goetz Berlin
- President Millard Fillmore
- Mary Talbert
- Canisus High School
- Bennett High School
- Meadille University/Sisters of St. Joseph Teacher's College
- Amherst Central School District
- Grand Island/ Niagara River
- WNY Waterfalls: Akron Park/Falls, Niagara Falls, Glen Falls
- Masten Street Armory
- Albright Knox Art Gallery
- Broadway Market
- Statler Hotel
- Erie County Fairgrounds
- General Mills Plant
- Shea's Buffalo Theater
- Parkside Candy
- Loblaws
- Crystal Beach Park

Pop Culture - Songs, Musicals, Movies

- Elvis Presley Buffalo Concert - April 1st, 1957, Memorial Auditorium
- Elvis Presley - *Love Me Tender* (1957)
- Buddy Holly - *Not Fade Away* (1957)
- Frank Sinatra - *Fly Me to the Moon (1954)*
- Frankie Lymon & the Teenagers - *Why Do Fools Fall in Love* (1956)
- Goo Goo Dolls Buffalo Concert - July 4th 2004, Darien Lake
- Goo Goo Dolls - *Iris* (1998)
- West Side Story - *Somewhere* (1957 Broadway)

- Music Man - *Wells Fargo Wagon* (1957 Broadway)
- Annie Get Your Gun - *Anything You Can Do I Can Do Better* (1946 Broadway, 1950 movie)
- Guys and Dolls (1950 Broadway, 1955 movie)
- East of Eden (1955 movie, James Dean)

The Literary Arts

- On Death and Dying - Elizabeth Kubler Ross
- The Silent Lover, Sir Walter Raleigh

Community Resources

- Crisis Services
- Camp Good Days and Special Times

About the Author

Julianna Woite (juliannawoite.com) is an educator and historian who is fiercely passionate about preserving the history of Buffalo and Western New York. A graduate research & writing instructor for Medaille University, Woite specializes in educational technology and serves the university as a digital learning technologist. Throughout her career as an educator, she has worked in classrooms and on the athletic fields with pre-school to high school aged youth and spent several years teaching adult education classes. With a degree in Psychology, professional development studies in adolescence and thanatology and numerous years working with youth, Woite is dedicated to promoting the mental and emotional health of youth and young adults. Outside of the classroom, she dedicates herself to the preservation and promotion of the history of Western New York. As the great great granddaughter of Michael Snyder, namesake of Snyder, NY, she has always felt both a desire and a responsibility to promote the area's past as well as a need to inspire everyone to take note of their own unique place in history. She has published several non-fiction history books through The History Press and Arcadia Publishing and offers presentations and walking tours on various topics of local history. She was a member of the Town of Amherst Bicentennial Commission and Erie County Bicentennial Committee. She lives in Snyder, NY where she and her husband have successfully raised four amazing children and several less amazing pets.

Also by Julianna Woite

Julianna Woite is passionate about preserving the local history of Western New York and telling the stories of the people and places that left their footprints throughout the region.

WNY and The Gilded Age

Born from the success of the Erie Canal, the communities of Western New York enjoyed a century of growth and prosperity during America's Gilded Age. Buffalo was one of the richest cities in America and dominated industry and politics, producing two presidents. Wealth and architectural opportunity enticed figures like Frank Lloyd Wright, while the events of the Pan-American Exposition and a presidential assassination and inauguration attracted the world's attention. Drawing on the natural resources of Niagara Falls and profiting from a friendly relationship with Canada, the people of Western New York enjoyed luxurious leisure time and documented their adventures in photo albums and postcards. It is these images and remembrances, beautifully reproduced in this book, that capture this charming time in Western New York's history.

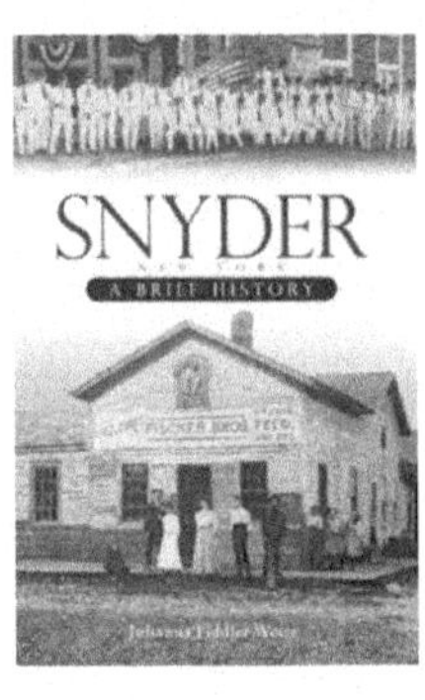

Snyder, New York: A Brief History

In 1823, the Erie Canal sparked visions of opportunity and fortune in many, including Abraham Snyder, who traversed to the land that would become his namesake. But when Abraham mysteriously disappeared in 1832, his son, Michael, became the "man of the family" and consequently became a one-man powerhouse of industry and generosity.

Michael Snyder's eponymous settlement became a hamlet of Amherst in western New York that boasts a rich history dating back to its origins. The Snyders and other early settlers established several town institutions and landmarks—including the first mercantile and band hall—that gave locals a sense of community. Further, because of their humanitarian spirit, residents cultivated a sense of generosity and tolerance, evidenced by the practice of donating instruments to schoolchildren and embracing the Seneca Indian tribe as equals.

Clarence

Located 12 miles northeast of Buffalo, Clarence is proud to be both a bustling suburb and the oldest town in Erie County. When the Town of Clarence was formed on March 11, 1808, it incorporated six settlements: Clarence Hollow, Harris Hill, Clarence Center, Wolcottsburg, Swormville, and East Amherst. Four years later, this area played a vital role in the War of 1812 by providing men for the American militia and housing refuges after the burning of Buffalo. During the 200 years since, Clarence has thrived as an agricultural community. Grown from such pioneer families as Van Tine, Harris, Ransom, Eshelman, Parker, and Lapp, Clarence remains home to 30,000 residents and has housed notable personalities like Wilson Greatbatch and Joan Baez. Clarence has featured the businesses of the National Gypsum Company and Greatbatch Industries and proudly boasts historical icons, such as the Spoor Hotel and the Goodrich-Landow Log Cabin.

Lutherans in Western New York

During the construction of the Erie Canal in the early 1820s, the population of Western New York increased 145 percent. Many of these pioneers were European immigrants, with a high concentration hailing from the German-speaking states. These immigrants brought their Lutheran ideals and continued to practice the religion in their new homeland. By 1827, the first official Lutheran church in Erie County had been incorporated as the German Reformed Church, known today as St. Paul's Lutheran Church in Eggertsville. Soon after, the need for mission churches arose, and by the mid-1800s, Lutheran congregations had been established in several Western New York suburbs. During the following century, the Lutherans in Western New York would undergo growth and change. While all congregations eventually abandoned German as their primary language, many struggled to further separate from their German roots during the Nazi regime. Today, there are nearly 200 Lutheran congregations in New York.

Made in USA - North Chelmsford, MA
1318335_9780578379777
06.14.2022 0813